CAPTAIN
of my Heart

CAPTAIN
of my Heart
NEW YORK BLIZZARDS HOCKEY ROMANCE

Mandy Fate

4 Horsemen
Publications, Inc.

4 Horsemen Publications, Inc.
1497 Main St. Suite 169
Dunedin, FL 34698
4horsemenpublications.com
info@4horsemenpublications.com

Typesetting by Autumn Skye
Cover by Niki Tantillo
Editor: Sienna Skye

Library of Congress Control Number: 2023945651

Paperback ISBN-13: 979-8-8232-0312-8
Hardcover ISBN-13: 979-8-8232-0314-2
Audiobook ISBN-13: 979-8-8232-0311-1
Ebook ISBN-13: 979-8-8232-0313-5

This one's for you, Mom. Thank you for indulging me in my crazy midnight ramblings about hot hockey boys.

Table of Contents

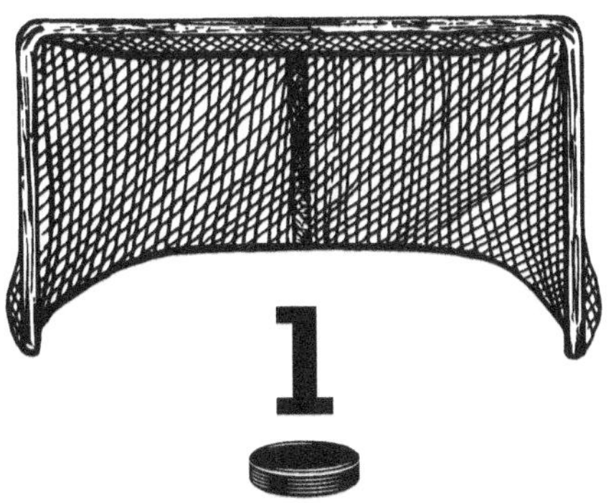

Milly

I was five seconds away from stabbing this guy with a freshly sharpened knife. It would be so easy; a selection of them was laid out between us. All I had to do was grab one before he could react, lunge across the stainless-steel table, and carve him up—easier than breaking down a whole chicken. And more satisfying.

Because if he didn't stop staring at me with his beady eyes as if he could read every thought in my mind, I was going to lose my shit.

Hell, I was already close to it.

Okay, so maybe his eyes weren't beady. In fact, they were a nice light brown. And okay, maybe it wasn't him I was actually mad at. But he was still freaking me out.

The guy looked like a kid, lean and fair-skinned, but had the thousand-yard stare of a seasoned veteran. Not a military veteran, though.

No. A culinary veteran. He had a face that said he had stood through raging chefs screaming an inch from his straight nose and indignant customers demanding unreasonable service.

The look was familiar. Months ago, I would have said I saw it every day in the mirror, but that was then. Now, I wondered if I still had a hint of it left deep inside or if it was something a person never really loses. Either way, I was okay with never seeing it again, on myself or anyone else.

I took a deep breath and rubbed my fingers together behind my back, trying to fight off the uncomfortable tightening that came whenever I set foot in a professional kitchen these days. Imagine that. A professional chef afraid of kitchens. Pathetic.

Yet here I was.

At the thought, the irritation that had been simmering on my back boiler overflowed, and my murderous rage was redirected from the chef in front of me to my so-called best friend, Thea. She would be so easy to hunt down; she was in this maze of a building somewhere, but she had been avoiding me.

Smart choice on her part.

I'd tried calling her as well, planning on begging off with an excuse about poisoning from a new food truck I tried, but the bitch refused to pick up. I couldn't be too mad, unfortunately. Thea didn't entirely deserve my rage; she was just trying to help me in her own overbearing and controlling way. She probably thought recommending me for *sous chef de cuisine* position at her workplace was the kick in the ass I needed. So, as much as I hated her for forcing me here, I wouldn't just disappear on her after she went through the trouble of pulling strings to get me to this ridiculous audition for a job I didn't want. Didn't mean I couldn't bitch her out later, though.

I grumbled to myself but kept my discomfort quiet from the three other chefs that stood in the presentation line with me. If only the guards who had practically stripped searched me at the entrance had turned me away, this would have been a non-issue. They seemed hesitant enough about me, and I would have been offended had they not been about to be my legitimate excuse for why I couldn't make it to the auditions.

It was like they had never seen a woman in black leather carrying a roll of knives before. Honestly. I wished people would stop saying I looked sketchy.

Sure, they may have had a point. But unless I wanted to become a smear on the unforgiving streets of New York City, the armored leather jacket, full-face motorcycle helmet, thick black jeans, and steel-toed boots were a necessity. Protection came before fashion. Still, I preferred "badass" to "suspicious."

The knives were both easier and harder to explain.

Thea must have been bribing the universe, though, because I was let through despite my being suspicious. But for all her universe-bribing, Thea only had so much control. I didn't want this job, so I would make sure I didn't get it. Simple as that.

The double doors to my left flew open, and everyone in the kitchen turned as one to look.

Unconsciously, I snapped to attention, straightening like someone had shoved rebar up my spine. But it wasn't the *chef de cuisine* that entered. Instead, a harried man rushed through the swinging doors and stopped nervously at the sight of the five people watching him. He was obviously not in charge of anything.

He looked at the group of us, and his eyes landed on me just as I recognized him.

"Shit!" burst out from him.

A smile cut across my face before I could stop it. I nodded at Adams in greeting and managed to hold in my chuckle with some difficulty.

The other chefs in the room couldn't have missed his expletive at seeing me if they were both deaf and blind. They looked between us with question marks in their eyes before the only chef who actually worked here cleared his throat. Our attention was yanked back to where he stood across the metal table from us.

He pointed toward the little hallway leading off from the swinging double doors that Adams had entered through. "Lockers and whites in there." Like it had when I walked into the kitchen, the man's voice startled me, clearly scarred from years of chain-smoking and at odds with his young looks.

With an indecipherable look thrown my way, Adams disappeared into the break room without another word, and the attention of the kitchen was left on me.

The line of chefs beside me—one woman and two men—flickered their eyes over me, trying to see what had Adams so visibly nervous. They wouldn't find anything. In the borrowed chef whites, I looked just like the rest of them. Well, mostly.

Where they looked like the definition of clean-cut chefs—their coats buttoned all the way up, sleeves sitting neatly at their wrists, and towels folded just so over their aprons—I was a disaster in comparison. My chef's coat gaped at my neck where I had left it unbuttoned, and my sleeves were rolled above my elbows. I'd tucked my towel into my back pocket instead of into my apron, and my steel-toed boots were noticeably different from their non-stick shoes. Then there was the bandana—bright red and distracting in the otherwise white and silver kitchen.

In the pristine, monochrome environment, it was my little rebellion.

Today, it was folded into a headband and pushing my blunt bangs back. The rest of my wavy, brown hair was tied into a French braid that hung down between my shoulder blades. I could already feel escaped wispies floating around my face, but I ignored them.

Still, all the differences between me and my young competition were negligible. They couldn't see my years of experience working in Michelin-starred restaurants in my looks. As far as they knew, I was just another mediocre chef.

I let them look until they dismissed me and went back to facing forward, trying to seem at ease while unsubtly sneaking glances at the main doors. While they all tried to project an air of confidence, I could see a tremor of nerves in each of them. The woman beside me was shaking so much I was afraid to let her hold a knife.

I located the bright red first aid box on the wall beside me. Just in case.

They were all extremely young. I would place the oldest man at about twenty-five. My mere thirty-three years of age suddenly seemed ancient.

I'd seen baby *stages* on their first round of apprenticeships be less nervous in the kitchen. It looked like someone had just come in here and threatened the lives of everyone they'd ever met. Their eyes kept flicking around, looking both terrified and hopeful.

They must have met the *chef de cuisine.*

Looked like my suspicions were true. This would be a no-nonsense kitchen with a mean, old chef who didn't take constructive criticism. My plan to throw the tryouts solidified. No way was I working in one of those kitchens again. Not when I just got free of the last one.

Adams emerged from the break room, dressed in clean chef whites, coat not fully buttoned, and came to stand on my free side.

"Fucking Milly Chambers," Adams spat my name under his breath, his sun-tanned face pissed.

I cracked a smile at the chef I'd first met in France nine years ago and had run into multiple times in kitchens around the world. I knew why he was disappointed at the sight of me, and I didn't take it personally. I wouldn't want to be my competition either. Thankfully for him, I wouldn't put up much of a fight today. In fact, I was glad he wanted this job. I would much rather lose to him than the kids on my other side.

"Damnit. Why the hell are you here, Chambers? Thought you would be working toward your first star by now."

My shoulders tightened before I forced them to relax in a semblance of a shrug. Six months ago, he would have been right. I had been working to get my own restaurant for the better part of a decade, studying from master chefs, practicing for eighteen hours a day, and living and breathing food. But when I was finally at the top of my game and seconds away from getting my own restaurant, Michelin stars in my eyes, I quit.

According to most in the business, I just fell off the face of the planet, probably to privately cook for some eccentric billionaire or in a basement, making the best menu in the world and devising my plan to take over the culinary world.

Ha.

More like I was eating my way through New York City for half a year.

And now I was here, in somebody else's kitchen—somewhere I'd never thought I would be again.

"Ehh," I answered with forced nonchalance.

"Oh, I get it. You're taking the job for the free games, right? I didn't know you were a hockey fan, Chambers."

"Hockey fan?"

His dark brows scrunched at my obvious confusion. "Yeah… Are you not? That's why the rest of us are here."

I looked over at the woman beside me who was eavesdropping.

She nodded. "I caught a glimpse of Mason Frey on the way in."

"Who?"

Adams sighed. "Forward for the New York Blizzards. You know, the home team for the hockey arena you're standing in?"

"Ok." Forward sounds like an offensive position, but I couldn't identify it further.

Adams shook his head but let my insulting lack of knowledge about his favorite sport go.

Something clicked in my brain. I lowered my head to Adams'. "Oh, is that why they're all nervous? Because they think they're going to see a hockey player?"

Adams gave the line of chefs on my other side a once-over. "Probably," he whispered back. "Why did you think they were?"

I shrugged. "Figured they met the *chef de cuisine*."

"What, you think this *chef de cuisine* is like Janvier?"

I almost shuddered. If this head chef was anything like Janvier, I'd leave a trail of smoke behind me with how fast I'd be out the doors, Thea be damned. Mention of the chef who was a driving force in my life and my decision to leave my career sobered me. And just in time.

"Welcome to the Snow Globe Arena," a voice spiced with Deep South announced as a tiny, middle-aged, dark-skinned woman came through the swinging double doors. She looked us over as she came to stand on the other side of the table with the scrawny chef with the thousand-yard stare. "Well, the Snow Globe Arena kitchen. It may not be the rink, but it's still darn impressive if I do say so myself."

Her accent was obviously south of the Mason-Dixon Line, but I hadn't been that far down in years and couldn't quite place it. The woman was dressed in chef whites, her sleeves rolled up to reveal toned forearms that spoke of her ability to easily break down whole animal carcasses. She had soft, aging features and chic white-and-baby-blue box braids the same colors as the concrete tunnels I had navigated to get here. They must be the team colors. Twined around themselves and piled on top of her head, the braids resembled a colorful toque. But she had no need for an actual toque; the whole kitchen could tell her rank without the classic white hat.

She was completely comfortable in the space, as she should be; she ran the place. And she wasn't a curmudgeonly old man. Unexpected.

The head chef placed her hands behind her back as she studied us. We snapped to attention. I held still under her searching eyes, years of working in kitchens stricter than the military smoothing my face into the perfect blank mask.

Never challenge a chef's rank in their own kitchen—it was the number one unspoken rule. But that didn't seem to be a problem. Instead of the hard expression I expected, a bright smile broke across her face, lifting her plump cheeks.

"Hey, y'all. My name is Odette LaBeux."

The Cajun French accent and name clicked in my head. She was from Louisiana. I was surprised it took me a moment to place, but the last time I had been to the bayou was eight years ago when a culinary school friend opened a restaurant a couple of blocks off Bourbon Street.

"I'm the *chef de cuisine* for the New York Blizzards. This here is Peter Nilsen." She gestured at the chef beside her. "He is my *chef de patissier.*"

I should have guessed. Looking closer, I could see the tightness of his coat over his arms. The fabric looked fit to burst. Pastry chefs always had the best arms. It was all the kneading and rolling they did.

Chef LaBeux continued her welcome speech. "The rest of the staff is out serving lunch, so we have free reign of the kitchen for a bit. Now, should you be hired, your job will be to make nutrition fun and enjoyable while still taking into account each player's special needs. You may think this job is just cooking bland chicken for athletes, but you're wrong. Your audition today will consist of one thing; make the healthiest, most original, delicious meal you can."

That, I would not be doing. And not only because I didn't want to.

I couldn't.

The word "original" was no longer in my vocabulary.

"I looked over y'all's resumes, and I was impressed. This is a great group to help us out." Chef LaBeux's deep eyes flicked to me for a second but shifted away before I could read them. "But I can only pick one of y'all. So, I hope y'all are game for a competition."

"Yes, Chef," we echoed in unison.

LaBeux immediately raised her hands, waving them as if to wipe away our words. "Heavens, no. Please just call me Odette. Or LaBeux. We are a relaxed kitchen, and there is no place for hierarchy here. This is an open space where everyone is meant to collaborate and work as one. That goes double for y'all. Should you get this job, you will not be working under me; you will be my equal. Just like the hockey team practicing down the way, we are a team."

I must be having a stroke. I subtly sniffed the air. No burning toast, just lemon cleaner and soap from the kitchen's last wipe-down. But what other reason was there? No chef who had spent their entire life crawling up the steep and hot oil-greased ladder of culinary hierarchy would willingly give their title away. It was unheard of.

Until now. Because my ears definitely heard that.

Che—LaBeux clapped. "Ok, that's all. Your hour and a half starts now. Show me what y'all got and pull no punches. Go all out."

With that, the chefs stampeded straight for food storage. I shuffled after them.

Shit. This is not going well.

I snuck a glance at the cutting board of the chef beside me and fought off my frustrated tears.

Come on, man. What athlete wants to eat a jellied sweet potato square?

Even with my advanced palate, I wouldn't want to eat that. Disgusting.

I looked to my right, hoping to see something better from the other woman chef.

Damnit. Those portions wouldn't sustain a toddler, let alone a full-grown man.

I'm going to win, I suddenly thought with horror. My hand stilled, the knife in it stopping in the middle of roughly chopping a head of cauliflower.

Then I remembered my only hope. I casually set my knife down, wiped my hands on my towel, returned it to my back pocket, and strolled across the kitchen.

The stainless-steel kitchen had a traditionally classic layout, something that surprised me when I had first seen it. I didn't know what I expected from a kitchen for a sports team, but it wasn't an industrial version of something I would have seen in a Michelin-starred restaurant. Coming in from the double doors, spacious steel counters with a few sinks ran along the back and right wall. Matching metal islands in the center of the room held the grill, burners, and more prep space. Vent hoods hung from the ceiling, and pots and pans were tucked under the counters and islands. Food storage was around a corner to the right, the break room to the left.

I made my way to the ovens stacked in the back left corner. I was the only one using them, the others sticking to the grill, stove, or—I let my shudder emerge—the emulsifier.

"Behind," I warned the others as I passed and slowed when I got to Adams' station, last on the L of counters.

Not bad. He was going the tried-and-true route with chicken, vegetables, and carbs, but was putting his own twist on the classic combination by making it Cajun. It was a risk, the flavors not to everyone's liking, but it would give him points with the Cajun head chef.

Or it could torpedo him. There was one thing that would secure him the win, but he would have to move fast.

"Make it a casserole," I whispered and continued past him.

I quickly checked on my salmon in the oven and returned to my station, feeling Adams' questioning gaze on my back the whole time. But I didn't get to confirm that he got my message, because I had a guest at my station.

Chef Odette LaBeux.

"I like what you're doing here," she said with a smile.

"Thank you," I replied hesitantly as I closed the last of the distance to my cutting board. LaBeux stood just out of the way, not invading my space as I picked up my knife again and continued to dismantle my cauliflower. I knew what came next and braced for it. Maybe she would say it in her Cajun French to make it more authentic.

I like what you're doing here, but...

Who taught you knife skills? A Parkinson's patient?

It's not 1950, update your recipe.

You'll never get a star with this kind of mediocre shit.

But nothing followed her compliment. Instead, she watched for a moment then moved on to the next chef beside me.

I kept an ear open as she commented on the uniqueness of his dish, but, once again, no cutting remark came from her. Thoughts churning like homemade ice cream, I went back to my vegetable and the boring dish I had made dozens of times over the past twenty years.

Forty-five minutes later, I plated my dish with slumped shoulders and presented it to LaBeux, the pastry chef, and another cook LaBeux had brought in to judge. I set the plate in the line of dishes served by the others and kept in my growl.

Adams hadn't turned his dish into a casserole.

I headed back to the line of chefs awaiting judgment, already knowing I won.

Fuck.

Ethan

I ducked my head as much as I could while keeping my peripherals open and jolted to the side, throwing the eyes tracking me off my rhythm. A rubber puck danced between the smooth chopping blade of my hockey stick. Speeding up, I left my opponents and my allies in the dust until only one person stood between me and my destination.

Mick Little, decked out in the same Blizzards' blue-and-white practice gear that I was, moved to intercept me. His too-tight grip on his stick made his movements jerk erratically, and his feet struggled to keep up with my speed. His one chance to check me and steal the puck was swept away under his fumbling skates.

There was only clear ice ahead of me. I doubled down, forcing more strength into my legs until I had almost grown wings. The goaltender's head twitched frantically, trying to both track the path of the puck and look for any tells on my face or in my body language about my next move. My impenetrable stone expression gave nothing away.

I dribbled the puck. Right. Left. Right. Left.

Fifteen feet from the goal, I cut to the side. My whole body read that I was going to shoot to the left. I tapped the puck, sending it backward through my legs, then whipped my stick to the right and slapped the puck before it got too far from me. The move was new to me, only having been trying to pull it off for the past couple of weeks. But luck was on my side because it sailed to the right, bypassing the goalie completely, and buried itself in the goal. The net billowed backward with the force of the shot, and the goalie whipped off her mask.

"Fuck, Jones!" Riley Warren, our backup goalie cursed. Her brown eyes glared at me as if I had scored the winning goal against her during the Cup final instead of sneaking in a lucky shot during practice.

"Sorry?" I apologized with no sincerity.

She snorted like an enraged bull, but I didn't take it personally. It wasn't me she was mad at; it was herself. Then, like the stubborn professional she was, Warren replaced her mask and returned to her default squat position in the net.

"Again," she demanded.

But Coach's voice rang out across the ice. "That's practice!"

Like someone pulled the plug from the rink, the electric atmosphere of energized athletes drained so much that a toddler just waking up from a nap would have more zip in them than the players on the ice. A collective groan of relief rose from the team. Only Warren grumbled, not wanting off the ice, but started gathering her equipment. The last drop of energy from everyone was put into getting their skates to cut across the ice to the rink door as fast as possible. The faster off the ice, the closer to showering and eating and getting home.

"Hey, Little. Wait up a sec," I called out and skated up to Mick Little before he could escape with the rest of the team. I caught the sympathetic looks a few of our teammates shot him as they disappeared toward the locker room, but none of them were going to come to his rescue. They knew better.

I was the captain, and there was no escaping my need to help. And while most of the rookies I'd mentored resented that at first, they grew to appreciate my unconditional support of all the players I was responsible for. Just like I was sure Little would. Although he might take more time than most to acclimate to my notoriously helpful personality. Because he wasn't a rookie. Far from it. He had been drafted over seven years ago, but he was new to my team. And he was playing like shit.

Little sighed and raked an irritated hand through his sun-bleached hair but stopped and stood to the side of the rink gate. The boys left until only he and I were on the ice. I came to a gentle stop beside him and propped myself against my stick as the last player disappeared down the tunnel that would take them to the players' lounge and then the locker room.

"Want to stay and slap some pucks around with me?" I asked.

Little copied my pose, leaning against his stick, and shot me an exasperated look. "No, I don't want to *slap some pucks around with you*, Jones. Not when you're just going to be asking me Psych 101 questions, trying to get to my gooey, soft center. I get that this is your *thing*, but can we just not?"

"No. I'm captain of this team, and it's my job to help out my teammates and be a confidant whenever they have problems."

"Like I've already told you a million times before, nothing's wrong. I'm not a lost rookie, and I don't need a confidant. Thanks, but no thanks."

I took a deep breath and pushed down the urge to pinch the bridge of my nose like my dad did whenever my brothers or I were pissing him off. "You may be new to this team, but I know the way you play, Little. So unless you've decided to completely throw in the towel on your career, something is going on with you. Your shots on goal have been absolute shit, a pre-teen could intercept your passes, and I'm honestly impressed that you managed to put on your gear correctly with how absentminded you've been."

It was the wrong thing to say. I knew that. But the words shot from my mouth like a forward on a power play with a puck and nothing but free ice in front of him. And … goal. Right where it hurt.

Little's back snapped straight, icy-blue eyes turning hard, and any chance I had of getting through to him was picked up and carried away by the cool air coming off the surface of the rink.

"Ah, shit, Little," I waffled.

"You know what, Jones? You need to chill the fuck out. We have two and a half weeks before our first game. Yeah, I maybe have a few things going on, but I'll be fine. Maybe you should get it through your head that you're just the captain of this team, not the coach. And you're definitely not my therapist." With that, Little shoved the rink gate open and stomped off as best as he could in hockey skates. He wobbled angrily down the rubber floor leading to the locker rooms and around the corner.

"Fuck," I grumbled. As loath as I was to admit it, the man did have a point; it wasn't *officially* the captain's job to butt into the lives of their teammates. Most captains in the league tended to just do their duties on the ice—mediate between teams, discuss with referees, and help out the coach when needed.

But I wasn't most captains.

"Yeah, that wasn't great," Warren deadpanned.

I whipped around, my heart jumping up a few beats per minute, to see Warren skating up to me, wiping sweat from her forehead with her shoulder, her hands full of gear.

"Jesus Christ, Warren. I thought you'd left with the team."

She shrugged padded shoulders and gestured with her goalie stick to the net at the end of the ice. "I was just collecting the last of the stray pucks when you guys started having your heart-to-heart. Well, maybe it was more of a heart-to-middle finger. I figured I should try to turn invisible until you finished your conversation. It seemed to have worked. You guys didn't even notice me."

I snorted softly as the familiar cut of her New York accent—mostly Manhattan proper but with the occasional hint of the rougher boroughs—drained the tension I hadn't noticed building from my traps. Warren lightly slashed my shin with the blade of her stick. I barely felt it through the pads.

"Cheer up, Cap. You'll get through to him eventually. You always do."

"Yeah?"

"Yeah. I mean, you got to me."

I shot her a smugly amused look. "I think Kingston got to you more than I did. Or into you."

This time, I felt the slash at my shin, but Warren was smiling along with me.

It was true though. While Warren had her issues when she first joined the team as our female goaltender, I never intervened. I didn't have to; my best friend and assistant captain at the time, Sebastian Kingston, was all over it. And all over her.

Unfortunately, as one of only two women in the NHL, Warren couldn't date a teammate. That shouldn't have been a problem, as everyone thought she was a lesbian, but Kingston found out that wasn't entirely true when she kissed him in an elevator. After a whirlwind of love and denial that I had to hear about in excruciatingly repetitive detail, my best friend decided to retire from the team so he could be happy with his girl-friend. And he hadn't regretted it since.

Just because he was no longer my teammate, though, didn't mean he wasn't my friend. Since he and Warren weren't out as a couple to the world yet, they tended to spend a lot of time at each other's house. More often than not, I was invited over also, and I had connected with Warren more than I thought I would. So even though I'd lost one friend on the team, I'd gained a new one in Warren.

For good measure, Warren hit me again. "Better watch it, Cap. I could kick your ass."

I couldn't help the incredulous double-take. "Sure. If you call up Kingston and Frey to back you up." All of them together might have a chance. *Might.* I may have the reputation of being one of the kindest people on the ice, but I grew up with two older brothers and was a hockey player. I could hold more than my own.

Her lips tilted up at the corners, satisfied, and I realized what she had done.

"Alright," I told her, imaginary fight forgotten. "I'm officially distracted from Little. Can we get off this ice?"

Warren grabbed her platinum blonde braid and ripped the rubber band off the end. She snapped it around her wrist then ran her fingers through the rope of her braid, breaking up the strands until they framed her pale face in sweat-slicked waves. "Good God, yes. I need an hour-long shower to get this smell off me. Haven't sweated this much since that first game."

I winced at the memory of Warren's first game with the Blizzards as she skated past me, opened the door to the rink, and stepped out. I followed.

I knew she didn't hold any resentment toward me or the rest of the team for that game, but I still felt guilty. I couldn't help it; knowing her as well as I did now, I would never put her in that position again. Although at the time, the crazy bitch had reveled in facing down an entire hockey team on her own. But she shouldn't have had to.

Riley Warren was the second female in the NHL, and our coach hadn't been sure she could cut it as a goaltender on our team. So he had us test her when she was traded to the Blizzards. In an infamous national show of sexism, arrogance, and plain disrespect, we, her fucking team, abandoned her on the ice. For seven whole minutes, she was the only person guarding our goal against the Pittsburgh Piranha's entire first line. Like total assholes, we did nothing to help. It was only when she got hit in the mask with a too-high puck and then picked herself up off the ice, proving her spirit and fortitude to our coach, that we were allowed to help our new teammate.

At the time, I hadn't disagreed with Coach Hansson; while the league already had a female goaltender in Vancouver, Rachel McCarthy, there was no guarantee that Warren wouldn't have flamed out. So we left her to fend for herself.

Now, thinking about what we did made me sick. It went against everything I stood for as a captain, as a hockey player, and as a man; you don't leave your teammates to the wolves. I didn't know how she had forgiven us after that. It was like it hadn't even fazed her. She'd let it go almost immediately. I hadn't believed her at first, but after checking in with her enough times to genuinely piss her off, I realized she was a saint. As a perpetual thank you, I'd promised to never again ask if she was sure she wasn't mad.

Still, the urge to double-check sprang up whenever she alluded to that game.

I held the tip of my tongue between my teeth as I followed Warren off the ice and down the tunnel, balancing our skates carefully on the rubber floor. We returned our sticks as we passed the rack that held them and heard the locker room before we saw the open door that led inside.

We stepped inside the circular area and split up to go to our lockers. The lockers were open, wooden cubbies that ran the perimeter of the room, interrupted only by four doors, spread out equally along the circumference of the circle. Two led to the main lounge area that the locker room sat inside of, one to the main rink, and one to the showers.

What was a large, open space felt significantly smaller with a couple dozen men—and one woman—in full hockey pads milling about. The wave of loud music and louder conversation had hit me first, but it was the second wave of potent sweat and body heat that almost knocked me out of my skates. I had never quite gotten used to the smell of a men's locker room, no matter how much of my life I'd spent in them.

Avoiding stepping on the Blizzards' logo in the center of the carpeted room, I headed toward the shower door, but instead of going through it like I was dying to, I turned on a skate at the last second and dropped down onto the bench seat in front of my locker.

Erik Berg grunted in acknowledgment beside me. I grunted back.

After Kingston left the team, along with a few other players for various reasons, the locker assignments were shuffled around. My new assistant captain, Berg, ended up to my left, taking Kingston's old cubby. Mason Frey, my old mentee, had his locker moved to the other side of Berg. But like always, he wasn't in his spot. Instead, he stood at the opposite side of the room, talking to his childhood friend, Warren. He would return to his assigned locker after Warren pulled the privacy curtain that encircled only her locker, closing the lone woman off from the group of men.

Most players undressed from the top down. But as soon as my ass hit the bench, I went straight for my skates. I had them off in a flash and splayed my toes out in my socks.

Ahh. That's nice.

Even after almost thirty years, balancing my significant weight on tiny skate blades still hurt my feet. No amount of support could completely stop the pain. But a good, warm soak could.

A moan almost escaped my throat at just the thought. Maybe I would break out of the bubble bath that my last girlfriend left in my bathroom over a year ago. Afraid that someone had heard my bubbly thoughts, I whipped my head up and around. But no one had developed telepathy in the past minute and was looking at me like I had lost my balls.

At my quick motion, Berg raised his eyebrow.

I pressed my lips together and tugged off my sweater.

He opened his mouth, but I was saved from any uncomfortable questions as Coach Greg Hansson appeared in the room.

I threw my sweater haphazardly behind me into my locker and absentmindedly undid my top layer of pads as the room quieted down, focusing on the mountain of a man that was our coach. Most would assume Hansson ran his team like a drill sergeant based on his shorn grey hair and unflinching stare that came from decades of staring down opponents while waiting for the puck to drop. And most would be right.

Coach was a no-nonsense kind of man, especially after having dealt with hockey players both as their teammate and, after his leg snapped in three places, as their coach. But while he didn't take our shit, he didn't give us any either. We all respected him, and he returned it tenfold.

Hansson clapped once, and everyone relaxed into their lockers, settling in for the foreseeable future. "Alright, lady and gentlemen, that was a good practice. I know we're only recently back from the off-season, but I need you to kick it into high gear and buckle down. If we're going to make a play for the Cup this season, I need you all in fighting shape. I won't stand for anything less. There will be no weak links on this team."

Hansson's hard gaze flicked to Little who was slumped over dejectedly in his locker, still fully dressed in his gear, then over to me. His whiskey eyes, surrounded by sun-damaged crow's feet, squinted at me pointedly. I pursed my lips.

No, I haven't had a breakthrough with Little that magically fixed his sudden desire to play like shit.

Hansson continued talking like nothing had happened, the boys none the wiser. But the woman who was trained to spot even the most minute facial variations caught on to the silent exchange. I flicked my eyes to Little. Warren followed my look, and her lips parted as understanding dawned on her face. Then a pitying look was being thrown my way.

A sharp breath escaped my nose, my nostrils flaring. I didn't need her pity. I knew I messed up, but I would fix it. My temper wouldn't get the best of me again, and I would get through to Little. I had to if I wanted him to stay on this team. And I did.

Little was a dependable player who had shown his ability to play under pressure for years. The times I'd played against him before he was traded to New York were memorable. He was a bastard to be up against, in the best way. When he was traded to our team a couple of weeks ago, I thought it was a fantastic move. But it seemed Little was determined to prove me wrong.

Of course, I wasn't the only one to notice; you would have to be blind to not see his mistakes. And Coach Hansson was not having any mistakes this year, not after the injury-fest of last season

Coach didn't have to say a thing before I was moving to befriend Little; it was obvious that he wanted me to intervene as I had done with multiple players before. From my experience, most struggling rookies just needed a mentor or a friend. And while not a rookie, I knew Little needed the same.

So I would keep coming at Little until he finally cracks open and spills his guts. Because if he didn't get his shit together fast, his future with this team would be bleak. Especially as Coach and management have been going on a trading spree, building our defenses and cutting out dead weight. But I believed Little could take this team to the next level, and I was willing to fight for him, even if he wasn't willing to fight for himself.

With a new surge of determination filling me, I turned my attention back to Hansson as he finished summarizing the schedule for the next couple of days.

"Now, for the last order of business before I pass out from the smell in here. There are a few reporters outside fishing for comments on the upcoming season. Who wants to volunteer to talk to the vipers while giving away no privileged information?"

All eyes immediately turned to me.

I grimaced at one of the only duties as captain that I disliked. But it was my job, so I stood. "I would love to converse with the fine media gentlemen and women outside."

Deep chuckles broke out around the room at my sarcasm, and even Coach joined in. "Once again, our captain takes one for the team. Can we show some appreciation for him?"

Cheering and chirps bombarded my ears from every direction.

"Hell, yeah, Cap!"

"Oh Captain, my captain!"

"We owe you a beer, Jones."

"All hail our savior!"

I smiled indulgently and patted the air placatingly, trying to calm the bunch of idiots.

It was the same song and dance. But I let them have their fun and took a bow for the room before I pushed open the door that would lead me into the pit of vipers that called themselves the press.

It took longer than I thought, but with some carefully worded and vague predictions about how the team was going to perform this season, and the occasional dodging of personal questions, the vipers slithered away, their bellies empty of any juicy drama.

At the thought, my stomach growled. Instead of finding the snack table in the players' lounge, which had undoubtedly been raided by now, or heading to the showers as planned, I turned and walked away from the room.

3

Milly

*A*s I looked around the unique room, I had to suppress the uncomfortable curl creeping up on my lips. I'd never seen an office look so much like a kitchen before. And that was saying something as one of my old *chef de cuisines* liked to drag a table into the kitchen to do paperwork in the middle of the chaos.

LaBeux, on the other hand, did the opposite and dragged the kitchen into her office. Her desk, a solid slab of stainless steel, was obviously a stolen prep table and had a mix of culinary and office equipment scattered on top. The rest of the room was a similar mess. The office was a comfortable size, but loads of cookbooks, stacks of administrative paperwork, and what looked to be a couple of crates full of kitchen equipment made it much more cramped than it should have been. Like a lot of chefs, LaBeux's training that kept her kitchen and cooking workspaces pristine didn't extend to areas outside the kitchen.

But with how much the office mimicked a kitchen, I was surprised at the mess. A half-boxed *sous vide* cooker sat sadly next to a paper shredder under LaBeux's desk. The *sous vide* cooker had obviously been used once and discarded. I wasn't surprised; while most high-end restaurants used the precision water bath to cook their protein, I doubted the athletes here would appreciate the non-charred, non-grilled taste.

But what commanded my attention most was the cutting board by the office phone on LaBeux's desk. A large chef's knife sat on the rubber board, a small basket of un-cut celery stalks beside it. I cocked an eyebrow.

Across her desk, LaBeux caught my glance. "I like to chop while I'm on the phone. Can't just be still," she explained. I nodded in understanding.

I usually just paced, but maybe I would try out her technique. A picture of me on the phone with my mother flashed across my mind, arguing once again about my career decisions, and I could practically feel the knife slicing through my finger as I suppressed the urge to yell down the line.

On second thought, I'd stick to pacing.

"So." LaBeux shifted in her chair. "Milly Chambers. I've heard of you, you know? And not just from the resume you sent in."

I hadn't sent in my resume. Fucking Thea.

"I became aware of your career while you were working in France under Marcel Janvier. A mutual friend of ours, Sophia De La Fontaine, raved about your creativity after she tried one of your dishes. It was rare. She doesn't usually do that, as I'm sure you know."

Of course. It was common knowledge that the only way you got a compliment from Sophia De La Fontaine was in a newspaper. And even then, the restaurant critic's ravings tended to be back-handed and reluctant. To hear she had liked my cooking enough to remember my name and mention it to her friend outside of an official review was a shock. "I didn't know you knew her."

"We met when she came down to New Orleans to write an article about the 'wannabe French cuisine of New Orleans.'"

"I remember that article. It wasn't negative at all."

"Of course not. I made sure to change her mind." A smug smirk flashed across LaBeux's aging face for a split second before it was gone. The kind, grandmotherly chef returned. "We've stayed in touch since, and your name has come up a couple of times, especially when you moved to the city last year."

My respect for her doubled. She'd managed to sway Sophia De La Fontaine's opinion. "I'm honored that you, and her, have followed my career." I managed to keep the bitterness out of my voice. That career was gone, along with the chef that had been able to delightfully shock one of France's best food critics.

"Yes. She was confident that you'd be working your way to your first Michelin star by now. So imagine my surprise when your resume lands on my desk months after you disappeared from the culinary world."

I gave her a tight-lipped smile. Oh, I could imagine; it would have been the same surprise I'd have had if someone told me years ago that I would end up interviewing to cook for a hockey team.

But here we were.

"I don't know why you tried out for this job, but I'm grateful we have someone like you on the team now," she said.

This was my moment. I'd had my speech prepared since she called me into her office immediately after the competition. It only had a few simple points, but I thought it was convincing. *Chef Adams' dish was just as good as mine. He actually wants the job here and is a fantastic cook. He would be a better fit for your team.*

Easy. Simple. And my way out of this place.

"And I'll definitely talk to HR about Dr. McKenna," LaBeux continued.

I paused. "What about Thea?"

"Well, since she recommended you, I'll put in a good word for that promotion she's aiming for."

I racked my brain until I remembered what she was talking about. The promotion that Thea had been talking my ear off about for months! Right. There was a position opening up for a physical therapist to travel with the team on their away games, and Thea had been working toward it ever since she'd been hired as one of the team's PTs over a year ago. Currently, she only worked with the players when they were in the city.

"You have the ability to do that?"

LaBeux's smug smirk was back. "Of course, dear. I'm friends with everyone in this arena. That old adage is right, you know. The way to a man's, or anybody's, heart is through their stomach. I could probably change the team's entire lineup with a pot roast."

Or torpedo their promotion if the person they recommended quit minutes after they were hired.

I sighed.

Looked like Thea would be getting her wish.

Damn that woman and her universe-bribing ways.

"Now, since you're part of the team, let's put your experience to use. I've got a proposition for you."

Wait. What?

A full menu overhaul? I thought hysterically as I made my way back to the kitchen through the blue-and-white painted concrete halls. Thankfully, LaBeux's office wasn't too far from the kitchen, or I would have ended up on the other side of the building in my daze.

I may have overestimated this job.

Scratch that. I definitely overestimated this job, because had I known what LaBeux had planned for me, I would have torpedoed Thea's career myself.

Instead of the regular sous position, I was now the team's creative culinary manager. I didn't even know if that was a thing or something LaBeux made up on the spot. Apparently, LaBeux was working on a journal article about sports nutrition and was traveling with the team this year to get insight on the menus of other teams. And while she was away for the majority of the season, she needed a stand-in to redo the outdated team menu, cater to the needs of the players, and basically be her when she couldn't be.

A wave of muscle spasms shook my hands, and I had to stop before I reached the kitchen doors and take a deep breath, hands clenching each other to stop the tremors.

Maybe I was being overdramatic. The job didn't seem that bad, and LaBeux was unlike any other *chef de cuisines* I had worked under. She was a relaxed chef that ran a friendly kitchen cooking nutritional food for hockey players.

I closed my eyes and tried to picture it. A fun, collaborative kitchen like the ones I'd only ever heard rumors about before. A new, exciting chance to create original dishes for an entirely unique menu. It was like a dream come true. Everything I'd ever wanted in a creative job, without all of the bullshit that came with cooking in a fast-paced, stressful environment.

Except... I opened my eyes and felt nothing.

No spark of anticipation, no cravings, and, most importantly, no inspiration.

My head was as empty as it always was these days.

I was a chef that hadn't cooked anything original in six months.

I growled under my breath. "So much for this city."

I'd thought New York would be different, the thrill of being back in the city I'd gone to culinary school in bringing new life back to me. Except it was the same as Lyon; inspiring no new ideas, just the overwhelming need to be somewhere else. But deep down, I'd always known the cities weren't the problem. Whether in one of the best culinary cities in France or in New York City, the place in which I'd invented more recipes than I could count, I had to face the truth—I was the problem.

So only three months after moving back to New York, I quit my new sous job. I suspected the *chef de cuisine* wasn't too torn up about it, considering the look on her face when I finally took off my apron after the fifty-second new dish I'd attempted was plated like a decaying piece of raw chicken on a bed of what looked like apple sauce.

I threw in the towel, literally.

Now, half a year later, the thought of cooking something I'd made and eaten dozens of times turned my stomach. Even *I* didn't want to eat my own cooking anymore.

Like the dish that won me the competition, I could only reproduce old recipes, never create new ones. I had become a passionless machine.

I suddenly wished I had my skates. The cement floors of the Snow Globe Arena tunnels, uninterrupted by seams or cracks, were the perfect surface. Build up a little momentum, and I would fly down the slick hallways, untouchable. I could circle the entire arena in mere minutes and escape this dreadful day.

Instead, I grumbled to myself and pushed open the swinging doors to the kitchen. A distant wave of discomfort and apathy washed over me at the sight of a room full of stainless steel. I looked at the counters and burners just waiting for something new to be cooked on them and felt … tired. And hungry.

"Casserole?" Adams asked as he leaned against a table in the middle of the kitchen, out of his chef whites and in a plain black shirt and blue jeans.

My mood lifted at the sight of him, and I walked up to my former co-worker. "Casserole," I confirmed.

Adams shook his head. "So easy. I should have seen it. A meal that you can bake in large batches with consistent taste. A bulk dish. So simple."

I shrugged. "You're a gourmet chef. You never go for the simple option. That's a good thing."

"Not when it loses you a job."

I patted my apron pockets, then my jeans. "Do you have a pencil and paper?"

Adams produced a tiny pen and a notepad. I flipped through the pages of recipe ideas with a bit of jealousy until I got to a clean page. That was what my notebook used to look like. Now it was as empty as my head.

As Adams watched, I jotted down an address and time.

"Here." I hooked the pen on the metal spiral and gave the whole thing back to him. "That's the address for Le Canard on Fifteenth Street. Their sous is going on permanent paternity leave. I'll let Chef Garza know you're coming to audition for the spot."

Adams' jaw dropped at Garza's name, and he looked at the notebook like it was his golden ticket. Perhaps to him, that piece of paper *was* a golden ticket. To me, it would be a death sentence. While Chef Garza was a fantastic chef and friend, he, like most of his rank and jaded experience, had a tendency to bawl out you and your family if you so much as julienned a carrot a millimeter too wide.

I was done with that. Done being yelled at by head chefs, hit in the face with spittle, and publicly humiliated. Some people may thrive on that kind of reinforcement, but I never had. And after over a decade of fighting for my sanity in loud, terrifying kitchens, I was never going back.

Then, I lost my passion, and I couldn't go back even if I wanted to.

I could tell Adams was curious why I was giving him the job tip when I could take the better-paying position myself, but he had never been one to look a gift horse in the mouth. He shot me a smile, thanked me, and was out of the double doors as if I would change my mind any moment and rip the precious paper out of his notebook.

I lifted my hand in goodbye even though he couldn't see. I'd run into him again in a year or so; I always did.

In the corner of the kitchen, Nilsen, the pastry chef, tugged on oven mitts and pulled two sheets of brownies from the ovens. Unhealthy treats in hand, he looked up as the doors swung shut, nodded at me in greeting, then went back to his brownies.

I headed down the walkway to the break room. My stomach grumbled in anticipation of the extra serving of food I'd set aside earlier. I hadn't eaten anything since I stuffed an overly sweet Pop-Tart down my throat that morning. I followed the smell of perfectly cooked salmon and … found it being devoured.

"What the hell?"

The half-naked man seated at the long table in the break room twisted his head around, his fork, full of my salmon, entering his mouth. "Hmmm?" he grumbled around the bite. His big brown eyes gaped at me like a confused puppy. My stomach overrode my usual politeness.

"What the hell?" I asked again. "Why are you eating that?"

He swallowed the bite. My eyes tracked it down his throat, the fluorescent lighting in the kitchen's break room catching beautifully on his dark skin as his esophagus contracted. Without my consent, my gaze drifted farther down over his huge bare chest, wide as a doorway, and down to the sculpted muscles of his abs, which were cut off by bulky, black pants. Knee-high white socks were pulled over the odd pants, and he wore no shoes. I pondered his socked feet for a second before his deep, grumbling voice brought my attention back to his face. His gorgeous face.

"Because I was hungry…" He drew the sentence out as if unsure if he was answering a trick question or not. He wasn't.

"Well, so am I."

Puppy eyes dropped to my chef whites then back up. His lips twitched, a hint of an adorable smile peeking through. He turned halfway in his seat. "I'm sure you could whip up your own meal."

"Yeah, I could. But I already made something for myself." I pointed to the plate of what was once a quinoa-stuffed salmon pinwheel on a bed of cauliflower mash.

He looked sharply at the plate on the table. The almost empty plate. "Oh shit."

"Yeah."

He dropped the fork to the plate with a clatter. "I'm so sorry. I thought LaBeux left this out. She always has an extra meal or two around for me."

"Or two?" I asked.

"Hey! I am a growing boy. I need to eat."

I gave him another once-over. A twice-over. I could see that. That was when I finally recognized his bulky, black pants were part of a hockey uniform. "Oh, you're a player."

It was hard to tell without the jersey. Not that I minded him shirtless. In fact, his brown skin, glistening with the traces of sweat, was making me forget that I hadn't eaten in hours and that he'd stolen my lunch. Suddenly, I was hungry for something else.

A perfect smile parted his dual-colored lips, the top one a darker pink than the bottom. I was right; it was adorable. "I mean, I like to think not. But I won't deny I've enjoyed my fair share of puck bunnies."

"What? I meant a hockey player." My brow scrunched. "What are puck bunnies?

The apples of his cheeks pushed into his eyes as he cringed. His plush mouth, framed by a close-cropped, dark beard, thinned in embarrassment. He pinched the bridge of his wide nose between his thick fingers, the move obviously unconscious. "I … never mind."

"But I want to kn—"

"So!" he interrupted pointedly, his hand dropping from his nose and his face relaxing with visible effort. "You must be new here. I know everyone in the kitchen, and I haven't seen you around. I would have noticed."

"Oh, yeah?"

The cringe returned for a split second before disappearing into the open curiosity of his defined face. "Sure. I know everyone who feeds me. You give me food and you have a best friend for life."

The last bit of irritation clinging inside of me disappeared as his mahogany eyes sparkled with innocence and pure intentions, turning him from an enormous and intimidating hockey player to a giant teddy bear who would like nothing more than a cuddle. Another grin took over his face.

I couldn't help it—the corner of my lips tugged up in answer. His joy was contagious.

"Well then. It's a pleasure to meet my new best friend..."

With a sharp jerk of his body, he turned the plastic chair he was sitting in to fully face me. The scraping of the legs against the tile floor produced a deafening screech. His face scrunched at the sound then smoothed out again into, what I was beginning to suspect was his default expression, a friendly smile.

He stuck out his hand. "Ethan Jones. But my teammates just call me Jones."

I stepped forward and shook his strong hand. Mine was just as strong from decades of knife handling, although more scarred than his from years of handling knives and hot pots and pans. A tiny spark of recognition flared at his name, but I couldn't place where I'd heard it. I hadn't been around hockey crowds much.

"Milly Chambers," I offered.

"The fantastic chef." He said it like it was my title.

I almost snorted. At one point in time, it would have been. But instead of the bitterness that always crept up at the mention of my old reputation, my smile never slipped off my face. How could it, with the beaming light that was Ethan Jones still grinning at me.

I let go of his hand and shot a wry look at the decimated plate of food in front of him.

"I must be. You seemed to enjoy my food."

I took a step back and reached around to untie my apron. With a few tugs, then a quick toss, the fabric landed in the hamper by the entrance to the break room. My borrowed coat quickly followed.

The long table that Ethan sat at took up most of the decently sized break room. He sat at the head of the rectangular table. In my black jeans and white shirt, I pulled out the chair to his right, angled it to face him, and sat.

With my new proximity to him, the scent of coconut filled my nose.

Ethan scratched at his head, and I heard a prickling sound as his short fingernails caught against the buzzed hair of his skin-fade haircut. "Ehh. It was okay. I would have preferred a steak."

He was obviously teasing, but I was too preoccupied to chuckle at his joke. I couldn't respond. Deep in my brain, gears started to churn, shedding cobwebs.

No, not steak. Pork loin—stuffed with shrimp. Placed in a bowl of seasoned rice with a honey garlic glaze.

I jumped out of my chair and rushed to the wall of lockers lining the back wall of the break room. I barely noticed Ethan grabbing my chair before it could fall over as I opened the locker I had claimed earlier, pushed aside my motorcycle helmet, and rifled through my leather jacket. The armored plates embedded in the jacket dug into my arm, but I ignored them as I pulled out the tiny notebook hidden in the inside pocket. The notebook I hadn't used since I bought it.

I took off the attached pen, opened the book to the first page, and jotted down the ingredients and measurements that were whizzing through my head. The recipe idea wasn't much, but it was something. Something new.

I finished my notes, carefully returned the notebook to its pocket, and turned back to Ethan in awe.

Ethan

Chambers looked at me with crazy in her deep-blue eyes, and I held my hands in the air. There was no threat here.

"I was kidding about the steak. The salmon is delicious. No need to write my name in your burn book."

The crazy seeped from her eyes and was replaced with confusion. "Huh?"

I nodded at the locker where she had returned her little notepad. "You obviously took offense to my joke and wrote my name down in your list of people to destroy."

A small unattractive snort escaped her petite nose, and her lips, painted bright red against her pale skin, curled. "It isn't a burn book."

Whatever intensity that had overtaken her faded slightly, her tight shoulders loosening as she strode back to the chair she had almost upended. As she once again sat, Chambers ripped the red bandana from her French-braided, brown hair, revealing a mess of blunt bangs that flopped across her forehead. She patted them down roughly then plopped her hands on top of the stainless-steel table, still clutching the bandana. She left the braid intact, though a mess of flyaways flittered around her full face.

She was obviously somewhere inside her head, her deep-water eyes looking unfocused in my general direction.

"Then what is it?" I asked tentatively.

She blinked. And blinked again as if coming out of a fog. "Oh, it's just a book to jot down recipe ideas in."

I puffed up my chest in faux pride. "So I inspired a recipe?"

She took another step back to reality. Her lips twitched. "Well, the beginnings of one, at least."

"Am I your muse now?"

She returned to the present, visibly shaking off the thoughts swirling around that brain of hers. Good. I was worried that steam would start coming out of her ears if she kept on thinking that hard. "Muses aren't real."

I cocked my head. "You don't think so?"

She nodded. "I know so."

I squinted at her.

She squinted back, daring me to challenge her. I would bet money that she was considering chucking that notebook at my head.

Silence.

My stomach was the one to break the stalemate with a growl. I patted my bare abs and caught her eyes flicking down to follow the motion. Then I remembered her look of hunger and disappointment when she came in and saw me eating her food. "I really *am* sorry about that, by the way. I wouldn't have eaten it if I knew it was yours."

She leaned back in her chair with a careless wave. "It's okay. Go ahead and finish it. I won't get mad."

Keeping an eye on her like she was looking to steal a puck from underneath my stick, I slowly picked up my fork, speared a piece of salmon, scooped up a bit of mashed potatoes that didn't taste like potatoes, and popped the forkful into my mouth. When she didn't make a lunge to grab the fork from me and stab my eyes out, I swallowed the food with a moan of ecstasy.

Now that I knew it wasn't LaBeux's cooking, it was easy to taste the difference. While not as spicy as LaBeux's food tended to be, her Cajun background slipping into everything she made, the food was full of flavors that were distinguishable on their own but worked so well together that I was going for a second bite before I finished the first.

The next time I looked down, the plate was scraped clean, and my stomach was finally full. I looked over to gush to Chambers about her talent but was brought up short by the bemused enjoyment in her eyes. She must have been watching me scarf down her food like an animal. I went to apologize for the hundredth time today, but she spoke before I could.

"I'm glad you enjoyed it. Even though it was sitting out for thirty minutes and was probably cold."

"Only a little. I tried to find a microwave but had no luck."

A look of disgust came over her face, reviving the spirit that had burst out of her when she first walked in, bawling me out. "This is a professional kitchen."

If she were a kitten, her hair would be standing on end. I bit down on my smile and echoed the conversation I'd had with LaBeux years ago. "... And that means no microwave?"

"Yes!" she almost shouted. As if realizing how crazy she seemed, her face flamed red, matching the color on her lips, and she shifted her weight in her seat.

"Well, it was amazing, even cold. I'm glad for whatever reason made a chef as good as you obviously are take a job here."

"Maybe I just really like hockey."

I searched her deep-water eyes then shook my head. "No. You don't know a thing about hockey."

She leaned forward the slightest bit, her bangs swinging sassily over her forehead. I matched her movements. "What makes you say that? The fact that I'm a girl?"

"No. The fact that you have no idea who I am, even after I told you my name."

Her lips pursed at being caught, then she grumbled, "Doesn't mean I don't like hockey."

"I guess that could be true. I actually think you'd make a great defenseman or maybe a goalie. You look like you wouldn't be horrible on skates. And you hold your weight well."

"Excuse me?"

I choked on the foot in my mouth. "No. No! I mean, your center of gravity is solid. You're balanced, and you stand firm. It would take a bit of force to knock you over. And you've got big..."

Stop fucking talking, Jones!

Chamber titled her head, considering me. Her eyes twinkled in obvious delight over my predicament. "Thighs?" she offered. She crossed said thighs between us.

I cleared my throat and didn't look at the legs encased in black denim. "Yeah. But I like them. I mean, they're good for hockey and ... stuff."

Damnit, Jones!

My face heated, and I was thankful that embarrassment wasn't as obvious on my darker skin. It wasn't like I was ogling her, but I'd gotten a good look at her when she walked in.

Even under the shapeless chef uniform and body full of tension, I could see hints of her curvy form that spoke of athleticism and a love of food. She was clearly strong, her legs and arms solid, but there was a healthy layer of fat over her muscles and stomach, softening her body and filling out her face.

Then she took off the uniform, and I was proven right.

"Yeah, well. They're not made for blades or ice. And neither am I. I don't like the cold."

My head bobbed rapidly, taking the segue. "Well, who needs hockey when you've got a talent like yours."

"I guess." The look I'd just managed to tease from her eyes returned until I could have sworn I was looking at Warren after she had let one-too-many pucks past her and was ready to put her body on the line before she allowed another one through. Chambers was a wall.

Then a crack appeared, like a damn holding back too much water.

What is going on inside there?

I continued to babble at her. "And, hey. If you ever need new inspiration for recipes, I'm here. I can even help you out with the food itself. Muse and taste tester all in one."

Chambers cocked her head, question marks flashing across her soft features.

"Milly!" The familiar voice bounced sharply around the kitchen.

As one, our heads whipped in the direction of the main kitchen as Dr. McKenna walked in and immediately locked onto Chambers.

"There you are," she said to Chambers, then noticed me, her bright red hair flinging around in her ponytail as she glanced in my direction. "Oh, hey, Jones."

"Doc," I returned with a nod.

"What are you doing here, Thea?" Chambers asked the doc.

A breath puffed out of Dr. McKenna's nose, and I braced.

One of the team's psychical therapists, Dr. Thea McKenna was as fiery as her curly, red hair and took no shit from any of the guys on the team. With her crazy mass of flaming hair framing a beautiful, freckled face and gorgeous green eyes, she'd had to shoot down countless attempts at flirting from half the players during her first week here. But she'd gained everyone's respect with her cool professionalism and, adding in the fact that she could make grown men cry with a well-hit pressure point, she was as much a part of the team as the coaches.

Though why she was in the kitchen break room, shooting her patented I-dare-you-to-tap-out glare at our new chef, I did not know, but I doubted it was anything good. Then something amazing happened—the doc's face relaxed, and the intimidating woman who I suspected liked when men cried on her therapy table was replaced by a caring and concerned friend.

"I wanted to see how the auditions went."

Milly spread her hands wide, encompassing the whole break room and the kitchen on the other side of the wall. A grin creased her face, but the crinkles around her dull, blue eyes spoke of pain rather than success. "Well, I'm still here. And it looks like I'll be staying for a while."

The grin from Chambers' face echoed onto Dr. McKenna's, but the doc's was sincere, oblivious to the falsity of Chambers'. "That's great. I was sure you'd win, but you never know."

"Sure. But your plan backfired."

"Huh?"

"Well, if you wanted to see less of me, getting me a job at your place of work was probably not the best idea." Brightness returned to Chambers' eyes as she teased her friend.

Dr. McKenna chuckled. "I guess not. But at least you're out of the kitchen in my apartment. I've already gained fifteen pounds since you moved back to the city."

Chambers gasped. "That is patently untrue. And just for that, I'll be feeding you overcooked okra for the next week."

The doctor's face took on a green tinge. "Just as long as it's not cauliflower. I still can't handle it."

"Hey. Ethan, here, seemed to enjoy my cauliflower mash."

"Wait," I cut in. "That was cauliflower? Impossible. I hate cauliflower, but that was delicious."

A hint of satisfaction flickered in Chambers' eyes, and Dr. McKenna looked at me like I was a particularly cute puppy who had managed to potty outside for the first time. "Aw, sweetheart, Milly can make literal dirt taste like ice cream. There are no dislikes with her."

"Unless you have an allergy," Chambers clarified.

I scratched at my beard, thoughts flying.

"Still, even *you* can't make me like cauliflower," Dr. McKenna said.

"Don't make me start trying again," Chambers shot back.

Fondness settled on Dr. McKenna's face. "I would actually love that."

Chamber's jaw ticked, and my eyes bounced between them like I was tracking a puck, trying to decipher the unspoken messages in their looks. I came up with nothing. Dr. McKenna's gaze flicked to me as I was studying her, and, as if realizing how soft she'd turned in the presence of one of the players she worked with, the sadistic therapist returned.

"Don't be late for practice," she suddenly snapped at Milly.

Milly took the change in attitude in stride and nodded. Then the doctor was out of the room, ponytail snapping like a whip behind her with each step.

Silence fell, then, "She was kidding."

I turned to Chambers, who was looking at my/her empty plate. "Huh?"

She gestured to the plate with a strong motion. "I'm a certified nutritionist. Nothing I make is fattening."

I hummed. "Are you sure? Because something that good can't be healthy. Not that that stopped me from eating the whole thing, but I figured a couple of extra miles on the treadmill would be enough to work it off."

She scoffed. "This is probably the most nutritious and healthy thing you've eaten all week."

"I don't know. It didn't taste like cardboard, so how healthy could it really have been?"

A horrified suspicion slowly crossed her face. "Please don't tell me you only eat brown rice, unseasoned chicken, broccoli, and sweet potatoes."

My gaze flicked to the side nervously.

"Oh, God, no. That's so sad."

I shrugged. "I mean, I eat better here, but at home, I just make the same thing. I can't cook."

"Anyone can cook."

I squinted at her, but her face was perfectly straight.

"What?" she asked.

"... Nothing. I was just waiting to see if you would whip out a talking rat and start speaking French."

Her stoic face broke into glee, and she switched to perfectly accented French. "*I don't have a pet rat, but the sentiment is true. And that movie is a masterpiece.*"

"*Je suis d'accord,*" I returned, my accent not as flawless as hers. *I agree.*

Her smile widened until my breath snagged in my lungs, taken aback. It was the first time she'd truly smiled, teeth and all. She was beautiful. Red-painted lips revealed perfect teeth, and her huge blue eyes sparkled with mirth. I needed to send a thank you gift to my old Canadian team-mate for teaching me his native language. If my horrible French got her smile lines to cut grooves that deep into her cheeks and temples, then I would speak in the foreign language for the rest of my life.

The skin of anxiety and fear had shed from her, and a confident, talented, strong woman peeked out to acknowledge me. "Well, it was a pleasure meeting you, Ethan. But I'm starving, and there's a fantastic dim sum place a block away. So…"

She stood from her chair, rounded the break room table, opened the same locker as before, and pulled out a jacket, motorcycle helmet, and some kind of canvas roll. She tucked the lot under her arm and made to leave.

"I told you to call me Jones."

She stopped halfway to the exit and turned, her deep-water eyes peeking out from her dark bangs. "No, you said your teammates call you Jones. I'm not your teammate. So I'll see you around, *Ethan*."

With that, she exited stage left.

"See you around, *Milly*," I called out after her.

Oh, I like that one.

Milly

"**M**uses aren't real," I argued for the second time that day as I plowed to a stop, toes pointed inward to slow my quad skates. My voice came out strained, and I held my side in pain, lungs heaving. Sweat ran down from my helmet and stung my eyes.

Continuing our conversation from before the suicide drills, Thea rolled up beside me, out of breath as well but not in as much pain. "How can an artist say that?"

I straightened as the rest of the girls finished their drills and dropped to their asses, sliding down the oval track that was banked like the sides of a wok with a flat bottom. Their skate-clad feet stretched out in front of them as they fought to catch their breath, and a few claps echoed down from the metal stands surrounding the outside of the track where a smattering of kids watched us.

Some of the girls brought their kids with them to practice when they had no one else to watch them after school. A few girls raised their hands in acknowledgment of the applause, but the rest were laid out flat on the track without an ounce of energy left in them.

I would have been right there with them, but looking like I got hit by a truck after just barely beating Thea at the drill would defeat the point. So I relaxed on my wheels and let out a long breath to force my lungs to slow.

"It's because I am an artist that I can say that. Passion for your craft comes from within. Sure, you can be inspired by someone, but only being able to create when you're with them?" I scoffed. "Please."

"Then how do you explain Ethan Jones?"

I chewed on my lip. "Ethan was an anomaly. An anomaly that didn't even work out."

But how I wished it did.

After I left Ethan in the break room, I skipped out on lunch to run to the store. But it was no use. Even as I stood in line with my new ingredients for the dish written in my notebook, I could already feel the inspiration draining. And with every red light I sat through, motorcycle revving impatiently under me, it drained more and more until I was in my apartment and felt like vomiting at the thought of trying to cook something new.

I ended up pan-searing the pork and shrimp like I'd done a million times before, then walking the whole thing, pan and all, next door to Thea, not able to stand the sight of it.

"But it was the first time in how long since you've had a new idea?"

"Too long."

"So what's the harm in testing this out further? If Jones could spark one idea, what's to say he couldn't do it again?"

I must have hesitated for too long. Mr. Hyde, the evil personality that was the inspiration for the "Dr. Jekyll" written across the back of Thea's derby uniform, came out, sensing blood.

"Oh, wait," she drawled, emerald eyes searching my face.

I hoped the flush from derby practice would mask the blush I could feel rising to my cheeks and throw Thea off the scent. No such luck.

"Wow, this is even more rare than you getting a new recipe idea. You have a crush."

The heat disappeared from my cheeks in a flash. I rolled my eyes.

"What?" she asked. "You think you can't have a crush?"

"Considering I'm not a twelve-year-old girl, yes."

Thea's mouth opened again but someone cut off her next comment. "Yo, Dr. Jekyll," one of the girls yelled. "We done for the day?"

Thea turned to fulfill her captainly duties. "Yep. Go ahead and clean up."

As one, the whole team moved, dragging their exhausted bodies to the cones and various equipment set up around the track. Glad for the excuse to get away from Thea's probing questions, I joined the girls and rolled over to pick up and stack the small orange cones in the middle, flat portion of the track.

"Hey, Chopkick."

I glanced over at the sound of my derby name. I hadn't picked it out, but I could agree that it fit well.

"Hey, Rockem," I greeted the tiny woman. Her full derby name was "Rockem Sockem." Her real name was … I actually had no idea.

She smiled at me, her almond eyes shifting around my head but not making direct eye contact. For a few moments, we collected cones in silence so thick even I would have trouble chopping through it. The tension wasn't coming from my end though, so I waited.

And waited some more as the team finished cleaning up and Thea called us into a group.

In the middle of the track, the team kneeled before our fearless leader. Rockem took a knee next to me and leaned back against the toe stop of her skate on the floor. As Thea began her traditional roundup of the day and plan for next practice, Rockem leaned closer to me.

I looked at her softly. "What's going on, Rockem?"

Her eyes flickered erratically over the other girls around us, but everyone was focused on our captain like we should have been. She dropped her voice. "What were your parents' reactions when you quit your job?"

I blinked. That was the last thing I expected her to ask, but I rolled with it. "Well, my mother is a professional chef too, so she didn't understand and is still a bit disappointed that I 'gave up my career on a whim,' but my father likes to disagree with her at every opportunity, so he supports me completely. That's the joy of a broken home, though. Why? Do you want to quit your job?"

A sardonic curl lifted her lips. "Yeah. But my parents are first-generation Korean immigrants. I've spent my own life trying to make them proud after all they sacrificed to make sure I had a better life than them."

Rockem was a robotics engineer, hence her name, and I couldn't imagine her family would be okay with her changing career paths after she had finished her master's only a couple of years ago. Especially if they paid for her education. If my mom had chipped in for my culinary school, she would have had a dozen more criticisms lined up for me when she found out about me "fleeing France in shame."

"I can't tell you to just quit. It's not that easy. But if your heart's somewhere else, I don't think there's much else you can do. As much as you want to please your parents, you have to be true to yourself. It may take some time, but eventually, they'll come to respect your decision and the courage it took to make it."

Thea cleared her throat and clapped, sending a sharp sound wave across the track. We snapped to attention.

"One last thing before we go." Thea paused to let the dramatic tension build. I almost rolled my eyes at the drama queen. "I got the promotion!"

The team erupted.

"Nice, Jekyll!"

"Fuck yeah, Jek!"

"Knew you would get it!"

I cheered with the team.

Well, that was fast. LaBeux must have made a fantastic meal for Thea's boss because it had only been a week since I accepted the sous job.

"Alright, alright!" Thea called out over the noise.

We settled down.

"Unfortunately, this means I'll be traveling a lot. So I have to cut my time on the team."

A wave of "aww"s rose from the team, but none had too much heat behind them. Roller derby was recreational, and we always understood that sometimes life took priority over the team. It was inevitable that some people had to quit or couldn't make it to practice or bouts. A lot of the girls only had so much free time and were only here when they could be.

Even I would have to miss a couple of bouts when they clashed with the Blizzards' home games. But I would be at practice whenever I could, even if I had just finished working a long shift. It would take some maneuvering, but I refused to quit the team. Not when it had been the only thing keeping me out of living in my bed for the six months I'd spent failing to rekindle my passion for cooking.

"We'll also have to pick a new captain who can be here more than me."

The roar that burst from the girls was less than accepting this time.

I was the loudest among them.

Two days later, I once again stood in the Snow Globe Arena and wanted to flee for my life as pastry chef Peter Nilsen scooped up a forkful of pureed chickpeas, stabbed a piece of chicken, dragged the lot through an avocado and basil pesto, then popped it into his mouth. He chewed. Swallowed.

"Good."

I wanted to stab something. I knew it was good. It had been good last night, good a month ago, and good a year ago. It was always good.

I forced a smile onto my face. "Thank you. Do you think it would go well on the team menu?"

"Maybe for some of the guys, but there are a few boys on the team who don't appreciate pureed foods. Texture issues."

"Do you have a list of the player's preferences?"

"Not written down, but there's no use trying to create something that will appease everyone.

Players get traded too often to have a menu too specialized."

There's an idea.

I hummed, and the socially shy pastry chef took my pause as a chance to escape. Nilsen nodded and disappeared around the corner leading to food storage.

Well, okay then.

I pulled out a new fork and used it to pull the ceramic plate closer to me by the rim. Nilsen had only taken a single bite before delivering his verdict. I used the side of the fork to tear off a piece of pesto-coated chicken, scooped up some pureed chickpeas, and swallowed it with a grimace.

Always the same.

The fork hit the plate with a sharp ringing.

I took out the notebook from my apron and marked out the recipe from the list of dishes I jotted down the other day. Dozens more awaited their turn on the chopping block, a hundred more than that stored in my mental Rolodex of dishes. I knew enough recipes by heart to create hundreds of menus. But nothing new. Never anything new.

I flipped to the first page of my notebook. The half-legible recipe idea from days ago stared at me in judgment. I stared back, hoping for that spark of excitement that I'd had when writing it.

Nothing.

I slapped the notebook closed with attitude and shoved it back into my apron. Then I followed Nilsen's lead and gave in to the urge I always had when in a kitchen these days—I fled.

The second I pushed open the double doors of the kitchen and was spat out into the concrete tunnels of the arena, a weight was lifted from my shoulders. It was as if I was in a fresh spring meadow. I leaned my head back and inhaled. Instead of daisies and grass, the only smells I registered were stale air and rubber. Still, it wasn't kitchen cleaner and food in various stages of cooking. I would take it.

I walked down a couple of hallways at random, getting myself lost. The concrete walls of the arena's underground were painted an icy blue up to shoulder height and white the rest of the way to the tall ceiling. My heavy-booted steps echoed around me as I veered further from the occupied spaces and found a relatively secluded hallway.

I leaned against a dual-colored wall, reveled in the silence, and ignored the itching in my fingers that begged for a cigarette. I'd started up ages ago when the stress of a particularly volatile French kitchen had become too much but quit the habit when I left for a new job. Still, the urge came back occasionally when I was stressed.

I rested the back of my head against the concrete and stared at the exposed ductwork as I breathed in the cold air.

"Come on, bud," I heard seconds or minutes later.

I straightened up from the wall and immediately found the source of the familiar voice. At the hallway intersection up ahead, Ethan Jones came into view.

My hand was already up in a wave, ready for me to call out to him, when I spotted the second person. I dropped my arm to my side and tried to sink into the wall, not wanting to interrupt.

Across from Ethan, an angry, blonde man stood with his fists clenched at his sides, an angry flush spreading up his tan face. He seemed to be on the verge of attacking.

I checked on Ethan, but he didn't look concerned about the other man's anger, though he must have seen it—it was impossible to miss.

"I'm not your bud, Jones. Just leave it," the man talking with Ethan said, his voice just on this side of growling. A dimple on his flushed cheek jumped with the flexing of his jaw, ticking like a bomb.

Ethan, on the other hand, looked as calm as a Zen master, body language open and honest, hands splayed disarmingly, and head tilted in concern. "It's my job to make sure everything is copacetic, Little. And as much as you don't want to talk to me, if you don't, your future on this team is not looking good."

Ethan's words were soft but unbending, forceful in their honesty. By the sudden slump to Little's shoulders, he knew it too. Not that he let the truth affect his anger.

I was about to turn the other direction to not eavesdrop further when Little beat me to it, storming off in my direction.

Ethan sighed, blindly watching the man rush past me, and rolled his shoulders.

I raised a hesitant hand. "Hey."

Ethan finally noticed me.

"Chambers." Ethan blinked, and I saw a hint of leftover anger as it disappeared into his big brown eyes. Ethan's usual smile broke out on his face. "I mean Milly. Hey."

He walked to me, and I met him halfway. We came to a stop in front of each other as I realized that we matched, his white sweatsuit reminiscent of my chef whites.

I watched as he gave me a once-over and recognized the same thing.

"You're official! They stitched your name onto them," he said.

I followed his gaze to my embroidered name above my left breast, then threw him a soft smirk. "And look at you! You have a shirt on. I guess there are surprises all around."

"Sorry to disappoint."

My smirk got stronger. A matching one creeping up on Ethan's face said he knew, despite my sarcasm, how disappointed with his attire choices I actually was. Silence stretched, tension filling the air as I held his playful stare. Once again, I caught the scent of coconut. Did this man just walk around all the time smelling like a piña colada?

I was the first to break our stalemate.

"So, what's that mean?" I pointed at the black "C" on his white-and-blue New York Blizzards branded hoodie. I hadn't noticed it on the clothes of any other players with their otherwise identical outfits.

He followed my finger then raised his chin, meeting my eyes with pride. "It means captain."

My brows rose. We didn't have that in roller derby. "Oh. That's impressive. I didn't know you were the captain."

"I know. You don't know anything about hockey, remember?"

My cheeks heated at his amused tone. "Hey. I know more now than I did earlier."

"Oh, yeah?"

"That's right," I bullshitted. "I asked my friend."

"And what did your friend say?"

I caught his challenging look. He knew something was off. To be fair, I tried to ask Thea, her being the obvious option to fill me in on the basics of hockey, but the bitch had just pulled up a Wikipedia page and sent me off. There was no way I was going to spend an hour reading the whole thing, so I got a questionable run down from one of my derby teammates.

In the end, I somehow knew less than I did before. But one thing stuck in my mind.

I pursed my lips then answered Ethan. "She said that if you wanted to watch a boxing match, you should go to a hockey game."

Ethan snorted out a laugh, and I had to press my lips together to fight off my answering one.

"Well?" I asked. "Was she wrong?"

"Unfortunately, no. But the league's getting better. Fighting has been decreasing every year, more so once we started drafting women. Of course, there are some Neanderthals who think the decrease is a bad thing and that we're all turning soft. But while I will agree that fighting has its purpose, overall, I'm glad it's being phased out."

"Yeah. Seems hard to play hockey if everyone's fighting all the damn time."

Ethan shot me a considering look. "Exactly. We're here for the game, not, as your friend would say, a boxing match."

"I don't know, that guy you were arguing with looked like he wouldn't mind taking a few shots at you," I said, casting a line into the water as my curiosity got the better of me.

Ethan's face turned sour, lips quirking like he'd bitten into a lemon. "Oh, I'm sure Little'd like nothin' more than to have a go at me, but I'm his captain and even he's not going to risk that. If he would only hear me out and let me try to help him, we would be getting along much better."

My mouth gaped open at his words. It had disappeared just as quickly as it poked through his basic American accent, but I knew I hadn't imagined the Southern twang. It wasn't Louisianian like LaBeux's but something softer.

Thankfully, he was looking off into the distance over my shoulder where his teammate had disappeared with annoyance and didn't see my astonishment. I quickly smoothed out my face, pushed down my delight, and cleared my throat, picking our conversation back up.

"Well, I'm sure you'll figure it out. I have no doubt you're a fantastic captain."

Ethan met my eyes again, curiosity swimming in the pools of mahogany. "What makes you say that?"

"I saw the way you were talking to that guy. You were patient and trying to help. Most of all, you were nice. People don't realize how important compassion is. And I know how to recognize a good leader. You're a good one."

I knew how to recognize a bad leader too.

A tender smile creased the corners of Ethan's eyes. "Thanks."

A hint of his accent peaked through with his sincerity, as sweet as apple pie.

Or apple sausage.

The thought popped into my head unbidden, and I paused, barely noticing Ethan's fitness watch ding.

The spark was back. My fingers twitched—not for a cigarette, but for a knife. It was as if I'd been electrified. Ingredients flew through my brain as I gazed up at Ethan. Was this his doing? What was going on?

"Shit. I have to get back," he cursed as he read his watch then walked backward away from me, waving. "See ya, Milly."

Then he turned the corner, and the swirling storm of ingredients and ideas ceased. It was as if he took them with him.

Shit. Are muses real?

I stared after Ethan as he turned the corner.

This needed to be tested. I needed to cook for Ethan Jones.

Ethan

*O*ver the decade that I'd been captain of this team, I'd never had someone as hard to crack as Little. It had been over a month since we started up pre-season practice, and he'd been a wall the entire time. Sure, a few of the guys I'd mentored or tried getting to open up had been standoffish, as was the nature of uber-masculine men, but even the toughest guy had a chink in their armor by now.

With Mick Little? Nothing.

And with Coach watching me, I couldn't afford to let Little's issues drag this team's and my chances down.

As I crossed the locker room, dripping sweat from practice, I detoured to pass by Little. He was bent over his thighs, skates and upper layers off, and was working on shedding his lower pads. I stopped in front of him, waiting for him to finish, but he never did. Instead, he shucked off his pants, kicked them behind him, then touched his bare toes as if he was stretching out his hamstrings.

I waited some more.

He stared at my skates, somehow knowing it was me even though he couldn't see past my knees. In the locker beside Little's, Ian Decker glanced between us. He met my eyes then was suddenly also busy taking off his pads.

I sighed. Say what you would about my stubbornness, but I knew how to take a hint. I turned to my locker.

As I crossed the room, I felt eyes burning through my pads and into my back.

Berg, having noticed my non-confrontation with Little, raised his eyebrows at me as I approached him. I widened my eyes at him but said nothing and dropped onto the bench in my locker.

I still felt eyes on me.

My hands went immediately to my skates. Torso bent over my thighs to reach my laces. I spoke out of the corner of my mouth to my assistant captain. "Is he looking?"

I heard nothing for a second, then saw Berg's body shift around casually toward Little's side of the locker room. "Yes. He's looking. Wait, is he…? He is! He's doodling your couple's name in his diary. I think he's going with Littones. No, wait. Ethick." The deep rumble of his voice sounded odd in whisper form.

I sat up, free of my skates, and counted on my fingers. "One, bless you. Two, our couple's name would be Jittle. Three, fuck off." With the last point, I stopped ticking off my fingers and threw up the middle one. Just to get my point across.

Berg smiled good-naturedly, his teeth, with a gap where his front right incisor should be, shining through his thick blonde beard that, were he to braid it, would make him look identical to the Vikings he was obviously descended from.

"Why are we gossiping like teenage girls with a crush?"

"Because this guy is pissing me off. Why won't he just talk to me so we can get this sorted out? He should have broken by now."

My gaze crashed into Little's. I smiled at him. He glared at me, stood, and turned his back to the room to take off the rest of his pads.

I turned back to Berg.

"Nice. Subtle, even." Berg scoffed out a laugh. "That's why he won't talk to you."

"What?"

"You're too eager, you fucking teacher's pet. Name me one person who doesn't find that perpetual smile of yours annoying."

"Milly doesn't," I said before I thought about it. *Shit.*

A hungry gleam shone across Berg's ice-blue eyes as he leaned forward, sensing the tea I was keeping to myself. His wide shoulders pushed into my personal space.

Little forgotten, I scooted back from Berg, but the frame of the entrance leading to the showers stopped my escape. Trapped. I threw him a pained smile. "Seriously, bud? I thought you didn't want to gossip like teenage girls."

A bushy blonde brow rose. "So, there's something to gossip about? Who is this Milly?"

He gave me a once-over like information was written on my practice sweater. I held perfectly still.

"Let's see…" Berg searched my eyes.

He ran a hand over his beard, and I could practically see the Sherlock Holmes hat he mentally put on. I rolled my eyes at him. His wife needed to stop making him watch true crime shows.

He began his brilliant deductions. "You haven't done anything out of routine in the past … decade. And you haven't gone clubbing without the team in just as long. It could be someone you met on the street, perhaps on the way to the store. But you haven't shown up in new clothes, and you get your groceries delivered. Hmmm. Maybe a new neighbor? No! Maybe a new coworker. Is it someone who works in the arena?"

I must have twitched, or Berg was more of a detective than I thought.

"A-ha! It is someone here. Oh, God, please don't tell me it's a reporter."

"It's not a reporter."

I paused. The response hadn't come from me.

I looked up, dread pouring over me, to see Riley Warren standing above us, a hungry look to match Berg's aimed my way. Already undressed from practice and in just her under-leggings and sports bra, Warren took a vicious bite from a protein bar. I never knew someone could *eat* smugly, but Warren managed to pull it off, smirking and chewing at the same time.

I groaned.

She knew.

"Fuck," I grumbled and collapsed inward, my shoulder pads dragging me down until I was practically disappearing into my locker. I wished to become one with the maple. Oak? Pine?

Berg whipped to Warren. "What do you know?"

Warren shrugged, too casually for me to buy. "Nothing much. Just that there's an extremely nice and attractive new team chef in the lounge who is asking for Jones."

I was gone before their heads could turn back to me, rounding the carpet seal in the middle of the locker room as I practically ran to the door of the main lounge area. I barely noticed Little as I passed by. Without any of the grace I regularly displayed on the ice, I burst through the half-open door and immediately spun around, searching the room like I had lost track of the puck and there were seconds left in a tied game. I came up empty.

The main lounge area, filled with couches and televisions, was empty of everyone except players. From my spot, I could see into the therapy and massage rooms that branched off the main room. No sign of Milly there either.

But Warren had said… Ah. Of course. Where else would a chef be?

A woman rearranged the buffet table in the kitchenette, her back to the door. She moved the basket of chicken sandwiches to the left of the ham ones, stood back to consider the change, then switched them back. She hummed, thumb and forefinger pinching her chin.

I leaned against the door frame. "No, no. You were right the first time. The chicken obviously goes on the left."

Milly whipped around, her fluffy ponytail flying through the air.

"Ethan." Her hand fluttered to her heart.

I almost copied her, my heart rate soaring at the way she had gasped my name. Images flew across my mind, pictures of her breathlessly moaning my name for different reasons. And I would give her many reasons.

With a sharp breath out, she dropped her hand and gave me a wry smile. Once again, her red lipstick was perfectly applied, the edges sharp and providing a gorgeous contrast to her deep-ocean eyes that were lined lightly in black. With her light brown bangs that cut straight across her forehead, the rest of her hair pulled back from her clear face, she looked like a classic French woman. All that was missing was a beret. Or her usual bandana that seemed to have gotten lost.

"You scared me."

Her words jolted me back. I cleared my throat, giving her my full attention. "Sorry."

She waved her hand through the air as if batting away my apology. "It's okay. But for a big man, you move silently." She looked down, and a smile creased her face. "Or maybe it's those."

I followed her sight line and found my socked feet. Clearing my throat again, I shifted my weight sheepishly.

"I noticed the other day too. Why do you just wear socks around the arena?"

I scratched at the back of my head, my skin fade prickling under my fingernails. "I swear it's not a habit. I've just gotten distracted the past few days right after taking off my skates."

A deep line creased her forehead as her brows furrowed. "Oh. I'm sorry. They said you were done with practice for the day. I didn't mean to interrupt."

"No, no. You didn't interrupt. I was just about to shower." I sniffed at my sweater and recoiled. "Sorry about the smell. I can go wash off and come back."

"It's fine. I'm used to the smell of locker rooms. And I like your socks. They're cute and they match the rest of your uniform. The blue is fun. I've looked up a couple videos of your old games. I like the white home uniform over the blue away-game uniforms. You all look like little Smurfs on the ice when you're wearing blue."

"I think we're supposed to be snowflakes actually."

"What?"

"Well, we're the Blizzards, right?"

She pressed her lips together, crinkles around her eyes, and nodded, already seeing where I was going.

I continued on. "And blizzards are made of snow. So when we do our warmup laps before games, we are a bunch of snowflakes skating in a circle. Also known as a blizzard."

Giggles slipped out of her before she slapped a hand over her mouth. It didn't do a thing to stifle her laughter though, and I joined in with a light chuckle.

"I'll have to sneak upstairs and buy a jersey to support the team during your first game. I've always wanted to be a special snowflake."

"Oh, I think you're already a special snowflake."

"Aw, thank you." Her hand rested on her heart again, this time with sarcastic gratitude.

"Of course. And they're called 'sweaters,' by the way, not 'jerseys.' Since you're a part of the hockey world now, you've got to know these things."

"You're saying I have to actually learn hockey things now?"

"Don't worry. I'll get you a *For Dummies* book."

An unattractive snort blew from her nose. If I was within her reach, I was sure she would have pushed me for that one. I was tempted to let her, to feel her hands on me, even if it was through my thick pads.

"Speaking of *For Dummies*. The reason I'm here." She moved to the side of the kitchenette, across the room from the snack table, and stopped at a rolling cart covered with finger food on shiny silver platters.

I cocked my head and followed her. The food was tiny. "I hope this isn't what you're going to cook for us. I would need about ten portions to get half full."

"Of course not. Have some faith. This is a testing arrangement. For dummies. I'm creating a new menu for the team and catering it to each players' tastes. So I need to get a feel for everybody's palates. Starting with yours, Captain."

My eyes widened. "Every single player? What happens when people get traded?"

Milly produced a clipboard from under the cart. "Then I get the new players' opinions and tweak the menu. The hardest part is getting it set up. After that, it becomes pretty self-sustainable. And to be honest, I doubt most athletes who have been on strict diets all their lives are going to want a bunch of crazy, gourmet concoctions."

I nodded, impressed, and looked over the food. I didn't recognize half of it.

"I just need you to try everything and tell me if you like it or not."

I shot her a smirk. "I thought you could make me like anything."

She answered with a smug look of her own. "Of course. But it's good to know what I'm working with first."

I reached for a tiny black square. "What's this?"

"Can't tell you. It's a blind test."

I shrugged, but before I could pop it into my mouth, a hand grabbed my forearm with surprising strength. I locked down the full-body shudder before it could run through me.

"Sorry. I've already gone over the kitchen records, but I just want to doublecheck that you're not allergic to anything."

"No allergies. I'm all good." My short, clipped sentences came out like I'd said them with a mouth full of rocks. But I couldn't help it. Just being in the room with this woman destroyed my equilibrium. And now she was touching me. I was about ready to float away in the wind. Maybe Berg was right; I *was* acting like a teenage girl—a teenage girl in full crush territory.

"Then go ahead," Milly said, dropping her hand.

I breathed in and then out, steadily and measured until my heart rate dropped a couple of points. Then I ate the mysterious black square.

This time, I couldn't control my reaction. I hummed in delight as I chewed, and my eyes fluttered closed. The black coating on the square had turned out to be dried seaweed that crunched under my teeth, the filling the expected rice, but I didn't taste fish. I would hazard to guess Cajun grilled chicken, but I wouldn't bet money on it. What I would bet money on was that I was going to love everything this woman put into my mouth. Everything.

"Good?" Milly guessed.

I opened my eyes blearily, lids heavy with satisfaction, and grinned at the proud amusement she was trying to hide, head ducked as she marked something off on her clipboard. "Very," was all I was able to get out before I reached for the next morsel, this one a tiny slider. I placed the whole thing in my mouth and was sent to heaven.

"Is that all?" I asked with a pout as I looked over the empty platters. My stomach demanded I check underneath the cart for more food, but I restrained myself for the sake of my pride.

"Yeah. That was perfect. You gave great feedback," Milly said.

"All I said was I liked everything except that soup-Jell-o weirdness, that foam thing, and that mini taco that was definitely not a taco."

She smiled fondly up at me, her doe eyes shining under the curtain of her bangs. "And that's great feedback. Thank you."

Now was my chance. We were alone, and she was buttered up by my very deserving compliments.

"How would you like to come over for food at my place?" I blurted then could have sworn I heard a record scratch in my head.

Jones, you idiot. Who asks a chef out to dinner? That's like someone asking me to go to a hockey game.

Not that I would entirely hate to be an audience member again, but not after just getting off work at an arena.

I could slap myself. But … an interesting expression was on Milly's face. I held my breath. Maybe I could pull off a win at the buzzer.

"Like a personal chef gig?" Milly asked.

What? I floundered, caught off guard. "Um, well…"

"Because I could use the money…" She trailed off, and a faraway look took over her eyes, something bitter shining in their depths.

Silence stretched.

My mouth opened and closed like a fish. A mystery sentence choked off in my throat.

"Okay. Here. Put your number in my phone. Text me whenever you're free, and I'll come over for a trial run. We can discuss the details later."

On autopilot, I took her phone, and when I finally felt like I'd woken up from a horrifying nightmare, I looked down to see myself handing it back to her, my number on the screen. I watched silently as she sent me a smiley face emoji, said goodbye, the wheeled her cart out the door.

I was left amongst the sandwiches and protein bars, a man who had lost his mojo.

"What just happened?" I asked a turkey sandwich.

This used to be easy for me, right? I'm Ethan motherfucking Jones.

Giggles broke out behind me.

I didn't even have to turn around. I ducked my hand, slapped a hand over my eyes, and growled. "Seriously? Will you stop eavesdropping on my embarrassing moments?"

Warren's giggles turned into boisterous laughter that rang through the lounge.

I sighed. Yeah, that's what I thought.

7

Milly

Four days later, with a skeptical look, the doorman let me into Ethan's fancy building. I tried to not look suspicious in my motorcycle gear as I hitched my helmet up under my arm and made my way to the shiny elevators. While I made good money, it was apparently nothing compared to a professional athlete.

The apartment building looked like a five-star hotel, all shiny marble and plush couches in the lobby. Despite his bubbly manner, I could see how Ethan would fit in with the sophisticated tenants that no doubt snatched up this prime real estate only a block from Central Park. The way he carried himself spoke of both physical and intellectual confidence. And I'd seen the way he handled the media; he could hold his own amongst the upper gentry of this city.

Not that I was going to tell him that. That would require me to admit that I'd watched a handful of his interviews last night. And maybe drooled over a revealing photoshoot he had done for a sports magazine.

Yes, I think I'll keep those details to myself.

The elevator arrived. I rode it to the twenty-fourth floor. As I ascended, I sighed. Those weren't the only details I was keeping to myself. I still hadn't told Thea I was here.

When Ethan had suggested wanting me as a personal chef, I'd jumped on the opportunity. Once again, I suspected Thea was bribing the universe, but I couldn't deny that she had been onto something at derby practice. I refused to call him a muse, but Ethan had sparked inspiration in me the other day. It was like my creativity had suddenly come flooding back after almost a year of abandonment.

I thought it had been an anomaly, but then it happened again in the arena hallway. Ideas had started flowing through me, only to be cut off the second he left. But today I was going to be in his apartment. He would have no reason to leave.

Thea would be pissed that I hadn't told her of my plan, but I was too embarrassed to say it out loud. Still, I wasn't too embarrassed to go through with it. I would do anything to keep ahold of the last of my passion that was slipping through my hands.

A woman on a mission, I stepped out of the elevator into a pale, pristine hallway and immediately found the apartment I was looking for; there were only two on the top floor. I walked to it and knocked, not allowing myself to hesitate.

"Holy shit," was the first thing out of Ethan's mouth when he answered the door.

The sight of him sent that now-familiar sparkle through me. His shocked eyes—big, brown, and kind—made the corners of my lips tick up in response. He was wearing a grey sweat-suit, and his pants hung loosely to the ground where his, once again, socked feet poked out from the hem. But my gaze caught on his chest where hard, umber skin peeked out at me from the half-zipped hoodie.

I only allowed my eyes a split second of indulgence before I glanced up to realize he was checking out my outfit too. His groomed eyebrows had risen until they hit the burgundy durag tied around his head, a bemused, pouty smile shining through his beard.

"You look badass," he said. "Is this Milly Chambers outside of work?"

I spread my arms. The steel-plated leather jacket hindered my full wingspan a bit, and the motorcycle helmet that I was using as a make-shift purse to hold my knife roll unbalanced me. But I tightened my core and let Ethan get a good look as satisfaction poured through me. "Yes, it is. And thank you for calling me badass. I usually get 'suspicious.'"

His head cocked. "I can see that."

I deflated, and my arms dropped to my sides, defeated.

He chuckled. "But I'll still let you in." He opened the door wider, stepped aside, and held out an inviting arm.

A question that had been tickling my brain since he texted me his address floated to the forefront of my head as I stepped over the threshold and ended up in a dark and minimalistic penthouse apartment that was the epitome of a bachelor pad. "Isn't twenty-four your hockey number?"

Ethan followed beside me.

"Sure is. It's my lucky number."

"Why?"

From the entryway, I could see the whole open-plan apartment. The living area in the center of the main floor was entirely taken up by an enormous grey couch that looked like three full beds arranged into a horseshoe, facing a towering entertainment center on an exposed brick half wall. I squinted at the television playing at a low volume. Soccer commentary? Seemed an odd choice for a hockey player.

To the right of the television, massive windows took up the rest of the back wall until they were cut off by what I assumed was a guest room or office. On the other side of the entertainment stand, a large wall blocked off the majority of the penthouse with a door that had to lead to the main bedroom. A fairly impressive home gym was set up against the corner behind the couch, and, with a look up, I found a maze of exposed ductwork intermixed with shiny wood beams.

I blew out an impressed breath. The empty space in the penthouse alone was worth millions of dollars in this city.

If I had to pick one word to describe the place: oversized.

He's big, but he's not a giant, I thought incredulously before my brain came to a screeching halt as Ethan moved past me and I finally got a view of the right half of the apartment.

"Holy shit! Now *that's* a kitchen."

In a trance, I walked into the spotless kitchen. As much as I disliked the stainless-steel, clinical hell of professional kitchens, I loved a homey, personal one. And like the rest of his apartment that I could see, Ethan's kitchen was definitely homey.

The grey cabinets that matched the rest of the monochrome color palette of the penthouse and the dark marble counters would usually feel too dark for my taste, but the enormous island topped with a solid slab of light butcher block warmed up the space, giving it a whole new feel. The east-facing windows on the back wall let the painfully bright 8 a.m. light in. The beams bounced off the steel appliances and subway tile backsplash, calling to me.

"Thanks," Ethan said. He paused. "Do people have reasons for their lucky numbers other than pure superstition?"

I barely remembered what he was talking about but answered him absently as I inspected his pristine stove. I opened the oven and inhaled deeply. "Sure," I said, leaning farther into the oven. My voice echoed around me. "My lucky number is thirty-seven because of the symmetrical asymmetry."

"Wouldn't that make it your favorite number, not your lucky number?" A thread of amusement was woven through his question.

I took my head out of the oven to see what was so funny.

Ethan met my gaze head-on, lips pressed together in a faux-deadpanned look. His brow rose in question, and I squinted at him. He may not be smiling—odd for him—but I saw the humor in his eyes.

"Maybe," I conceded, still searching his face. I found nothing that gave away what he found humorous and gestured to his oven that didn't have a single crumb in it. "You have a very nice kitchen. Do you seriously never cook, or do you have a professional cleaner?"

"Both."

I hummed. "I wasn't sure when you first told me, but now I believe you. I bet you only use three things in here—one pan for chicken, another for veggies, and a pot for rice."

A guilty but not apologetic shrug. "You forgot the blender for smoothies."

"That begs the question of the kitchen, though. Why get an apartment with such a huge one if you never use it?"

Ethan's pouty mouth pulled up into a predatory smirk. "I'm holding out hope that one day a woman will make good use of it."

My breath hitched, caught in my lungs, and I was suddenly very glad that everything in this place was sized for a lion because the colossal island separating us was the only thing that stopped me as I took an instinctive step toward him. Ethan clocked the step, but I played it off by resting my hands on the counter as if I had not just thought about climbing over the stupidly huge island and wrapping my legs around his waist. My nails dug into the butcher block.

No, Milly.

I scraped my professionalism out of the gutter my libido had thrown it into and forced a wobbly smile onto my face. "Well, you have me in the meantime. So why don't we get started?"

Ethan blinked. "Sure."

"To be honest, I've never been a personal chef before, but I know what you like and your nutritional needs, so I don't think you'll be disappointed."

"Your food could never disappoint me, Milly."

My back tensed, and like someone had flash-frozen me, keeping my professionalism was suddenly as easy as breathing. No, most people were never disappointed in my cooking. The only one consistently disappointed was me.

"Do you mind if I rifle through your drawers and fridge to see what I'm working with?" I asked stiffly.

He waved a hand, encompassing the kitchen, pulled out a stool from the island, and took a seat. "Go for it."

It only took opening the first three cabinets for a disturbing pattern to emerge. As I had said, I knew Ethan's nutrition regiment and knew that he ate four protein-and-carb-packed meals a day when training—less on rest days—but this was ridiculous. I turned back to him, eyebrows furrowed.

Ethan's semi-permanent smile had gained a teasing cut at the corners of his lip as if he knew what I was thinking. I must not have been the only one to have done this. But instead of tired and irritated, Ethan looked almost anticipatory of the scolding he knew he would get from me if this pattern persisted.

I side-eyed him as I opened the last of the cabinets and then made my way to the double fridge that was wider than I was tall. I was almost afraid to open it but took a deep breath and persevered.

"Ethannn," I dragged out his name as I let the fridge door swing closed.

He held up his hands in defense, and I snorted out a laugh that was quickly cut off.

What the hell?

How did this man break my moods so fast? One second, I was lamenting to myself, and the next I was laughing. I felt like I had emotional whiplash. And he hadn't even said a word. My shoulders had relaxed without me noticing, untucking from my ears as if they have never been there. As if my hackles had never raised at his innocent comment.

I wasn't sure if he recognized the mood shift and adjusted accordingly or if his naturally friendly disposition just lightened everything in the room, but I knew one thing—I was right about him; he must be an amazing captain. Instead of fighting the shift, I rolled with it, surprised to find myself this happy while standing in a kitchen. That hadn't happened in far too long.

Embracing the light-hearted atmosphere, I leaned against the enormous fridge and shook my head at Ethan who had rested his chin on his hand, ready for whatever I came out of the gate with.

"Honest question; are you a robot or some sort of cyborg that runs on grilled chicken? Because that's really the only thing that makes sense here."

And it was the only option. Or he had no tastebuds. But I'd seen his reaction to my cooking. Back to cyborg it was. A cyborg that ran on chicken, a few varieties of carbs, vitamins, a handful of spices, frozen vegetables, and non-alcoholic sugar-free beer. Because those were the only things Ethan Jones had in his enormous kitchen. I was inexplicably glad that he had the beer, even if it wasn't the fun kind. Maybe he knew how to cut loose sometimes.

"I don't snack."

"Do you also not have fun?"

He chuckled. "I play a *game* for a living. Of course, I have fun. Just not usually with food. Food is fuel."

I shook my head in despair. Even at the worst of my creative rut, when I basically subsisted on frozen dinner meals, I'd never stopped loving food. "Dear Lord. That's just so sad. We have to fix that."

"By all means. If anyone can make me love food, you can, darlin'."

Heat flooded me at the southern term of endearment, and a shy smile tugged at the corner of my lips. A bubbly feeling started up in my gut. Then, as fast as the heat had come, it drained from me until I felt as if I was in the middle of a snowstorm.

Oh, shit.

I stared across the island at Ethan in dawning horror.

I knew I liked him—it seemed impossible not to with that smile of his that made you feel as if the sun had found a hole in the clouds on a rainy day and was shining down on you in one perfect beam. But I had thought it was friendly.

Right. Because friends wax poetic about their friends' smiles. Come on, Chopkick.

I flipped myself off in my head. Hindsight and all that.

But I didn't have time for those kinds of feelings. Not right now, and not with my potential muse.

Damnit! He is not my muse!

I rounded the island with sudden determination and came to stand beside Ethan. With him sitting down, I was finally the same height as him. I met his questioning eyes with determined ones and held out a hand.

Without question, he placed his hand in mine and allowed me to pull him up. I wouldn't have been able to move him without his permission and assistance.

"Where are we going?"

"Grocery shopping."

Ethan

"What about Vespas?" Milly asked, looking over her shoulder at me as she walked ahead, her gait faster than I expected.

"Nope."

On the chilly New York sidewalk, Milly stopped dead, turned to face me, and shook her head and disappointment like she had when she discovered the contents of my kitchen.

"And I thought your diet was sad. But this … this is devastating."

"Even if the league *did* allow it, I still wouldn't have gotten on your motorcycle. I'm not trying to get smeared across the street."

She rolled her eyes good-naturedly and flipped her hair over her shoulder as she spun and continued her brisk walk. I put a dash of pep in my step to catch up to her but stayed a half-beat behind to watch the way her loose hair swung across her back with each stomping stride of her black boots. It was the first time I'd seen her hair out of a braid or ponytail, and I was mesmerized by its movement, waves of brown shot through with natural highlights that jerked with each step, just as sharp and militant as Milly.

Her curtain of hair shifted as she glanced at me again. "We would only have been going a couple of blocks."

"Nah. I wouldn't even travel a foot on a motorcycle."

She pursed her lips at me, and I grinned back.

I couldn't seem to keep them off my face around her. Even when she was obviously thinking about something dark or not in the mood, just being in her presence made the corners of my mouth pull up.

I may have the reputation of being the nicest person on the ice, but this much joy was odd even for me. Our destination came into view after the next turn, and I caught Milly by her upper arm, afraid she would stomp right past it. As if made of water, she flowed with my slight movement and turned to the store as if knowing where I was going to direct her before I said anything.

We entered the grocery store, and I shivered at the warm blast of air. It was just getting chilly in New York, but my black Texan ass didn't do well with the cold. Back home, the weather would still be in the nineties.

As the door shut with a jingle behind me, Milly stopped in the entryway and looked over the store as if memorizing the layout. I got the feeling she could tell me where every speck of food in the store was better than I could. And I shopped here all the time. Again, before I could direct her, she was off, but her chunky movements from outside were replaced with long, fluid, strides.

My comment about her in ice skates from when we first met came back to me. She wouldn't be bad in them.

I grabbed a shopping basket as I passed the rack and caught up to her. She circled the store in the opposite direction I would have, starting with perishables, but knew exactly where she was going. I followed as the basket in my hand grew heavier.

"I have coconut oil," I said.

"Is it in your bathroom?"

"...Yes?"

"Then it's not for cooking." She tossed the jar into the basket and continued on, marching through the aisles like she was invading the store.

My smile had yet to leave my face, and my cheeks gained the pleasant ache of thoroughly used muscles. I loved a woman on a mission.

Humming along to the soft music coming from the overhead speakers, I trailed her around the meat section where she only got one portion of some kind of fish and no other protein. She must have planned to use the pounds of chicken I had in the fridge. But wait...

"Is that enough?" I asked.

She looked at the fish she'd placed carefully in our basket. "According to the team nutritionist, that's enough for you."

"What about you?"

Her eyebrows furrowed, and I knew the frown line of her forehead was popping under her bangs. "What do you mean?"

"What are you going to eat?"

Her harshly confused expression eased up but didn't disappear. "Nothing. I'm your personal chef, Ethan. I just cook for you, not myself."

I deflated like a leaky balloon, disappointment escaping me in a silent wheeze.

I knew Milly didn't see my interest in her. If she had, she would have assumed my invitation from days ago was a date, not an offer to hire her. But I'd been holding out hope that she was just missing it. I didn't want to think that she was ignoring my interest on purpose, but it might have been time to stop deluding myself.

She couldn't see my feelings for her because she didn't return them.

Well, shit.

Usually, this wasn't a big deal. I'd had my fair share of girlfriends and flings in the early days of my career, and I played the dating game just as well as I played hockey. But a year of being single must have been getting to me because I had a feeling that this rejection wasn't something I would be able to shrug off as easily as the others.

Maybe it was time to head over to Kingston's house and decimate his full-alcoholic beer stash as I kicked his ass in an Xbox tournament. We hadn't done that in a while; especially not with the first game of the season in two days.

But it was only the beginning of the season. *A beer or two couldn't hurt, right?*

The second the thought crossed my mind, I beat it away.

Yes, it could hurt. It could hurt a lot.

I wouldn't let this rejection affect my game or distract me. I couldn't afford it. At my age, any deviation from my routine could be my downfall. So I was sticking to the rules that made me one of the best forwards and captains in the league.

I would just have to get over Milly without the help of alcohol. It shouldn't be too hard. Or it wouldn't have been if I hadn't just hired her to come over to my house twice a week and cook for me. On top of that, I was sure to see her around the arena occasionally.

For once, I wished my rules about alcohol during the season were less strict.

Biting a corner of her bottom lip, Milly considered me from under her bangs.

"Well, maybe I can make an extra plate for myself while I'm over if you would like company every once in a while."

Her words reflated me, pumping me so full of helium that my voice raised a few octaves as I grasped at the straw she was offering. "It's a date," I blurted.

Pop.

Her jaw dropped open and mine clenched.

Seriously, Jones? What kind of idiot are you?

The ghost of Warren's laughter rang through my ears, and I blamed it on Milly. This woman had taken all of my game and flambéed it to a crisp. All I had left were the burnt remains of what once was my ability to pull any woman I wanted.

"I mean—" I started to backpedal but cut myself off.

There was no use; the veil over Milly's eyes that blinded her to my interest in her had lifted.

I braced, looking resolutely over her head and into the abyss of the cursed deli section. This was going to hurt.

"Oh," Milly breathed out.

I clenched my jaw.

Silence reigned until I forced my mouth open with a creak of bone hinges. "Sorry."

Someone had shoved sandpaper down my throat.

My apology wasn't about having feelings for her, but about making her uncomfortable with them. Unfortunately, I could barely look Milly in the eye, let alone expand on my apology. Words had escaped me.

The need to back away, making myself smaller and less of a threat, was strong. I barely held off, keeping my feet glued, shoulders forward like a defenseman was flying across the ice to break through me and steal my puck.

"Ethan," Milly said softly, and I refused to tilt my head down the few inches to meet her eyeline.

The rejection was painful enough; I didn't need her pity as well.

"Ethan," she said again, her voice insistent.

I dropped my stubborn chin an inch, but not enough to see past her fluffy bangs.

The sound of heavy boots and then a squeeze on my forearm sent electricity through my limbs.

My head dropped like my string had been cut and my eyes crashed into the sparkling, searching gaze of Milly Chambers.

For the second time in as many minutes, my heart soared, given wings by the confusing chef.

Because those eyes, along with the slight smirk, weren't ones of rejection.

Her hand loosened then ran down my forearm until it dropped back to her side. The grumble in my chest felt startlingly like a purr. I should be ashamed of the things I would do to get this woman to touch me again. I wasn't.

Then another detail hit me.

That wasn't the look of newly realized and curious attraction. The forward tilt of her head combined with the way she bit into her apple-red lips spoke of known desire.

My breath hitched. Was it possible? Could Milly be just as gone on me as I was on her?

I opened my mouth, words finally returning to me, and a man as large as me wedged between us, cutting off my view of Milly.

"Holy shit! Tank! No way!"

A muscle in my jaw ticked, and I cringed internally at the nickname I'd been saddled with for my whole career. But I tucked away my irritation and grasped the dark-skinned hand the man had thrust between us. His hand clamped down, and he pulled me into a bro hug.

I met Milly's eyes over his shoulder in silent apology as we slapped each other's backs before I stepped back from the fan, releasing his hand.

"I'm a huge fan," the man said.

"Thanks, man."

"Sucks about Kingston. Didn't see that one coming. The team won't be the same without him."

By the time I had exchanged a few more pleasantries with the man and posed for a picture, Milly had snuck another portion of fish into the basket I was still holding and was wandering off into the produce section. I jogged after her.

"Sorry. It's part of the job, you know?"

Milly nodded absently as she studied a head of lettuce, and I was glad she didn't seem angry. In fact...

I squinted at her, waiting. I didn't have to wait long. Her lip twitched up again as she kept the lettuce and continued through the store, the basket at full capacity.

Was she... Was she *laughing* at me?

I shook my head as I caught up to her again. It seemed like I would be chasing this woman for a while longer.

I came to a stop beside her.

She held up a stalk of Brussels sprouts.

"Do you like Brussels sprouts? Some people say they're subpar cabbages, but I love them."

I thinned my lips at her, not buying her innocent act for a second.

The corner of her lips spasmed, clearly remembering what the fan had said to me.

I didn't respond to her question. She didn't need my opinion; like Dr. McKenna had said, Milly could make you like anything.

She nodded. "You're right. It's not fresh enough."

She was determined to keep her smile to herself. She either didn't want to offend me, or she wanted to hold on to the humor to needle me with later. From the few hours I'd spent with her, I knew the correct answer. But I didn't want to wait for her jokes later, I wanted to crack her and bring out her rare laughter now.

"...always wanted to build a greenhouse to grow fresh herbs, but I've never had the space," Milly was saying, putting down the stalk of Brussels sprouts.

I couldn't take it anymore. "It was over a decade ago."

Her blue doe eyes blinked at me.

"Tank, my nickname. My high school teammates gave it to me fifteen years ago and—"

At the nickname, another giggle broke free from her, cracking her face from the picture-perfect blank look. Her bangs shook with the tremble in her chest. I made a valiant effort to not look at what else shook with her laughter.

"It's a sports thing," I defended myself.

Through her laughter, she waved me off with a flapping hand, then managed to pull herself together. "Oh, I know, I know," she said, only one more giggle escaping her. "But 'Tank?' Really? It's a little cliche, no?"

I shrugged and flicked my eyes to the floor. "It was originally to make fun of me. I'm not naturally this bulky. It takes a lot of effort to keep my muscle mass up. I was a scrawny kid in high school, the runt of the family, and my teammates weren't the nicest."

It wasn't like I was the smallest kid on the team at the time, but with my three older brothers already massive by eighteen, I was obviously the odd one out. When you add in the fact that I was the only black kid on the hockey team in a state where football ran supreme, it wasn't only my family that I stuck out from.

In a snap, Milly sobered. Then her lips quirked up savagely. "Well, look at you now. Did any of your shitty teammates make it to the NHL?"

"No."

"Of course they didn't. Because anyone who wastes their time and energy bullying others when they could be practicing doesn't have the discipline to make their dreams come true."

I scratched at the back of my head as I stared at the woman with an armful of produce. I'd never considered that.

"And don't worry about the nickname. It's uncreative, sure. But I've heard a million worse ones."

"Oh, yeah? Are there a lot of nicknames in the kitchen? What's yours? *Petite cuisinère?*"

Mock offense took over Milly's face. "So now *I'm* the talking, animated rat?"

I held up my free hand in case she was about to chuck the head of lettuce at me, but she just scoffed, not fully hiding her smile, and turned back to her produce. I dropped my hand and followed her with the basket, beaming in delight as she went on a mini rant.

"And 'little chef?' Not only am I not small at all, I'm pretty sure I'm older than you."

"Done?" Milly asked from the stove without turning around.

I was surprised that she hadn't jumped at my sudden arrival like she had in the lounge's kitchenette, but my loud, heaving gasps must have given away my presence.

"For now. Please tell me you have food for me."

Because if she didn't, I would have to chew off my own arm. As small as my home gym was, it was stocked with the best equipment, and the workout I could get in my living room was as intense and effective as what I could achieve at a regular gym.

At my desperate plea, Milly turned around to find me leaning against the island and watching her cook.

Immediately, I clocked the way her gaze dipped to my torso, my abs peeking out through the low-cut muscle shirt I'd changed into when we got back to my apartment. If I flexed a little to carve out the lines of my obliques, well, no one could prove it.

Nor could anyone prove that lust flashed across Milly's face, hungry and intense, but I knew it was there.

Just as I knew that she was not just attracted to me physically. I hadn't made up the looks in the grocery store. Milly wanted me just as much as I did her. But she hadn't brought up the moment or made any advance in the hours since, so I backed off, happy to take it at her pace.

There was no need to rush when you had already snared your prey, especially when they had snared you right back.

Milly cleared her throat, dissipating the starving look in her eyes, and gestured to the fish on the stove with a spatula.

"Can you wait a bit for this fillet, or do you need something now?"

I sat on an island stool and folded my hands on the butcher block like a schoolboy. "I can wait. I'm very patient, you know."

She squinted at me.

I smiled back.

Suddenly, Milly stepped back, and I watched in confusion as a spark seemed to go off in her cerulean eyes. Her spatula twitched, and she jerked back to the stove.

I opened my mouth to ask if she was okay, then shut it as she almost sprinted the short distance to the fridge where the meals she had prepped for me while I was working out waited.

She dug past a wall of glass containers, and I bent over to catch a glimpse of the meals that waited for me in the coming week. I hadn't caught much except the smell of cooking chicken and veggies while I was doing my lifts, but I knew whatever she made would be good.

Milly pulled the top half of her body out of the fridge, one hand holding half a head of lettuce, and skipped back to the stove.

I could recognize a person in flow when I saw one, so I let her do her chef thing while I got up to retrieve a glass of water, then buried my nose in my phone.

Thirty minutes later, I looked up as Milly set down a plate in front of me and joined me on an island stool with an identical plate.

"I thought it would just be a normal fillet," I said as I looked at what was definitely not a fillet on my plate.

She shrugged wordlessly.

I hummed before taking my food off my plate with my bare hands. The lettuce wrapping crunched under my hands as I picked up the large, burger-shaped food, and I wondered what was inside. It must have been the fish, but I couldn't see inside the lettuce. The only smell I could discern was something spicy.

I held it up slowly. Milly's eyes tracked the food like she had never seen it before, let alone made it.

I took a bite and ascended to another plane. Rice, fish, and chipotle sauce burst across my tongue, more complex and delicious than anything I could make with the same ingredients. The lettuce stole some of the spice from the chipotle sauce that I knew Milly had to have made from scratch because I didn't have any, and we didn't buy a bottle. Every flavor complemented and enhanced the others.

"Dear Lord, this is amazing," I said on a moan through the mouthful of food.

"Thanks," Milly said, sitting down with an excited smile. "It's a new recipe."

Milly

"**N**ow what?" I asked the empty arena kitchen as I glared at the two dishes in front of me.

One was a perfect recreation of the turkey-wrapped faux sushi creation that I made Ethan days ago, the other... Let's just say, turkey balls and couscous weren't supposed to look like that.

So the experiment at Ethan's had worked. I made something new for the first time in almost a year. *Yay. Great*, I thought acidly. Except for the fact that it had failed spectacularly. Because the minute I left his home, on a mission to cook up a storm in my kitchen, all the creative energy flowed out of me like a freshly tapped keg. I'd forgotten about that part. You know, the part where I needed Ethan to feel like the chef I once was, who had ideas spinning through her head like a hurricane, just waiting to pick one out and use it to create the most amazing dish you have ever seen.

Now, I couldn't even make turkey balls without burning them to little crisps. And don't even get me started on the couscous. It was supposed to be simple; a tiny variation on an easy recipe that I'd made dozens of times.

I looked at the mess of a dish that looked like a toddler had clapped charred dirt and mashed potatoes between their hands and plated it. The lettuce wrap, on the other hand, was exactly what I'd made for Ethan. The recipe had been added to my mental Rolodex where it would stay for the rest of my life.

If only I could do it again.

But maybe I could.

I considered the wrap before me.

All I needed was Ethan, right? If my experiment was to be replicated, I just needed him in the room while I cooked. And any new recipe I made with him would be forever in my memory bank.

Maybe that wasn't a terrible idea.

A concern tickled the back of my brain, but I shrugged it off.

"That looks great." LaBeux appeared by my side, and I almost jumped out of my chef whites.

When I got my heart rate under control, I gave my boss a short nod of thanks.

"But that one…" she trailed off as she looked over the bowl of Mediterranean couscous topped with turkey meatballs.

I winced. "Yeah, that one…"

"May I?" LaBeux asked.

I dug out a clean fork from my apron and handed it over. She cut off a corner of the square lettuce wrap with the side of her fork and popped it into her mouth. Ecstasy took over her face.

"That's darn good," she said, her New Orleans accent drawing out the words.

I offered her a tight smile. "Thank you."

LaBeux looked at the mess of a dish in the other bowl.

I shook my head.

With Southern grace, she set the fork down, not going for a test bite.

Good call.

LaBeux looked over the empty kitchen pointedly. "You know you're off shift, right? The food is out for the end of the game, and nothing else needs to be cooked. You're good to skedaddle. Go home. Or stay and watch the end of the game if you want. There's only one period left, and we're up by two."

I gladly cleaned up and then took the chance to flee from the kitchen, but I didn't go home to review my derby playbook like I'd planned to this morning.

It was time to see what this hockey thing was about.

"Oh, shit," I whispered as I walked through a door and ended up in a tunnel, the sounds of cheering and screaming echoing off the blue concrete walls before being absorbed by the black rubber flooring. I cringed at the volume. I didn't know where I was, but I was not supposed to be there. The wall of sound came from the brightly lit end of the tunnel, so I turned in the opposite direction.

"Milly?"

I paused mid-stride, barely hearing my name over the deafening crowd outside the tunnel, and turned to see Thea pushing off the wall she had been leaning against. She was dressed in a fitted black-and-blue New York Blizzard tracksuit and sneakers—her uniform when she was on duty as one of the team physicians.

I immediately bounded up to her, relieved to see anything familiar in this hell maze.

"What are you doing here?" she asked.

I looked around the brightly lit tunnel that smelled of sweat and rubber. "I have no idea. I don't even know where 'here' is."

Thea's smile pushed her freckled cheeks into her emerald eyes, and she walked toward the noisy end of the tunnel, waving for me to follow. I cautiously did, her swinging, red ponytail guiding the way.

"This is where you are."

At the edge of the tunnel, the light became blinding, a hundred industrial lights reflecting off the white ice rink. Tall glass panels rose before me, circling the rink and protecting the audience that roared as streaks of white and red battled across the ice, a black circle ping-ponging between the players. The two team benches in front of us partially obscured our view of the ice.

I looked up, and my mouth dropped open. I'd never been to a professional sports arena before, and I was taken aback by the size. In comparison to what must be thousands of audience members, I felt like an ant.

"Wow," was the only thing I could say.

Thea looked over the arena with me. "I know, right? It dwarfs our derby track ten times over."

Not that that was hard. A kiddie pool could dwarf our rink.

"So, did you ever learn the rules?" Thea asked.

My cheeks heated in shame.

"Really? Girl." Thea shook her head.

"Well, since my hoe of a best friend won't help me out because she likes to see me embarrassed in front of the hockey players, I haven't been able to find the time." It was a lie—the time part, not the hoe best friend part.

"I guess you *have* been busy, what with your new job and all."

Right. Because it was so hard reproducing dishes that I could make in my sleep, I thought with vicious sarcasm.

Thea's soft look of understanding tugged at my heartstrings.

"About that. I actually have two new jobs," I blurted out.

Thea's brows furrowed, and she leaned forward like she wasn't sure she heard me right over the noise of the rink. "What?"

I cupped my hand over my mouth and spoke into her ear. "I took your advice about Ethan."

"You tested it out? Did it work?"

"Yes! I cooked for him. And guess what." I paused for dramatic effect, drew back from her ear, and held my arms open. "I made something new!"

I caught Thea as she barreled into me and hugged me for dear life.

"That's amazing, Milly. I'm so happy for you."

My heart raced with excitement just remembering the feeling. My plan could actually work. Sure, it wasn't what I pictured when I moved back to New York with the plan to get my passion back, but I also didn't think it would take this long either. At this point, I would take what I could get.

And I like Ethan. He was fun and nice. Cooking for him wouldn't be a hardship.

Thea drew back from our hug. "Wait. Where did you cook for him? In the arena kitchen?"

"No. And that's the best part! He asked me over to cook for him, and now I'm his personal chef. I'm going over to his house twice a week to meal prep for him. I mean, I doubt he'll be there every time I cook, but when he is, I'm going to make so many new recipes!"

I about danced in my boots.

Thea's ginger eyebrows scrunched. "He asked you over? Are you sure he wasn't—"

An ear-piercing alarm shook the arena. The audience erupted into cheers. The Blizzards' players on the bench jumped to their feet, fully blocking our view of the rink. Thea's head snapped up at the sound, and she let out a sharp whistle. I cringed back then whipped around to see what the hell had happened. The answers were found on the jumbotron above the ice. Ethan had scored a goal and was playing air guitar on his hockey stick beside a goal net.

I clapped with the crowd and watched as Ethan celebrated with his teammates, patting them roughly on his shoulders and smiling as widely as a Cheshire cat. Even in video form, his attitude was infectious, and I found my face stretching into a grin along with his, a soft feeling invading my chest at his joy.

I shook my head at how he was able to turn my mood around on a dime. The man must have been some sort of witch, and I was extremely glad for it.

He was the happiest man I'd ever met, mouth stretched into a permanent grin at all times, and I wanted to—

I froze, my hands lingering in the air mid-clap.

I wanted to kiss those smiling lips.

Shit.

My palms twitched with the need to slap myself, but Thea was worried enough about me. Suddenly hitting myself would be the final straw. I would undoubtedly be in a mental hospital by midnight.

Maybe that was where I needed to be, actually. Because who forgets they're attracted to someone?

Especially someone as sexy and charming as Ethan fucking Jones?

I wasn't usually this stupid, but with the excitement of my new plan and the resuscitation of my almost-dead passion, I had other things on my mind.

I studied the celebrating team on the jumbotron, easily picking out Ethan among the crowd of players on the ice with unerring accuracy. It was as if my eyes were drawn to him.

My lips twisted.

I may have to finally accept it—he was my muse.

And there was the kink in my plan.

Because if I was using Ethan to kickstart my imagination, I couldn't act on my attraction to him. I already felt uncomfortable with the notion of using someone to inspire me like some kind of parasitic vampire, feeding off Ethan's passion.

I couldn't also sleep with him, could I?

Could I?

I watched absently as the players on the ice broke apart and returned to the middle of the ice, giving me the perfect view of the back of my … muse.

On his white, snowflake uniform, his last name stretched across his shoulders in black, his lucky-slash-favorite number sitting underneath.

"Kingston?" Thea suddenly called out beside me, bringing me out of my head.

I turned to follow her enthusiastic waving and found a man in jeans and a brown leather jacket walking through the tunnel.

He spotted us—not hard with Thea's red hair glowing under the fluorescent light like a glow stick—and adjusted his trajectory.

"Hey, McKenna. Nice to see you again. And I'm retired, so I think it's about time to call me Sebastian." The man's voice was soft but strong, and he gave off the vibe of a veteran soldier, always keeping an eye on everyone and everything around him.

I half expected a knife-wielding ninja to drop down and try to do battle with him. I would have put a hundred bucks on Sebastian, but Thea's next comments destroyed my soldier theory.

"Right. So, *Sebastian*, how are you here? You're not part of the team anymore," Thea said playfully with no indication that she wanted to have the man thrown out of the arena for trespassing into a staff-only area.

"Hey. I basically ran this team for years. I just walked through the doors like normal, and no one stopped me. Although, it is weird to be here as a spectator and not on the ice."

Sebastian looked over our shoulders toward the rink, a longing look in his grey eyes.

"I saw you on the jumbotron. Why are you in the stands and not a private box?" Thea asked. "You about caused a riot."

Sebastian shrugged. "They're special seats to my family."

Thea's face creased in confusion, but if Sebastian saw it, he chose not to elaborate. Instead, he turned to me.

"Sorry. Hello. I'm Sebastian Kingston."

"Milly Chambers," I introduced and took his offered hand.

As we shook hands, a gleam of recognition sparkled in his eyes.

Odd. By the context clue that Thea had so helpfully provided, I believe I was supposed to be recognizing him, not the other way around.

"Oh, shit. Where are my manners." Thea glanced between us as our hands separated. "Milly, Sebastian was the team's assistant captain until he retired last season. Sebastian, Milly is the team's new—"

"Chef," Sebastian cut in.

Thea and I looked at each other, then back to Sebastian and his knowing smirk. He shouldn't have known that. I'd taken my chef whites off as I left the kitchen. In fact, in my leather jacket and jeans, I looked more like him than anyone else.

Thea opened her mouth in confusion before I could, and *buzz.*

I barely managed not to cringe at the loud alarm. Damn, that thing was annoying.

The crowd and the sitting Blizzards erupted again, and I watched as hundreds of people whipped the hats off their heads and then flung them over the glass panels and onto the ice. Ethan, who had apparently just scored a goal, held his arms wide open as if flowers were being rained down upon him after a spectacular figure skating routine. Instead, the white-and-blue hats poured down on the ice like it was snowing. Talk about a blizzard.

I backed up, not wanting to be hit by a stray cap. Retreating was a good call too because as dozens of hats collided in mid-air, one ricocheted in my direction. A white ballcap landed at my feet where it would have hit me in the face had I not fled. I hesitated then bent to pick it up.

My confusion must have been clear on my face because Sebastian chuckled and snatched a flying hat out of the air as easy as catching a baseball lobbed to him, this one Blizzards blue. "Jones scored his third goal of the game." He spun the hat in his hand. "It's called a hat trick."

Understanding flooded me. "Hence the hats."

Sebastian nodded. "Hence the hats."

I laughed, swept my bangs apart, and pulled the hat on, glad I'd taken down my hair from its traditional braid after I'd left the kitchen. My hair poofed into a brown cloud around the rim of the hat. I patted it down until it settled.

Thea, who had retreated farther into the tunnel to avoid the snowstorm of hats, stepped back a few more feet. "And I think that's my cue," she said. "The game's over. I should be heading back to get ready. I'll see you later, Milly."

With that, she disappeared into the tunnel in a blink.

"How does she do that?" Sebastian asked, shaking his head.

"She likes to think she's Batman," I answered Sebastian with a chuckle and turned back to the ice.

"She might be," Sebastian said with a look that spoke volumes about who Thea was underneath her angelic appearance.

He should see her during a bout.

Without me realizing it, the players' benches had emptied, and the teams were forming lines across from each other on the ice. Then the lines of hockey players began to move. As they skated past the opposing players, they shook hands, and I appreciated the sportsmanlike gesture despite the stereotypically violent nature of the game.

Then the men separated and headed back to their respective benches. But they didn't sit. Instead, they headed through an opening in the panels that led them right toward Sebastian and me.

Whoops.

I quickly moved out of the way of the line of heavily padded hockey players. Sebastian stepped back but didn't practically press himself to the wall like I did.

"Your Majesty!" a handful of the players called out. It took me a minute to realize they were talking to Sebastian. As they got closer, the players raised their hands, and Sebastian slapped palms with each of them as they passed me, greeting each one.

Without permission, a tiny giggle escaped me as they waddled past us on their skates down the rubber-floored tunnel like little penguins.

"What do we have here?" a penguin asked, and I sucked in my giggle in a sharp inhale as the two players bringing up the end of the line stopped before us.

10

Ethan

I squinted at the scene before me.

"Hey, bro," Kingston greeted casually, but I saw the glint in his eye.

I squinted harder. I didn't like this. He looked more evil than usual.

"Hey, Kingston," I said cautiously.

Kingston pursed his lips. "Seriously, *Jones*?"

Warren left my side to stand beside Kingston, arms full of her goalie gear and chuckled at her secret boyfriend's irritation. "Don't know why you try anymore, Seb. He's never going to use your first name."

Kingston pouted down at his girlfriend.

I blinked. I still hadn't gotten used to the playful expressions that Kingston showed around Warren. Even though their top-secret relationship wasn't even a year old, I was constantly surprised at how much happier and carefree Kingston seemed.

I had played with Kingston for the vast majority of my career, and I'd known for a long time that he didn't love hockey as much as I did. Sure he was good, but that was mostly because of his natural athleticism and relentless practicing. The one thing he didn't have though was passion for the game. Or passion for anything.

Then he met Riley Warren, the first female goalie on our team, and was a goner. I'd felt sorry for him at first; falling in love with a lesbian wasn't ideal. But falling in love with a fake lesbian was more so.

After a roller-coaster romance that ended in a secret relationship for months because the press would eat a woman alive for dating a teammate, they were finally ready to come out to the world as a couple. So the two perfectionists made a plan. One that was right on track.

Kingston had retired from the league and Warren had come out as bisexual, both resulting in the expected mixed reactions from the press. The next step involved Kingston and Warren being seen more in public until the final stage where they blow the hockey world apart with the news of their relationship. Then, presumably, happily ever after.

That was if they could complete the plan successfully. With how gushy they were around each other, I was surprised the entire country didn't know by now. As it was, I was pretty sure Milly had clocked them.

Her eyes bounced between the two lovebirds as they had some sort of telepathic conversation, gazes locked in a loving embrace. Then, Milly's eyes pinged to mine.

I kept a straight face.

Milly's stare was relentless.

A beat.

I winked, and a teasing smile fought Milly's lips, red as always.

After another bit of silence, I cleared my throat. Warren and Kingston flicked to attention.

Like nothing had happened, Warren finally saw Milly.

"Oh, hey," Warren said. "Miley, right?"

"Milly, actually," she said.

Across the women, Kingston's lip twitched the slightest. I followed his eyes to Warren and saw the faux-innocent look on her face.

Damn it all. Warren has told Kingston about Milly already. Those gossips.

Warren continued her act. "Right, right. How is the menu coming along? That palate tester you gave me was amazing. I wouldn't mind having everything again. Except maybe that foam thingy."

Milly smiled. "Most people don't like that one, even me, if I'm being completely honest. It was mostly to test consistency sensitivity."

"Well, the rest was delicious."

"Thank you."

Kingston crossed his arms. "Now I'm jealous. Had I known the team would be getting Milly this season, I would have waited a year before retiring."

I snorted.

Sure, bud.

Nothing in the universe could have stopped Kingston from retiring when he had.

Warren's brow rose—a habit she'd picked up from Kingston—at the comment, knowing just as well as I did that it was complete bullshit.

Milly beamed at Kingston, one of her rare, full-teeth smiles. A ping shot through me but dissipated when Milly's hand lifted and patted me over the heart, the sensation almost non-existent through my chest pads.

"If you're ever at this one's house while I'm cooking, I'd be happy to whip up an extra portion for you."

Fuck.

Warren and Kingston's grins morphed into identical toothy smiles. They resembled hungry sharks smelling a drop of blood.

"Reallyyyy," Warren dragged out.

Kingston was more subtle than his psycho girlfriend. "Oh? You're cooking for him?"

Not realizing what she'd done, Milly's hand dropped from my chest. Warren and Kingston's eyes tracked the movement.

"Yeah. Twice a week," Milly said.

"Are you cooking for his party on Saturday?"

Milly looked at me.

"No," I answered for her. "I was going to cook."

Silence.

"Okay. I was going to order in. Whatever."

"Actually, I would love to cook," Milly cut in.

I shook my head. "That's not necessary, Milly. Some catered sandwiches won't kill these Neanderthals."

Distaste squeezed Milly's face for a second before a lightbulb seemed to go off somewhere in that brain of hers and an excited gleam settled into her deep-water eyes. She stepped closer to me, reached out, and settled her hand insistently on my bicep. "No, really. I want to. In fact, I insist."

Twice. She's touched me twice in a row. In full view of my friends. The doubt that had pricked at the back of my brain since she hadn't brought up the moment in the grocery store settled. I wasn't sure if she was aware of it, but she was broadcasting her interest for the whole world to see.

So I did the only thing I could as Milly released me, giving me back function of my tongue. I nodded and croaked out a "Sure."

Warren clapped. "Great. I can't wait. Seb, you're going to love it."

Kingston grinned, the scar on his lip cutting through his dark stubble, twisting in amusement.

I leaned back on my stick until I was out of Milly's view and flipped both of my asshole friends the bird.

"Jones, Warren. Let's go. And Kingston, get the hell out of here," Coach Hansson's voice echoed from the other end of the tunnel.

Not even looking back, Kingston raised a hand and waved it through the air, batting away Coach's throw-away order.

Warren was less blasé. Juggling her gear, she grabbed me by my still-gloved hand and tugged.

"See y'all," I called to Milly and Kingston and fought to stay balanced on my skates as Warren towed me away. I could do nothing but try to keep up; the woman was strong.

She was also a bitch, as she proved by her parting comment before Milly and Kingston were out of earshot.

"Bye, Milly! Can't wait for Saturday!"

She pushed open the locker room doors, forced me inside with one last tug, and then dropped my hand as the doors closed on Milly's friendly and Kingston's amused faces.

"I hate you," I mumbled. Frey, Warren's best friend on and off the ice, chuckled in solidarity at his locker.

The next afternoon, I helped Milly put an ungodly amount of food into my fridge, replenishing it from the barren state it had slowly regressed back into since Milly had last meal prepped for me.

Chapter 10

"Oh, by the way, I'm going to text you the code to my place so you can get in on Tuesday," I said as I closed the fridge and turned to Milly, who was putting the last of the ingredients into the cabinets. The food she'd purchased—with my card—was for today and a couple of days from now when she would be coming in to cook for my meals after I got back from our first road trip of the season. We would be flying to the west coast for a few games, and the thought of Milly's cooking waiting for me was the only thing that kept me from bitching about the long trip like I always did.

I loved playing against the West Coast teams, but living out of suitcases was not for me. The long-ass away games were the only downside of this job.

Though an even better consolation prize would be Milly herself in my kitchen instead of just her cooking. But I would take my wins where I could get them in this slow seduction.

Still, I couldn't help but step on the gas pedal just a little. And giving her the electronic key to my place was a revving of the engine that she couldn't ignore.

Milly looked over from putting away quinoa with raised brows.

I waited for a refusal, but none came. Instead, a soft smile creased her lips. Her eyes searched mine.

I let my affection shine through.

Her red lips parted, and I took a step forward.

A metallic knocking sounded from the front door.

I pinched the bridge of my nose, eyes scrunched in pain, and felt it like a lost limb the moment Milly stepped back.

I opened my eyes to see her looking at the front door with an interesting mix of emotions written across her face. I could pick out annoyance, relief, and more than a hint of leftover lust.

I stalked forward. Milly watched me approach her, turned to lean back on the kitchen counter, and crossed her arms, leaving me ample room to pass between her and the kitchen island to get to the front door.

But I was a big guy.

"Excuse me, darlin'," I murmured deeply as I brushed by, my hard body rubbing against hers. As professional athletes are wont to do, I couldn't quite keep my balance and had to reach out to steady myself against the nearest surface.

The nearest surface being Milly. My hand landed on her waist, and she pushed back strongly to brace against my weight. A flush so red it almost matched her lipstick spread up her pale cheeks, but she kept the rest of her expression softly amused. Her lashes fluttered around her deep-ocean eyes, teasing me.

I squeezed the small of her waist. As I suspected, her body had a layer of give before I felt hard muscle that spoke of years of athleticism. The arms crossed over her chest, showing the same strength as her core, brushed against my pecs as her fingers flexed into her biceps. A hum escaped her throat. I answered with a grunt but kept on moving. With more strength than I knew I had, I let go of her waist and crossed the rest of the kitchen.

I felt her tracking me as I strode to the door and stopped the incessant knocking by almost ripping the slab of metal off its hinges.

A smug Kingston and Warren smirked at me.

"Took you a while," Warren said, suggestion dripping from her words. "Hope we didn't interrupt anything."

I almost growled at her, but Kingston held up a case of beer, condensation dripping off the cardboard. No doubt it was full of sugar and alcohol, unlike the bottles in my fridge. In his other hand, he held a six-pack of wine coolers for Warren.

"It's okay. I brought the good stuff to drown your sorrows."

I pointed at Warren. "You weren't this much of a smartass before her."

Unoffended, Warren pushed through the door, already peeking toward the kitchen. She must have seen Milly because her face lit up and she abandoned us to go bug the chef.

"I know. Isn't it great?" Kingston said.

I grabbed the beer and wine coolers from him. "Fantastic."

We joined the women in the kitchen. Milly already had a pan on the stove, strips of turkey bacon sizzling away. The oven light showed it was pre-heating.

Kingston joined Warren at the island, taking a seat to the left of her, while I dropped off the beer and wine coolers in the fridge. I grabbed a couple of each then let the door close. After handing Kingston and Warren's drinks to them, I held up the last beer and wine cooler.

"Want something?" I asked Milly.

Her eyes landed on the blue wine cooler, but she hesitated.

"Go for it," Warren cut in. "I'm only having a couple tonight. Big game tomorrow."

"Then, yeah. I'd love one."

I handed off the bottle, letting my hand, cold from the drinks, brush across her warm, strong fingers. The contact sang through me, and I had to mentally shake myself as I stepped away from her to join Warren and Kingston at the island.

The hold this woman, who I haven't even kissed yet, had over me was honestly embarrassing. But what was more so was the knowing looks from Warren and Kingston.

I held my beer on the edge of the island, slammed my hand down on top of the cap to pop it off, and slumped in my seat beside Kingston. Like Warren, I wasn't planning on drinking much today. This would be my only alcoholic beer. Then I was switching back to my boring, sugar-free, non-alcoholic brew.

"Hello, again, Sebastian. I know about everyone else, but you don't have any allergies, do you?" Milly asked.

Kingston shook his head. "Nope. All good here."

With a decisive nod at that, Milly turned around, grabbed three avocados from the counter, dropped them on the cutting board, and whipped out a deadly-looking knife.

In seconds, she had the avocados split in half and pitted.

"Do you need any help?" Warren asked Milly but was looking at me pointedly.

I held up my hands, knowing what Milly's answer would be from when I offered the same thing.

"No, no!" Milly insisted, turning her head to face Warren but kept her body facing the cutting board, chopping without looking. Her face was sincere and insistent. "I've got it all. You guys just do whatever you usually do. No need to keep me company."

She, to my great relief, turned her eyes back to her knife. She finished dicing the avocados, took a bowl from the cupboard, and scooped out the avocado's insides. We all watched, transfixed, as Milly produced an onion, garlic, tomatoes, and jalapeños, then promptly dismantled them, turning the vegetables into tiny, perfect cubes. They went into a bowl, got sprinkled with sea salt and lime juice. Then the turkey bacon was chopped and added. After a quick mashing and stirring, the bowl was shoved into my hands. A bag of chips followed into Kingston's hands.

"Out of my kitchen," Milly commanded with a horrible British accent and took a satisfied first sip of her wine cooler.

I sputtered into my beer, and Warren burst into laughter.

"Yes, Chef." Warren shot from her stool as if she was a contestant on a cooking show and saluted Milly. Then she took off toward the living room.

Kingston followed her with the chips, but I hesitated.

Milly shot me a softly exasperated look and dropped her British accent. "Honestly, I'm fine. Go."

"If you need anything…"

She pointed over my shoulder.

"Alright, alright."

I took my beer and the guacamole to the couch where Kingston and Warren had turned off the lacrosse commentary I had been studying and were starting up the Xbox. Before I could set the dip down, Warren grabbed a chip from the bag and scooped a hunk of the guac into her mouth. She hummed around the bite, and I quickly put the bowl down before she chopped off my hand to get the rest.

More knocks echoed through the apartment, and I went to let in Erik Berg and Mason Frey, our last two guests.

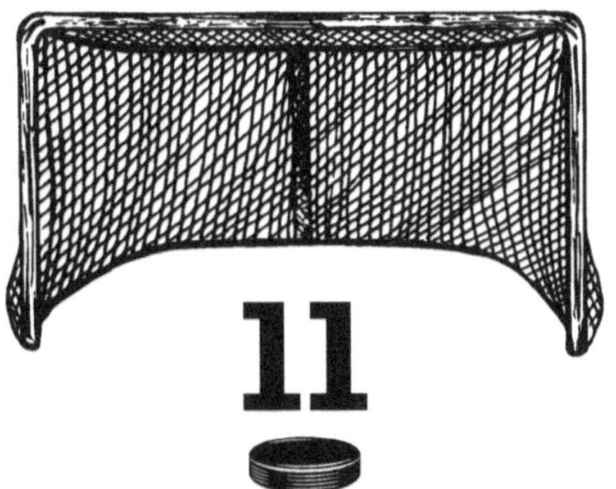

11

Milly

"**D**ie!" one of the boys screamed from the living room. The sound was then accompanied by multiple people shouting and the plastic crack of game controller buttons being slammed.

Two more hockey players had joined Ethan's little party, both of whom I recognized from the team and were reintroduced to me as Mason Frey and Erik Berg. I'd exchanged pleasantries with Erik, whom I'd discover had a fantastically sophisticated palate while he was trying out my testing spread, and shook hands with Mason, whose tastes I had yet to test.

As another shout ripped through the apartment, this time a female voice, I chuckled. Video games were never my thing, but anything that could get these intimidating athletes fired up must be fun.

"Sorry about them."

The sudden, deep voice almost made me drop the pan of cauliflower bites, but I managed to recover and placed them gently onto the counter. Then I turned to Sebastian Kingston.

After our introduction the other day, I'd looked him up and was unsurprised that he was an impressive hockey player. In the arena, he had carried himself with a confidence that just bordered on arrogance. According to the internet, that confidence was well earned. Now, stealing another beer from the fridge, he seemed too relaxed to be the hockey god that had commanded attention in the tunnels of the Blizzards' arena.

I remembered what he had said as he came into the kitchen and scared the shit out of me. "They're fine. I'm used to screaming, although usually it's an angry chef yelling in my face."

Sebastian turned to me, pried off the top of his beer on the edge of the countertop, and took a sip. "So those shows are real? With the chefs screaming at each other and being dicks?"

I winced, but I was the one who'd brought it up. "They can be. Not all kitchens are like that, but enough of them are. Especially in Europe, where they can be a little old-school."

I shook off the thoughts, not going through the door that would take me back to the place I had escaped from.

Sebastian stepped closer, looking with familiar curiosity at the buffalo-coated cauliflower bites.

I picked one up and handed it to him. "What do you think? Should I sprinkle some cayenne on them, or no?"

The answer was no, but I let him pop the piece into his mouth, wondering what he would say.

A single eyebrow rose on his lightly tanned face, and his stubble shifted as he chewed.

"Those are awesome, and I think they have just the right amount of kick. Anything more and Mason would combust. He can't handle too much spice."

So far so good. "What about a spicy vegan ranch dipping sauce?" I tested further.

"Hmm. Maybe one spicy and one regular?"

"Sure. I can do that." I took out two bowls from the cupboard. "Do you cook?" He had the hungry curiosity of a chef—the same thing I seemed to be missing.

Sebastian shook his head. "No. I love food, so I gave it a try, but it's so stressful. Doing everything all at once is too much."

I skirted around Sebastian, who stepped out of the way, grabbed the vegan mayo from the fridge, and returned to my spot. "A lot of people say that. They don't know that the secret to enjoying cooking is in the prep. Get as many ingredients chopped and prepared beforehand as you can. It leaves you time and space to be creative and passionate."

Sebastian sipped his beer thoughtfully. "I'm finding passion hard these days."

I paused while scooping mayo into two bowls and remembered something I'd read while looking him up. "Because you quit hockey?" I asked tentatively.

He didn't even hesitate. "No. Quitting hockey is one of the best things I've ever done. But now I have a bunch of free time and nothing to do with it. While hockey was never my one true love, I'm waffling without something to focus on."

"I get that." I paused, then shrugged and emptied the last of the mayo without care. "I quit my job about seven months ago in Lyon, France, right before I was about to open up my own restaurant and came back to New York. Everyone thought I was crazy, but I just didn't feel passionate about it anymore."

"Cooking or cooking there? Because for someone without passion, your food is amazing."

I shot Sebastian a thankful nod as I side-stepped to the newly designated spice cabinet and retrieved an armful of unopened little bottles. "I thought it was about cooking there."

I left it at that.

Sebastian didn't push, seemingly comfortable in the silence.

I ripped the lids off the spices and broke the seals before I added them into the bowls, only sprinkling cayenne into one bowl. Then I swept the cauliflower bites onto a plate and stuck two spoons into the bowls of ranch after a couple of quick stirs.

Sebastian grabbed the plate, but his gaze was off toward the living room. "A piece of advice? Passion doesn't come around every day, so hold on tight and fight dirty when you find it."

I followed his eyeline and landed on Riley Warren. Maybe it wasn't hockey he was missing at the game a couple of days ago but playing with a certain someone. I kept my mouth shut as I collected the dipping sauces, and we walked the food to the coffee table in front of the couch.

"And I think that's about it," I said as dropped the dips next to the platter of bites and clapped my hands together, making sure to stay out of the way of their—I glanced at the screen—hockey game. The coffee table, as large as everything else in the penthouse, was completely taken up by food platters. From every finger food you could think of to full meal portions of salads and sliders, I had cooked enough to feed an entire super bowl party.

Or five hungry hockey players.

And feed they did. The plates and dishes were decimated. It looked like a pride of starving lions had attacked them. Luckily for them, I knew what I was doing, and the food was relatively healthy. Of course, it wasn't completely clean; I wasn't a magician. But, compared to the recipes that I'd tweaked, the food was fit for Olympians.

And I'd made every single dish before.

My theory was trash. Even with Ethan within eyesight, a single new idea hadn't come to me. It was official, I was washed up.

I thought about Sebastian's comment in the kitchen. He was right; passion didn't come every day. And it looked like mine had dried up.

"I'll just show myself out."

At my self-dismissal, Ethan, who was lounging furthest from where I stood off to the side of the U couch, came out of his video game trance and dropped his controller into Erik's lap, who immediately scooped it up and picked up the game where Ethan had left off. His avatar raced across the ice.

"No, don't go, Milly. Stay. Eat some of the delicious food you made for us." Ethan looked at the destroyed plates. "Well, what's left."

"Yeah, stay," Riley chirped in loudly as Sebastian dropped onto the couch between her and Erik, throwing her slightly off balance. Her plan to only have a couple of wine coolers had gone out the window. She draped herself across her obviously secret boyfriend.

Mason, still invested in the game he was now playing against Erik, fumbled for the cauliflower bites near him, dipped one into the spicy ranch, and popped it into his mouth.

"Oh, wait," I tried, but I was too late.

"Ahh," he screamed and dropped his controller to lunge for his beer. He gulped it down and grabbed for another bottle when his was empty—one of Ethan's non-alcoholic beers. Mason made a disgusted face around the neck but continued chugging.

"That was the spicy dip," I finished with a wince.

Sebastian broke into laughter, Erik quickly following. At least Riley had the decency to hold in her giggles as she drunkenly crawled across the couch to her friend and patted him on the back while he panted for relief around the beer bottle.

"See," Ethan said. "You can't leave us just yet. At least not Frey. Look at him. He's helpless."

Mason had finished Ethan's beer and seemed to be calming down, but a deep-red flush had spread across his lips until it looked like he was wearing my lipstick. Beads of sweat began to roll down his face, and I started to feel genuinely concerned.

I hadn't made the ranch that spicy, had I?

Then he stuck out his tongue in a futile attempt to cool it down, and I understood. He had a geographic tongue.

Ouch.

But while he would suffer a little, Mason would be fine.

I made a mental note about Mason's sensitive tongue for future meals and turned back to Ethan, who was pouting at me. Pouting! Sure, it was subtle pouting, but still!

I squinted at him, waiting, but he held his ground, brown eyes big with pleading while Mason panted beside me, adding a pathetic soundtrack to Ethan's cute, pillowy pout. I shook my head in exasperation at the man using his friend's suffering to coerce me and dropped onto the couch beside Mason. Eyes still locked with

Ethan's across the coffee table, I joined Riley in patting Mason's back.

Ethan's mouth twitched and turned up just slightly, but I read the victory and satisfaction in it still.

On the screen, one of those annoying goal alarms went off, and Erik whooped at his victory over an incapacitated Mason.

"Who's next?" Erik asked. "Chambers. You game? Jones has every game ever invented. If hockey's not your thing, we could kill some zombies."

I looked up in surprise. Had I told him my last name? I couldn't recall. But I didn't begrudge the hockey players their tendency to only use each other's last names. Someone in my sport didn't have a foot to stand on when it came to nicknames.

"I'm not really a gamer," I said and held up my hands. I wiggled my fingers. "These are more for chopping vegetables than decapitating zombies."

"I don't know," Riley said on the other side of Mason. "I've seen those cooking shows, and I'm sure you could carve up a carcass like a butcher."

I beamed at her. She wasn't wrong.

"How about something we can all play together?" Ethan suggested.

Riley's eyes lit up. "Poker!"

A chorus of groans reverberated through the penthouse. Even Mason pulled himself together enough to roll his eyes.

"Oh, come on! I've been practicing."

"Not enough," Sebastian mumbled, and Riley swung to him in betrayal.

Fire shot from her eyes, and Sebastian's hands went up to show he was unarmed.

Ethan must have caught my bemused look because he turned to me. "Warren is a great goalie and can spot a tell across half the ice. She knows that a twitch of an eyebrow means someone is about to pass, but reading faces at poker is her kryptonite. She gets too competitive, and all her perception goes out the window."

Mason, mostly recovered, chimed in. "And without her goalie mask covering her face, she is stupid easy to read. Which wouldn't be terrible, but she's too stubborn to ever fold. We had to stop playing with her. Taking her money was just too sad."

Riley finally butted into her roast. "No, seriously, guys. I've been practicing. I'm getting better."

Out of her view, Sebastian shook his head.

Silence.

"How about Monopoly?" Ethan asked.

"No. Milly, put that down!"

I carefully set the precarious stack of plates onto the counter by the sink and turned. "Huh?"

Ethan's metal front door shut with a metallic clang behind his friends as he stormed back into

the penthouse and toward the kitchen. Midway, he stopped, detoured to the living room, grabbed the last of the dirty dishes from the coffee table, then stomped carefully to me.

I watched him in amusement. He had obviously never been a waiter because every single plate was on the verge of shattering on the floor into a million pieces. But he managed to get to the kitchen with no casualties.

"What are you doing?" I asked and grabbed the dishes from him before he could attempt to unload them himself. I shuffled the plates onto the counter beside the sink which was already filled to the brim with half-rinsed off bowls and platters.

Hands free, Ethan stepped forward. I backed up to make space for him and realized the position he had put us into. He was effectively blocking me from the sink, obscuring the piles of dirty plates, bowls, and cutlery with his wide torso.

The intoxicating smell of coconut invaded my nose.

"I'm taking over. You're not doing the dishes after you spent hours cooking. My mama raised me better than that."

His accent snuck through and melted something in me, turning my insides into liquid. Used to the feeling by now, I didn't react externally.

Then I paused.

I cocked my head in consideration.

My experiment had been a bust, theory shattered on the floor like Ethan's plates almost were. It was official—I was burnt out. My passion had been blown out like a candle in a dust storm. The thought came with a strange wave of relief. I could finally stop fighting.

Because, of the dozens of delicious appetizers, snacks, and finger foods I'd whipped up today, not a single one of them had been a new recipe. The inspiration that had come to me while making Ethan's meal prep must have been a fluke. And I knew of no way to reproduce it.

A knot somewhere inside me loosened.

It was time to stop grasping at straws and just accept the glaring truth that I had been avoiding for the better part of a year. There were no more straws. Hope did not spring eternal. I was done.

During my silent contemplation, Ethan had crossed his bare arms over his pecs, as if bracing for a barrage of protest. His chest puffed out under his forearm until he was three times my size, both in height and width. He was ready for another standoff, knowing I would fight with him to do the dishes. He would have been right at any other time.

He glared steadily down his wide nose at me.

I should have been intimidated—having a large man looming over me like he was. I should have wanted to run in the other direction or lower my eyes in submission. Instead, I reached up and placed my palm on one of his flexing biceps, and watched as the stern image he was projecting crumbled. The big, buff man that could knock full-grown men to the ice with one punch—I'd seen a video—softened until he was as threatening as a teddy bear. And just as cuddly.

Watching carefully, I moved forward, taking back the feet I'd put between us, and slid my hand further up his arm. And ... there—the reaction I had been waiting for.

His mahogany eyes, the color the exact shade of his skin, widened, and his plush mouth parted, his pink bottom lip separating from the darker-colored upper lip in a puff of air. Under my hands, his crossed arms unwound and dropped to his sides, knocking my grip off on accident.

I wasn't blind; I'd seen the way Ethan froze every time I touched him, as if I was made of static and he was getting addicted to the touch. And he wasn't the only one. The difference this time? I could finally act on the desire. Nothing was holding me back anymore. He wasn't the key to my success anymore. He was just the man I wanted with every molecule of my body.

Like my permission had let up on its choke collar, my hand shot back up as I closed the last of the space between us, grasped Ethan by the corner of his jaw, his beard soft and curly under my palm, and pulled myself up to him.

A breath of surprise burst from him, but he put his reflexes to work and leaned down to meet me halfway. In a crash of hungry lust and tortuous gratification, my lips slammed into the soft pillows of his. The contact tore a wounded sound from my throat, and I wrapped my free hand around the back of Ethan's neck, opening my mouth to let his tongue in. It ran across mine and lit up my every nerve in its wake. While I enjoyed the height difference between us, it was getting on my nerves now. I tugged on his neck, and my fingers became claws on his bearded jaw.

He got the message.

Warm arms snaked around my sides and back until I was fully enveloped by him in a bear hug, the strong fingertips clenching through my shirt as he straightened, pulling me up to his level. For the first time in my life, I was glad for the padding that came with trying out every restaurant and food truck and bakery I came across because my not-so-small waist was the perfect fit for him.

I moaned into his mouth as I teased his tongue into a game of cat and mouse. He pulled back slightly with a groan. My protesting sound came out as a squeal as Ethan hiked me up in his arm until I was sitting in his arms. That was one way to fix the height gap. In fact, now I was about a head taller than him.

He looked up at me, and I smiled down at him as I wrapped my dangling legs around his waist. My thighs, strong from years of skating and running off restaurant calories, squeezed his waist like I was trying to pop a watermelon between my quads. Instead of the squeal I was trying to draw from him in retaliation for breaking our kiss, a delicious grunt tore from him.

"Fuck, darlin'," he growled, a spark igniting in his eyes. It wasn't the only thing that ignited. The steadily growing length under my ass was too much to resist. I loosened my grip on his neck and ground my weight down.

His biceps flexed under the new weight they held, and he stumbled forward with an aborted thrust. A rough groan came out of his beautiful, dual-colored mouth, and the next thing I knew, I was over the kitchen countertop, head banging lightly against the grey cupboards. His arm disappeared from under me, and I landed on the marble countertop. I kept him close with my boa-constrictor thighs in case he wanted to flee.

He didn't.

Instead, he pressed closer and thrust the stiff length of his cock against my pussy. I grunted and silently cursed the clothing between us. As it was, his navy slacks looked fit to burst against the significant weight of his cock, and I wouldn't be surprised if my jeans and panties melted from the heat and wetness emanating from my pussy.

I ground against him and reached for his jeans. As if eager for my touch, the silhouette of Ethan's cock quivered. The hands I hadn't noticed slipping up my shirt yanked at my waist, bringing me closer still to Ethan. And throwing me off balance.

Mistake.

"Shit!" I shoved back further onto the counter and caught a glimpse of his baffled look before I whipped around.

I lunged and caught the toppling tower of plates just in time. Then Ethan caught me before my uneven weight could drag me off the counter too. We quickly dismantled the tower into a more manageable structure, and Ethan huffed.

"I think we're destined to always be interrupted," Ethan mumbled, then reached for me again.

I leaned back just a millimeter, but it was enough for Ethan to notice.

He backed off, literally and figuratively, shifting his weight to edge out from between my thighs.

"What's up?" he asked.

I glanced around the kitchen, clocking every dirty dish, the scraps of food on various surfaces, and the mess of knives and cutting boards in the sink that I had yet to clean. If any of my old bosses saw the deplorable state of the kitchen, I would be on prep duty for the next month.

Ethan followed my look. Then he rubbed his knuckles over his jaw. A muscle in his cheek twitched in amusement.

"You need to clean the kitchen, don't you?"

I winced and hopped off the counter. "Yeah."

"Let me help, at least."

Before he could move, I shot my hand out, fingers spread in the universal sign for 'stop' inches from his chest.

"No!" If he had gotten any closer to me, I would have ripped his jeans to shreds to get at his cock. "You stay there while I finish these dishes. I'm sure you're already hungry again."

He paused, and his look, too aroused to be sheepish, told me I was right. Then he looked around, and I realized the problem. Only scraps were left on the various platters here and there.

Suddenly, I was moving.

As if I were outside of it, I watched as my body walked around the kitchen, swiping the remaining leftovers onto a clean cutting board until it was back where it started. My hand whipped out a knife and went to town on the pile of scraps consisting of cauliflower bites, vegan sweet potato skins, a buffalo chicken skewer, and the last turkey slider. Once everything was diced, my hands drizzled spicy vegan ranch onto a spinach tortilla stolen from the fridge, stuffed the tortilla with the diced and shredded filling, and wrapped it like a burrito.

I came back to myself just in time to hand over the cauliflower-turkey-buffalo chicken-sweet potato spinach wrap.

I looked on in hopeful horror as Ethan ate the unique wrap—something I had never made before.

Oh, shit.

I cleaned the dishes in a daze then fled Ethan's apartment like a demon was chasing me.

12

Ethan

I stole the puck from a Winnipeg Wolves forward, did a sharp one-eighty, turning away from our goal, and shot toward the other end of the ice. Blurs of grey and navy blue flew past me before they realized I stole the puck and turned to intercept. They were too late.

The puck ping-ponged between the blade of my stick as I used it to corral the little rubber disk. My legs pumped hard, blood rushing through them, and I ate up the yards between me and the opponent's goal on a breakaway. No one stood between me and the goaltender. I looked around, hoping to spot Berg and turn this one-on-one between me and the Wolves' goalie into a two-on-one. Except the snowflake I spotted wasn't Berg but … Little.

I had almost forgotten Coach had put him on this line, trying to see where he fit best within the team. Despite my faith in the player I knew he could be, he might fit best on the bench. At least for a bit. Over the past few weeks, he had been getting better, but he was nowhere close to where he needed to be, not for a professional hockey player.

He knew it; I knew it; Coach knew it. But we also knew what he could do when he wasn't in a funk. His skills could shoot this team into the championships if only he could get his shit together. And if only he could stop trying to fight my help.

I considered my next move for all of half a second, then passed the puck to Little. He got control over it easily and passed it back, making the goalie readjust and confusing him. Perfect. I played with the puck as Little and I got closer to the goal, then passed it back at the last second. Little drew back his stick then let it rip.

The puck flew through the air like a tiny black missile, and I watched as it headed toward the top right corner of the net. The goalie lunged for it, and I moved to intercept should the puck ricochet off the goalpost. With a dull ping, my precaution proved necessary.

My eyes struggled to track the trajectory, and I shifted my weight as I readied myself to lunge. But the puck didn't come to me. Instead, it redirected to the left and zipped into the back of the net.

The goal alarm ripped through the air with a piercing sound. The crowd, mostly filled with

Winnipeg fans, groaned as a victory pop song started playing after the goal sound, and I wanted to groan with them. Because it wasn't Little's skill that got us that goal; it was pure luck. And by Little's face, he knew it too.

Our teammates on the ice stormed Little and almost tackled him in celebration. I followed at a calmer pace and gave Little a pat on the shoulder. He shrugged off my hand and headed to the bench for the line change without a word.

I sighed.

Why is everyone running from me lately?

The second the thought appeared, I shook it off. I was in the middle of a game; it was not the time to be thinking about Milly and our interrupted night.

My brain didn't agree.

I just didn't understand what happened four nights ago. I thought we were having a good time. She had met and gotten along with my friends, then we shared a kiss that rocked me to my core.

I wasn't blind; I knew she was a little apprehensive about a relationship right now. The way she had run out of the door after she finished the dishes spoke of a much larger issue. One I wanted to address.

But that was a problem for later.

I shook myself out of the funk I had dipped into and skated to the bench for the line change.

"Whenever you have some free time, I want to talk to you," I read aloud. My thumb fluttered over the button for a second before I pulled up my big boy pants and pressed send. The message whooshed off to Milly.

Like a teenager who had just sent his crush a first text, I immediately closed my phone and put it in my pocket. I loosened the knot of my tie with a quick tug.

"That Milly?" Warren asked on a long yawn as we stepped off the bus.

I grunted noncommittally, and Warren was thankfully too tired to dig further. She hummed and went to collect her bag. Frey appeared by her side, his own bags in hand, and they walked off to his hideously green Jeep to carpool home.

My stomach growled, and I couldn't wait to get to my apartment. As much as Milly had been avoiding me, it seemed she wouldn't let me affect her work. My security system had alerted me when she used the electronic guest key I gave her to get into my apartment yesterday afternoon, then again a few hours later when she left. I could only imagine the delicious food awaiting my arrival.

I had only just gotten my own bag when my phone buzzed in my suit pants.

It was Milly.

I blinked. I hadn't expected her to answer me so soon. Hell, it was two in the morning. I figured she would just get back to me when she woke up.

I cautiously swiped across the screen to open the text and was greeted with an address and nothing else.

Curiosity wiped away the exhaustion in my bones that came after a four-day road trip. Heaving my duffel over my shoulder, I headed to my SUV and put the address into my navigation system.

"What the fuck?" I mumbled tiredly as I pulled up to some sort of market near the Manhattan docks.

I found a place to park amongst the sea of cars, opened my door, and was immediately hit by a pungent wall of fish. I guessed I knew what they were selling.

As I worked my way toward the dock, the sound of crashing water mesmerizing me and bringing back a twinge of exhaustion, I wondered how I would find Milly in the crowd. But my worry was unnecessary. I walked into a maze of a fish market, vendors set up in a big open-air area by the water and found Milly immediately, talking to a seller by the entrance.

She was in her usual motorcycle get-up but must have left her helmet on her bike because in her hand was instead a red cooler that she was placing a paper-wrapped package into.

I walked to her, squinting as the bright flood lights that lit up the market reflected off the early morning dew in the air and into my eyes.

"Hey," I said as I came up beside Milly. "Why are we at a fish market?"

Milly's head came up, and my breath caught.

Her bangs were plastered to a face that was more flushed than normal, and her mouth, clean of lipstick for the first time since I'd met her, pulled up into a smile. But what threw me was her eyes; the deep-water blue had a spark to them I rarely saw. They shined like someone had thrown a handful of diamonds into the Atlantic, and I could only wonder what had caused the new-found light in her.

"Why else would someone go to a fish market? We're here for fish."

"At 3 o'clock in the morning?"

Milly nodded at the vendor who had been watching me with recognition, closed her cooler, and hooked her arm through mine. I went liquid and followed her as she dragged me farther into the market.

"Of course. That's when they're open." Milly leaned back and gave me a once-over. "The better question is why are you wearing that?"

I looked down and found myself in my game-day suit. I grimaced. The people around me looked like they had either rolled out of bed or off a boat.

"Game day," I explained. "Didn't have time to change."

"Wait. Did you text me right when you guys got back?"

"Yeah. I wanted to talk to you. Although, I didn't expect a response until tomorrow."

The playful smile that I had only seen on Milly's face a few times lost some of its intensity. Her grip on my arm loosened but didn't fall away "Right. You want to talk. About what happened the other day, I guess?"

"Yes."

Her lips pursed, and she glanced around the market. "Alright. But first, urchins."

"Huh?"

I was towed toward the vendor selling sea urchins.

I looked suspiciously at the piece of food before me and fought the urge to poke at it like a toddler.

"It's not going to bite you," Milly said, a laugh dancing in her voice.

"I don't know. It's not still alive, is it?"

"No."

Well, that was a relief, although not much. "I've just never been a fan of sushi."

"Have you ever had it?"

"Sur—"

"Not from a grocery store or gas station, I mean. From an actual chef?"

I sighed, knowing I'd lost the battle. "No."

On the other side of her kitchen island, Milly pushed the plate with a spiked shell on it toward me. It struck me again that I was in Milly's apartment. When she'd run away after our kiss, I'd thought my chance of ever seeing the inside of her apartment had vanished with her.

Had I known the first time I set foot in her place, I would be forced to eat raw sushi, I would have thought twice when she invited me over after the fish market to talk. But I really wanted that talk.

I picked up the fork, gripping it like my life depended on it, and stabbed at one of the pink strips of meat in the shell.

"Who craves sushi this late at night?" I grumbled one last time then popped the urchin in my mouth, chewing quickly.

A fresh burst of sea spray filled my mouth, salty and sweet at the same time.

My jaw stuttered then slowed down. I swallowed and blinked. Immediately, I went for another piece, taking my time to savor the flavors, and wasn't even embarrassed by the soft moan I let out.

Across the gleaming white island, Milly took a bite of her own urchin, a little smile playing around the tines of her fork. She chewed and swallowed, a hum escaping her lips.

"I can't take credit for this one," she said. "It's an all-natural flavor. All I did was crack them open, rinse them off, and squirt some lemon juice on them."

The rice cooker dinged as I finished off my last piece of raw urchin. I pointed at the cutting board that Milly informed me held tuna—which I'd never seen outside of a can—with my empty fork.

"That what you're going to do with those?"

"No, I always preferred my fish in a roll, never by itself. And I've got plenty of stuff for us to use."

Wait. "Us?"

A smile with a hint of evil creased her face. "Yes. Us. I'm off the clock. I'm not cooking for you. Pull your own weight."

"Oh, I'd love to." I stood and rounded the island, stopping a good distance from her. "And I could hold your weight too."

Under her bangs that looked black in the low light of her apartment, Milly's deep-water eyes grew intense, rolling with waves of challenge and lust. I shifted my weight to one leg to adjust the sudden hardness in my slacks. My exhaustion had come back as I followed Milly's bike back to her place, but apparently, I wasn't *that* tired.

Then the reason I was here came back to me, and I sobered.

I cleared my throat. "What do you want me to do?"

As if coming out of a daze of her own, Milly blinked, turned, and handed me another cutting board piled with a variety of vegetables. "Julienne these," she ordered.

"Julienne?"

"Cut them into slivers."

"Yes, Chef."

A muscle twitched in her face, and she turned to the laid-out fish.

I retrieved a knife from the cutting block and set up shop beside Milly on the island. Milly's knife was bigger than mine.

For a moment, the only sounds were our chopping, Milly's slices lighter and more rhythmic than mine. Still, I held my own. I may not have been the best cook in the world, but you didn't grow up in my house without learning how to help Mama in the kitchen.

"I'm glad you texted," Milly said, and I jolted out of the lull the rhythmic sound had sent me into.

It took me a second to process what she'd said. I snuck a glance at her and found her engrossed in her cutting board, fully focused. I'd seen her slice and dice vegetables without even looking before.

"I'm glad you answered. And that you invited me over."

She finally looked up from the fish that she was just moving around the cutting board at this point.

"This time, you can't run away since we're in your apartment."

Milly's lip twitched sardonically, and I realized how that came out.

"Oh, God. That was a creepy thing to say. Sorry."

Milly snorted, and her steel knife gleamed under the kitchen light.

I had the feeling that Milly could hold her own, especially when she had a knife on her. And if I remembered the strength of those thighs of hers correctly, which I most definitely did, I was sure she could knock someone on their ass with one well-placed kick.

My slacks tightened at the thought, and I cleared my throat, turning my eyes back to the cucumber I had been cutting. I sliced off a few more strips as thin as I could.

A metal cling drew my head back up. Milly had placed her knife on the board and stepped back, her full attention on me.

I straightened and copied her, placing my knife down and leaning a hip against the island.

She spoke first. "What are you looking for out of this, Ethan? Are you just flirting? Do you want a fuck buddy? A relationship? What?"

I liked her bluntness, so I gave it back. "I want a relationship with you. I like you, and you like me too. I want to see where it goes. If that's not what you're up for, I'll back off. But fair warning … I won't settle for anything less than a monogamous relationship. I won't be your fuck buddy or your situationship. If you decide to do this, you need to be fully committed, Milly."

Milly searched my eyes. I let her see my sincerity.

She blinked. "I'm not sure you know what you're asking of me, Ethan. I may not be ready for a relationship right now. With you or anyone."

"I know you've got issues, Milly. Hell, half the time I'm with you, you seem off in another dimension." A flush reddened her cheeks, but I held up my hand before she could open her mouth. "It's okay. I get it. You obviously have things going on. But I still want you. And if you choose to have me, maybe I can help you out with those things you've got rolling around in that head of yours."

"Oh, yeah? You want to be my therapist?"

"No. I want to be your boyfriend."

Still, she didn't answer, back in that far-away world of hers, and I was starting to get nervous. My hand twitched, eager to rub itself over the back of my head, but I held in the tic. I couldn't hold in my babbling, though.

"If the whole 'I'm technically your boss' thing is a problem, I can fire you. You wouldn't have to keep meal prepping for me. Or, if you say no, I won't fire you. Wait, that—"

"Okay."

My breath tried to strangle me. "Okay? Okay, what? You don't want me to fire you?"

Milly smiled. "No. Well, yes. But no. I meant 'Okay, I want to see where this goes.' But may I make a request?"

"Of course. Anything."

"I'll exclusively date you, but can we hold off on the 'boyfriend' 'girlfriend' labels for now?"

I chewed on my lip. "Just for now?"

Milly nodded.

"Alright, I can deal with that. But we'll be revisiting this conversation later," I promised.

Milly stepped toward me. I could only watch her as she closed in, afraid to wake up, realize this was a dream, and find her gone.

"Deal." She reached up and pressed a sweet kiss to my lips.

A smile shoved my cheeks into my vision, and a surge of relief brought my exhaustion back. It was a miracle I didn't collapse onto the kitchen floor.

"And you're barely my boss, by the way. I consider myself more of a contract worker. Now go sit down before you fall over and let me finish this."

I grinned tiredly as she shoved me out of the kitchen, and I shuffled to the other side of the island to fall into a stool and watch her work.

Sometime later, a whole un-cut roll of sushi was placed in front of my hooded eyes.

Exhausted, we ate our sushi rolled like corn-dogs at 4 o'clock in the morning. They hit a weirdly satisfying spot.

My eyelids drooped.

"Come on, big guy. Let's get you to bed."

Her hand in mine, Milly guided me to her room.

Milly

I woke up in my bed and immediately missed the warm body that had been my personal space heater through the night. From the other side of my closed bedroom door, the sound that had woken me echoed through my apartment again, the clang of metal on metal.

Was Ethan in my kitchen?

I stretched and sat up in my bed. My grey duvet fell into a puddle around my waist, and I tucked my hands into the sleeves of my pajama top.

I stared at the door.

What do I do now?

I knew the second I'd handed that leftovers-stuffed spinach wrap to Ethan after what happened moments before that I'd fucked up. I wasn't supposed to get involved with him while using him to stoke the fires of my love for cooking. But when I kissed him, I thought it was a non-issue.

I was wrong. I was so fucking wrong. The first time in his kitchen hadn't been a fluke. Ethan Jones was officially my muse.

I dropped my face into my hands at the thought, cringing. Thea would have a field day with this; she always liked proving me wrong.

With a groan, I rolled out of bed.

Five minutes later, with an empty bladder and clean teeth, I emerged from my bedroom and found Ethan "I can't cook" Jones over my stove, shirtless. The curtains were drawn back from my windows, letting the late morning light in, and baseball highlights were playing quietly on my television.

At the padding of my bare feet against the cold concrete floor, Ethan looked up from the skillet where he was making—I sniffed—eggs and bacon. His smile lit up the room, as bright as the sunbeams streaking across the floor of my apartment.

"Perfect timing. I know it's probably not up to your standards, but I wanted to make something for you. Figured you'd like a break from cooking all the time."

I stared at him.

Unlike Ethan's kitchen, with its earthy tones and warm feeling, my kitchen more closely resembled a professional one. The open cupboards and steel countertops that reminded me of my favorite kitchen in London were one of the main selling points of the apartment. The similarly steel island between us with an overhead rack that I hung my pots and pans from reflected the morning light harshly. It all just looked so … clinical. Or it should have.

But like last night, when Ethan sat at that same island, warm and sleepy, looking cuddly even in his pressed suit, Ethan lit up the room. He filled the cold steel space with light and warmth. Just being in his presence was like being wrapped in a blanket fresh from the dryer. It was no wonder I had agreed to start a relationship with him.

And watching the tall, dark, and absolutely fucking gorgeous man in my kitchen flip an omelet, I couldn't bring myself to regret the decision that my sleep-deprived, tired-from-practice self had made last night. Plus, she had made a fantastic point when considering Ethan's offer of a relationship.

Plenty of artists sleep with their muses, right?

A pang deep in my stomach, under layers of muscle and sinew, told me this was different. Heat crawled up my chest, reminding me why I'd asked Ethan to hold off on the labels. I didn't want to be a shitty girlfriend. And I couldn't do that if I wasn't one, right?

I forced a smile onto my face and walked through the living room to the kitchen. "It smells perfect."

I came to a stop beside him and peeked into the pans on the stove. In one sat over-cooked turkey bacon. The other held a wonky omelet, folded in half the American way rather than in thirds like the French did.

"This one's yours," Ethan said, pointing at the omelet with a spatula. "I was going to make mine without the egg yolk and cheese. You know, the fun stuff."

The muscles in my cheeks lost the forced tightness. I nudged him with my elbow. His side was rock solid. "Come on, Ethan. Unlike some of us, you have the day off. Eat the yolks. Live a little."

He grinned, turned off the range, grabbed a plate he'd set on the counter, and served up my omelet. A couple pieces of turkey bacon quickly joined my omelet on the plate.

"Isn't it your job to make sure I'm eating healthy and all that jazz?"

I took the plate from him. "Thank you. Also, yes, that is my job. But a yolk here and there isn't going to kill you."

Ethan hummed, and the rumbling of his bare chest caught my attention.

The morning light bouncing off the steel appliances and white countertops caught on the ridges and dips of Ethan's torso. Shadows settled into the creases of his wide pecs and contracted beautifully against the hardwood of his skin. I followed the light down his stomach, the swells of his abs like rolling waves, and found my gaze halted by the Blizzards' blue sweatpants that Ethan had retrieved from his car last night.

A throat cleared.

I looked up and felt heat spreading in my face. My eyes flicked down. "Sorry."

A warm finger settled under my chin, and I followed its guidance up until I was looking back up at Ethan. His semi-permanent smile had gained a softly amused edge. "Don't apologize. Here, look your fill."

With that, he stepped back, dropping his hand from my face, and spread his arms, giving me a full unobstructed view of him. His hands went to his hips, and he looked up into the distance as if hearing cries for help from a damsel in distress.

"Alright, Superman. Put on a shirt."

The serious face he'd put on cracked, and his teeth shone through his dark beard.

I smiled back, glad the awkward moment was over.

I didn't know what the rules between us were. Sure, we were "dating," but we'd done nothing more than kiss. And sleeping in the same bed counted for nothing; we were both unconscious the second our heads hit the pillows and had stayed firmly on our own sides of the bed.

"Does that make you Lois?" he asked.

Before I could answer, he was back in front of me, almost on my toes, and grabbed me by the waist.

"Ethan," I squealed as he lifted me.

The next thing I knew, I was being deposited on the island. The cool metal shocked my bare thighs, my pajama shorts not covering much. Then he was slotting himself between my thighs.

He took the forgotten plate that I'd somehow managed to not spill away from me and placed it out of the way.

My lips quirked up, and I propped myself up on the island with two hands behind me. A confidence that had been frustratingly absent since I woke up infused me. My thighs, strong from months of roller derby, tightened around him lightly and drew him closer to me.

He stepped forward with a grunt, closing the last of the distance between us, and his center found mine. I braced one hand against the island, ground my rapidly wetting pussy against his cock, and reached for him. With a grip on the side of his neck, I pulled him to me. His hands landed on either side of me like anvils, and his large chest hovered over me as our lips crashed together. Our mouths immediately opened for each other, and our tongues met in a slick dance. A rough hand moved up to tangle in my hair. I moaned as his fist tightened, the sharp pain in my scalp just right.

Fire licked up me, and my hips moved of their own accord, circling against the front of his sweatpants, searching for pleasure. They didn't have to search for long. A palm gripped my outer thigh, and Ethan tugged me closer to him in a half-thrust, letting me feel the full, thick length of him. I mewled in delight and threw my head back.

As if his lips couldn't stand being separated from me for a second, they immediately fell to my clavicle and kissed their way up to my ear. I titled my head, giving him better access, and continued my slow grind against him, his hard body a furnace against me.

"Damn, darlin'," he moaned into my neck.

I shivered at both the vibrating sensation and the southern accent that peeked out.

Then both of his hot hands were gone. I let out a soft noise of disappointment that was quickly cut off as they returned to me by pushing up the hem of my pajama shirt. His fingers played over my stomach and up my ribs, teasing and dancing along as he continued to nip at my neck, his beard scratching against me beautifully.

It wasn't enough.

I leaned back, ripping him from me, and whipped off my top.

Ethan blinked. His lips were puffier than usual, and I could only imagine what mine looked like.

"Well, good morning," Ethan mumbled, his brain obviously not fully present.

I couldn't help it; I laughed. "Are you talking to me or my tits?"

He blinked again, coming to. A shy smile crept up his face. "Both?"

I snorted. "Liar. You were talking to the twins."

"I couldn't help it. Look at them." He cupped them, and they filled his palms perfectly, overflowing from his fingers just a bit. "They're so happy to meet me."

And they were. In fact, my nipples, dusky pink and in the middle of large areolas, were practically saluting him. Ethan greeted them in return with a little pinch, and my back arched, pushing further into them. Then his mouth descended with devastating effect as he went straight for a nipple. He pinched the bud between his lips, the pressure just right, and played with my tits. I moaned and grabbed the back of his head, keeping him where he was.

He had no intention of moving.

Unfortunately, the universe had other plans.

A *ding* brought me out of my lust-induced haze, and my head turned absently to locate the sound. I found the source.

"Your phone," I panted into the air.

Ethan growled and switched his mouth to my other breast.

"It could be important," I said on another moan but kept my blunt fingernails digging into his hair.

Ethan pushed my tits together, kissed each one, then came up for air. His brown eyes were filled with lust as they met mine, and I knew I had the same crazed look in my eyes as well.

"It's probably just Warren looking for a practice buddy. The woman is a machine, and Frey, her usual practice buddy, can't always keep up with her."

"I thought you guys had the day off."

"We do, but Warren's crazy." He paused. "Do you have to go in today?"

I grimaced. "Yep."

He frowned even as he petted my ribs absently. "When?"

I leaned to the side and saw the time on the oven clock. My head collapsed onto Ethan's hard pec, and I sighed. His nipple pebbled from my breath, and his pec twitched under my forehead.

Hypnotized for a moment, I ran my hands down his torso then picked my head back up. "I've got to get to the arena in a couple hours to work on the menu." I sighed. "What did you say the other day? We're destined to be interrupted? Sounds about right."

A sharp smile suddenly cut through Ethan's beard. "Interrupted? What are you talking about? We've got thirty minutes to spare."

Ethan dropped to a squat off the edge of the island.

My mouth dropped open in shock, and I moved loosely with him as he grabbed me by the calves and pulled. My ass slid to the edge of the counter until I was millimeters from falling off. Ethan looked up from between my thighs, eyes as predatory as an alligator, and I watched in slow motion as his hand reached up, settled on my bare chest, and pushed.

I followed his silent direction and ended up on my back, the cold metal island shocking against my over-heated skin. I groaned in the back of my throat at the sensation. Then I felt the hands on my calves run up my legs and decided I needed to see this. I propped myself up just as Ethan reached my hips and caught onto the band of my grey pajama shorts. He yanked and suddenly my shorts and panties were on the floor of the kitchen. Then my legs were spread, and I watched eagerly as Ethan teased me with light kisses to my inner thighs.

I could already feel the slickness sliding down my thighs, and if Ethan didn't stop teasing me soon, I would have to take care of myself. In a half-warning, half-plea, I reached down to him and cupped the corner of his jaw.

"Please," I pleaded with a gasp.

Ethan grinned, placed a strong kiss to the center of my palm, and went to work.

With another yank, my ass was off the edge of the island and a tongue was on my clit.

"Fuck," I shouted at the sudden shot of pleasure and let out a moan as Ethan abandoned the clit to explore the rest of my pussy.

By the time he got around to inserting one of his thick, rough fingers inside of me, I was writhing on the island in ecstasy, my hands having dropped from underneath me and clutching uselessly in my own hair.

"More?" a lust-deepened voice growled.

"Yes!" I about shouted. "Please, dear God, yes."

A dark chuckle vibrated my clit, and my next breathless moan was cut off as another finger joined in on the fun.

"Fucking hell," I groaned out.

Then Ethan was back on my clit, and I was circling my hips frantically as I was pushed toward the edge of my orgasm. I tugged at the hair wrapped around my fist, the sting in my scalp adding another layer to my pleasure. Then I was shattering, shaking apart around Ethan's fingers and riding the flat of his tongue. Flashes of light burst behind my eyelids as I squeezed them shut and panted desperately at the ceiling. Ethan held still as I rode out the last of my orgasm on his face then pulled back when I finally went limp.

I opened my eyes blearily to see him get to his feet, a satisfied smirk gracing his handsome face.

He caught my gaze and, holding my eyes, brought his slick fingers to his mouth. I watched, lust already building again, as he popped them into his mouth and a pink tongue appeared between his fingers, lapping up every trace of me.

"Oh, darlin'," he purred and got the last of my taste from the pad of his thumb. My taste buds tingled in response. "You really do make the best meals."

I shot up with a curse and was reaching for him before I even recognized I was moving, but he caught my hand before it could touch the hard tent in his sweatpants.

A soft confused noise escaped me.

Ethan let out a pained huff, his smile more of a grimace.

"We're out of time, darlin'," he said.

I checked the oven. He was right. I had to get going.

He released my hand, and I considered reaching for him again, risking running late. But as if he read my mind, he grabbed me by the waist, pulled me off the counter, set me down, then took a significant step back.

The tent in his pants twitched, and I bit my lip, looking up at Ethan through my lashes.

"You"—he smacked my ass—"need to eat your breakfast before it gets cold."

Giving in with a pout, I rounded the island on shaky legs and scarfed down my room-temperature omelet in the nude, suddenly ravenous.

Ethan watched me with eyes just as hungry before he turned around to start his own breakfast. Well … his second breakfast.

Ethan

I burst through the swinging doors of the arena kitchen and was met with the bored eyes of Peter Nilsen. He saw me, dismissed me, turned back to the ovens in the far-left corner of the kitchen, and pulled out a pan of something. I raised up on the tips of my sneakers to get a look. It was a tray of his famous vegan protein brownies I'd heard about from another team cook. My stomach growled, but I ignored it. I had more important things to do.

"LaBeux's not here today," Nilsen said without looking up from inspecting his brownies, no inflection in his words.

"Actually, I was looking for Mil—Chambers." I didn't know if Milly was comfortable sharing our relationship with her coworkers, but I wasn't going to out us if she preferred to keep us on the down-low.

Nilsen didn't even blink. "Fridge."

With a nod of thanks that Nilsen didn't see, I took off toward the industrial fridge that sat behind the right wall of the main kitchen area. Two large metal walk-in fridges sat side by side. I opened the first industrial door, found it to be the freezer, and checked the next one.

"There you are."

Milly turned around, her usual braid swinging with her sharp movement. "Ethan? What are you doing here?"

"I'm feeling peckish."

"Okay. Let me whip something up."

I chuckled and slumped my shoulders dramatically. "I'm kidding. You were supposed to say 'Really?' and then I would say 'No, I'm here for you.' It was going to be really romantic, but you ruined it."

Her lips, juicy red as always and matching her bandana, twitched. "Sorry. Do you want to leave, come back, and try it again?"

"No, I want to take you on a date."

Her shocked expression made up for the false start. "A date?"

"Yes. A real one. One where you're not cooking for me."

She pouted, but I saw the amusement behind her eyes. "What? You don't like my cooking anymore?"

I snorted. "Never took you for a fisherman."

Her smile finally broke through.

"I'm serious, Milly. I want to do this for real. I know both of our schedules are crazy, but I can't wait any longer. So, what time do you get off today?"

Milly looked around the shelves full of produce and meat in thought. Then she turned to me, an interesting spark in her deep-water eyes. "I have to test out one more dish for the team menu, but then I'll be free for the afternoon."

"Great. I can wait."

"Or you can help me out. I'll even make an extra portion for you because I know you weren't actually kidding about being peckish."

I chuckled. She already knew me so well. The thought sent a wave of pleasure through me.

"You want *me* to help?" I asked incredulously. "I know that omelet I made you was delicious, but that's where my skills in the kitchen begin and end."

The lines around her eyes crinkled. "Okay, how about you pick out some random ingredients for me, and I'll see what I can come up with."

I finished off the cranberry chicken with one last hum.

"I've got to be honest. I didn't think you could pull it off. I mean, chicken and fruit? Who would have thought they would go together?"

Milly took a bite off her own plate, a satisfied smirk decorating her red lips. Her lipstick hadn't budged while eating, and I wondered what I would have to do to make it smudge across her face.

"I guess you just inspired me."

"When you said you would be taking me on a date, I thought we would at least be leaving the arena."

I chuckled as Milly wobbled through the dimly lit tunnel.

"We're always in a kitchen when we're together, so I wanted to show you where I work," I said and offered her my arm as a crutch again.

She threw an offended look at me and straightened on her hockey skates, the picture of stubbornness. Shoulders back and knees bent, she had a decent skating posture, and I was confident that she wouldn't immediately collapse like a newborn deer when we stepped onto the ice. Probably.

"Are you sure I'm allowed to be here?" she asked her skates, her attention focused on keeping her balance.

"Sure." I paused mid-step. "Unless you're worried about being seen with a player."

She halted with me and looked up, the frown line on her forehead popping under the red bandana that she'd kept on. "Is that against the rules? Staff fraternizing with the players?"

"No." I'd checked.

"Then it's fine. I don't care if people know we're together."

My cheeks ached with the smile that broke out on my face.

Milly smiled back, and we started our slow journey again.

It took a second, but we made it to the ice without incident. The arena opened up before us as we exited the tunnel, and Milly looked up and around the thousands of empty seats with awe.

"It's weird to see it empty," she breathed out.

Glancing around the arena myself, I soaked in the silence. For all I loved the screaming fans during a sold-out game, the quiet of an empty arena always had a certain magic to it.

I walked on my skates to the home team bench, opened the door that led to the rink, and held out a hand to Milly. This time, she accepted my help and grabbed my hand. I helped her over the lip of the rink and onto the ice.

"Shit!" she squealed.

Her feet immediately flew out from under her. One hand still holding hers, I lunged onto the ice and took her full weight into my body as she crashed against me. She immediately turned to cling to me, and I couldn't help the chuckle that bubbled from my throat. Milly immediately pulled back and punched me in the chest for making fun of her.

"Hey! I don't have pads on. That hurts," I lied, cringing away but still keeping a hold on her.

She snorted. "Yeah, right."

Then she straightened up, using me to balance, bent her knees, and let go of me.

She didn't fall over.

Carefully, she pressed off a skate and glided forward, arms spread at her sides.

"Good," I said and followed her easily. "Are you sure you're not a skater?"

She chuckled, attention back on her skates. "Not an ice skater. But I've been known to shred in some roller skates."

Her voice had more amusement in it than the comment warranted as if she had told an inside joke. I didn't get it but hummed out a light laugh anyway.

As we slowly rounded the edge of the oval rink and came up on the straightaway, I edged behind Milly. "Ok. You ready?"

She tensed, wobbled on her skates, then tried to relax. She wasn't successful. Her eyes flickered erratically around the ice like someone was about to ambush her. "For what? What are you doing?"

"Relax. I got you." I settled behind her and rested my hands on her curvy waist. "Trust me," I whispered.

Then we were off. I pushed off my skates and we launched forward. The *shick shick* of my skates cutting into the ice was drowned out by Milly's squeals. Thankfully, they were squeals of delight, not terror.

She grabbed at my hands then changed her mind, let go, and spread her arms like we were on the bow of a cruise ship. The brisk air coming off the ice whipped her braid into my face. I gave her a good push as I let go and watched her fly down the ice.

"Ethan!" she shrieked, laughter in her voice.

I put some pep in my step and flashed forward to catch up to her. I reached her in milliseconds, maneuvered in front of her, turned to skate backward, and caught her hands as she reached for me. Not needing to look behind me, I pulled her along the perimeter of the rink, watching as she started to push off her skates by herself, excitement and joy swimming in the oceans of her eyes.

She quickly got the hang of the basic movements. Must have been her roller-skating background. But even when she was fairly stable on her own, she didn't let me go, letting me pull her around the rink again. By the time we circled the rink for the half-dozenth time, I was a barely used crutch as she held her own.

We came to a gentle stop by the benches.

"Okay," she panted lightly. "That's fun."

"Better than a roller rink?"

"Colder, for sure." With that, she tucked her hands into the oversized Blizzards hoodie I'd lent her while I'd tied up her skates in the locker room.

Her cheeks were flushed a rosy red. "Are you too cold? Do you want to head in?"

An evil smirk pulled up her lips. "Hell no!"

She took off down the ice. Well, if you could take off that slowly.

My laughter echoed through the empty arena. She reminded me of myself the first time I'd stepped onto the ice when I was a kid. I cut through center ice to join her mid-way through her lap.

She gasped as I came up beside her and smacked me lightly, almost losing her balance. "Hey. You're cheating."

"Guess I'm disqualified then. You win the race."

A viciously satisfied grin shot my way. "I usually wouldn't take that and demand a fair rematch. But I think I'll make an exception this time. If only so I don't humiliate you on your own ice."

I interlaced my fingers with hers as we continued our lap, the cold air suddenly feeling blissfully warm.

I sliced my hockey stick through the air, tapped the puck, and sent the rubber disk skidding across the ice. Milly scuttled to the side and thrust her stick in the puck's path just in time. The puck bounced off the blade of her too-large stick and ricocheted away from the net she was guarding. Then the stick was waving erratically above Milly's head.

"Ha! Blocked. Suck it, Jones."

I shook my head, ducking to hide my smile.

In the short time since I'd pulled out a couple of sticks and some pucks from the benches, I'd learned a few important things about Milly Chambers. One, she must be killer on wheels because she was one of the quickest studies on hockey skates that I'd ever seen. Two, she was a natural athlete. Even though I was going easy on her, and she was obviously no Riley Warren, she could hold her own in the net. And three, Milly was just as competitive, if not more so, than me.

Just who was this woman? Because I'd never met anyone else like her. She was stubborn, sweet, and down to try anything. Add to that she was beautiful and knew how to cook, and I was done for. It was sort of embarrassing how far gone I was on her, but I wasn't fighting it. Not that I had much before.

I skated up to my not-yet girlfriend and came to a stop by the net.

"Well, it's good to know you're a sore winner."

Instead of being ashamed, Milly's chest puffed up under her/my hoodie. "Yep," she chirped.

I chuckled.

She glanced around the enormous arena, a contemplative look on her face. "I have to admit; I didn't really get the whole hockey thing. But this is fun. I can see why you enjoy it."

Standing on a giant hunk of ice, I just about melted. It wasn't often that someone outside of athletics understood the joy of playing a game for a living.

"Did you always want to be a hockey player?"

Suddenly, I felt the chill of the ice like I was laying directly on the rink.

I thought about giving my usual answer to the question. My bland, vague comments usually went over well with the press. But, as I looked at Milly's innocently curious face, a weird urge swelled in me. I wanted her to see the real me, not the facade I gave the world.

My warring thoughts must have shown on my face too much because the crease in Milly's forehead was out in full force. She glided forward the tiniest bit, looking like she wanted to reach out to me, but stopped before she got too close.

Her mouth opened, but I spoke before she could.

"Actually, I wanted to be a football player when I was a kid."

The crease in her forehead softened but didn't disappear. "What changed your mind? Were you no good at football?" she asked, voice cautious.

I laughed at the question, but a hard edge took out any humor in the sound. "No, I was a fantastic football player, even when I was a kid. So were my brothers. The game was quite literally in our blood. My father was one of the best running backs in the league. He took Texas to the Super Bowl a half-dozen times during his career, and my brothers and I wanted to follow in his footsteps."

Her jaw dropped. "Your dad is Ezra Jones?"

I gapped back at her, somewhat offended. "You know football, but not hockey? I thought you grew up in the north."

"I did. Upstate New York born and raised. But my father is from Tennessee. He has a game on the television every day during the season, and he still watches your father's post-game commentary. Wait. You have brothers in the NFL, right?"

"Yeah. Liam plays for Tampa and Isaac for Los Angeles."

"Wow." Milly blinked. "Then how did you get into hockey if your whole family bleeds football?"

I smiled. "My mom."

"Is she a hockey player?"

"Figure skater. Retired now, obviously."

"Was she any good?"

"Well, we have an Olympic medal hanging in our family trophy room, so I'd say yes, she was good."

A bemused look took over Milly's face as she shook her head, her braid swinging lightly. "Family trophy room?"

I shrugged and grinned back.

"So, your mom got you into hockey then?"

"Yeah. She had quit skating professionally by the time I was born and became a stay-at-home mother. I had never actually seen her skating until I was about ten years old. My dad had to come to New York for a charity thing around Christmas time, and my mom took me to the Rockefeller Center. It was the first time I'd ever set foot on the ice."

Most of the guys on the team probably couldn't remember the first time they'd strapped on a pair of skates, having started as soon as they could walk, but I was a little different. That trip to New York was only the second time I had seen snow. And the first time I ever saw my mom having so much fun.

My older brothers had stayed with my dad to go to his charity gala, but my mom had stolen me to go see the giant Christmas tree. I had known about it from movies and wanted to see it in real life. But instead of the tree taking my breath away, something entirely different caught my attention.

The memory of my and my mom's New York Christmas adventure played like a movie in my head. I'd known my mother was a figure skater; she'd shown me videos of her favorite routines and the one that had won her an Olympic bronze medal. But until that Christmas when she skated around the huge sparkling Christmas tree, arms spread wide like she was soaking in the freezing winter air, I had never seen her skating in person. Bundled up in a thick coat and her afro flying with how fast she was skating, she was like a Disney princess. Then she was tying skates on my tiny feet, and I was swept across the ice in her arms, my blades barely touching the ground.

"And you were hooked, weren't you?" Milly guessed and propped a hip against one of the net's goalposts.

I copied her on the other post. "Immediately and forever."

"Do you ever miss football?"

The moment we got home to Texas, I begged my dad to let me go to a rink. It took some convincing from both me and my mother, but he eventually acquiesced and signed me up for skating lessons. There, I eventually joined the local hockey team, and I haven't looked back since.

"Not even once," I said. "But you know what's it like to find your passion. The second you know what you want to do for the rest of your life, you forget everything else. Nothing else matters when your very destiny is on the line."

Milly broke eye contact with me, her lips pursed. "What about when you retire?" she almost whispered.

My brows furrowed at the sudden change in atmosphere, but I shrugged and kept the smile on my face.

"Hey, I'm not that old, yet. Don't jinx me. I've still got a few seasons left in me. But I've already got something lined up."

That seemed to bring her back to reality, and she smiled up at me.

"I'm sure you will be fantastic at whatever you do, Ethan."

15

Milly

I collapsed on the bench in the middle of the derby track and clapped as the new string of blockers took their places at the starting line. My plastic-padded palms made a sharp clicking noise with each clap. The warehouse containing the banked oval track roared with cheers as the girls from both teams settled into their positions. The rest of our team and our opponents joined the noise of the crowd surrounding the track. The warehouse practically shook with the sounds.

Thea skated up, dropped onto the bench beside me, and we both hunched over, forearms on our padded knees, to catch our breaths. That last jam had gone on for almost a minute—an eternity in roller derby—but we'd managed to score seven points before our jammer had called an end to it. Our team, the NYC Killers, was now tied with the Island Injuries.

On the track, our defense, four blockers crouched at the ready, intermixed with the Injuries' defense. Behind the pack of ladies, two women, one from each team, were in classic runners' poses, muscles bundled tight in preparation for an explosion of movement. The stars on their helmets marked them as the jammers, the offense.

The warehouse got suddenly quiet as if everyone collectively held their breath.

The first whistle blew, and the pack took off. Moments later, the second whistle blew, and the jammers raced to catch up to the blockers. Rockem Sockem, our jammer for this jam, was the first to reach the pack of defensemen and plowed directly into the dense group of women.

"Come on, Rockem," I screamed past the mouthguard I was chewing on.

Thea grimaced at my high-pitched screech but clapped along with me.

As Rockem worked her way through the pack of girls, our team helping her maneuver her way past, I could feel Thea's stare. I turned on the end of the bench to watch the girls go around, conveniently turning my back on Thea. Rockem was the first to break from the pack of blockers and was marked as the lead jammer, the only one who could call off the jam. I clapped, hoping to drown out the question I knew was coming.

No such luck.

"So, you haven't slept with him yet?"

Our coach, Sheila, shot a narrowed-eyed look at us before turning back to watch the track. Undeterred, Thea scooted closer until she was practically glued to my sweaty side.

"I can't wait until you're gone," I shot at her, but there was no sting in my words.

"Bullshit. You're gonna miss me so much."

Unfortunately, she was right. While this was our first bout of the season, it was Thea's last. Since she was quitting the team to travel with the Blizzards, she wasn't a full member of the Killers anymore, but she wanted to play one last game as our captain before she gave up the title.

So, I was stuck with her nosey ass for the hour we had left of the bout. I knew I should have waited until after the bout to fill her in about what was going on with Ethan instead of telling her in the locker room while we were dressing. Still, it wasn't like I could avoid her forever. Hell, she was my neighbor.

"When are you two going to fuck, Milly? Because I need to know when I'm going to get the juicy details.

I turned to her. "To be honest, I think I'm going to break it off with him."

She blinked, emerald eyes bewildered. "But I thought you liked him. And what about your cooking? How are you going to make new recipes without him?"

"That's exactly why I need to cut him loose, Thea. Because I *do* like him. I feel like a parasite. He's a great guy, and I'm just using him. I'm like a vampire, sucking out his passion to use as mine. I can't lead him on like this if I don't return his feelings."

I had been okay with the plan before, but now that I was getting to know him, everything was changing. I may need him to continue to create, but I wasn't going to use him like that when he obviously had real feelings for me. I wasn't cruel.

Thea's confused face turned to exasperated stone. "Milly, you emotionally stunted idiot, you *do* return his feelings."

"Thea," I said slowly. "I think I would know if I returned his feelings. Sure, he's one of the nicest men I know, and he's stupid hot. And I may get some fuzzy feeling around him, but that—"

I cut myself off.

The crowd cheered as Rockem called off the play with more points in the bag for us.

I barely heard them.

"Fuck. Do I like him?" I asked the air, already knowing the answer.

"Yes. You do."

"Shit. Now what do I do?"

I barely had time to finish the question before Thea launched into her plan.

Two days later, I shuffled out of my apartment building, my boots falling heavily to the lobby tile. I'd had a hard day at work, where I cooked

up a storm of recipes to test which went best together to make a cohesive menu. But I'd managed to get a good chunk of the main menu put together. And because of the two-day break the Blizzards were enjoying before another road trip, the arena staff had been let off early. I could have spent the rest of the day in bed, but I knew it wouldn't have been restful. Not with Thea's words banging around my skull.

Of course, Dr. Thea McKenna had suggested another experiment; she was a scientist at heart. But I couldn't argue with the results of the last time I went along with her suggestion. I may not have wanted a muse when she'd pitched it to me, but it seemed to be what I needed. So, with a pounding heart and trembling fingers, I'd texted the man who had been turning my life upside down since I'd met him.

I didn't know what Ethan was to me exactly, but he was something. Whether he was my muse, my boyfriend, or simply some guy who had come around just when I was getting my groove back was what I was going to figure out tonight.

Sudden determination filling me, I strode from my building on steady legs and immediately saw the large man lounging against his car.

"Hey," Ethan boomed and shot off the side of his SUV like an overexcited puppy. His large frame, legs bulging in his black slacks and rippling brown biceps one flex away from bursting the seams of his brightly colored short-sleeved button-up, didn't take away from his golden retriever personality.

He skidded to a stop in front of me. I answered his bright smile with one of my own, not able to stop it if I wanted to. And I didn't want to.

A tension I hadn't noticed I held released from my shoulders. We hadn't seen each other since the afternoon on the rink, and I hadn't realized how much I missed him in that short time. Being around him now reminded me of a feeling I hadn't experienced in almost a year. He felt like walking into a kitchen and being at home.

My smile faltered as a sudden breath rushed from me. A wave of emotion flooded my body, and I knew, as surely as I knew how to wield a knife, that tonight's little experiment was going to ruin whatever plans I'd made. Well, that was fast.

I suddenly wanted to slap myself for not recognizing that I'd had feelings for Ethan this whole time. Now that I was on the lookout for them, they were as obvious as a neon sign. No wonder Thea had looked at me like I was an idiot when I denied them.

I thought about fleeing inside; it wouldn't be hard to make up a quick excuse about food poisoning or something equally unquestionable. But if there was one thing I'd learned in the years spent grinning and bearing the violent chaos of a professional kitchen, it was to adapt or die. So, this was me adapting.

Ethan gave me an obvious once-over, and a spark of desire flashed across his irises. "You look like you could kick my shit in, and I absolutely love it."

"Aw. That's sweet." And it was. The usual discomfort I would experience from receiving a compliment on my looks didn't even register under Ethan's sincerity that hit all the right buttons.

I struck a little pose, hands on my hips, and let him look his fill. I'd debated dragging out one of the two dresses I had in my closet for the night, but instead of the gorgeous, dusty pink, body-con dress I'd bought on a whim, I'd stuck with what I knew—pants and boots. Although I spiced it up a bit for our first date outside of work.

Instead of my usual jeans, I dug out the black leather pants that a derby teammate had convinced me to buy for a night out with the girls. They fit like a glove, the tight matte material hugging every curve I had and propping my ass up to perfection. On my top half, I wore a white long-sleeved crop top with a peek-a-boo slit cutting across the top of my chest to let in the cooling New York air and show just a bit of tit. I threw on a little more makeup than usual for the date, going with a smokey eye and my usual red liquid-lip. For the *pièce de résistance*, I wore my usual motorcycle boots to tie the outfit together and add just a hint of badass. Or maybe more than just a hint.

I ran a hand down Ethan's silky button-down, noting the hard muscles under the shirt with an inaudible hum. I would have been worried that he would get cold later, but I knew how much of a heater he was. He was like a walking sun.

"You look great too."

Tendrils of bright colors decorated the black of his shirt, the jewel-toned blues and reds contrasting beautifully against his umber skin and bringing out a warmth in his dark eyes. He'd trimmed his beard in the days that I hadn't seen him, and it was shorter than I was used to, cropped close enough to his jaw that I could see his skin through the soft stubble.

Ethan's hand came up, took mine from his torso, and brought it down to our sides, entwining our fingers. He gave a light tug.

"You ready?"

I squeezed his hand. "Lead on."

He did, and as we got to his car, he broke away from me to get the passenger door.

I smiled at him as I stepped in and ran my fingertips gently over his bearded jaw in thanks. He pressed a kiss into my palm then closed the door behind me. He joined me in the driver's seat, and the cloud of coconut scent that always accompanied him filled his car. I inhaled the intoxicating scent subtly as he started the car and then steered us toward Queens.

For the first time since I decided on this date, I was looking forward to it with anticipation instead of dread, because I had the overwhelming feeling that so long as I was with Ethan, everything would be alright.

The thought should have scared me more than it did.

"Fuck," I muttered, staring up at the hole-in-the-wall ramen restaurant slapped on the end of a row of buildings and the sign informing us that the place was under construction.

Ethan chuckled. "Well said. I was looking forward to trying the 'best ramen in the city.' If it received that kind of praise from you, it must be Michelin-star worthy."

I turned to Ethan, incredulous. "You know what a Michelin star is?"

I couldn't be sure in the dying light of the day, but I thought his cheeks darkened the slightest. Then his gaze flicked to the ground, and I knew whatever was about to come out of his mouth would be bullshit.

"Yeah," he choked out. "I watch tv."

Well, I could have spotted that lie even without all of his tells. The only thing I'd seen him watch on his huge television were reruns of hockey games.

"Ethan." I dragged out his name.

He cleared his throat. "Fine. So maybe I looked up cooking things."

"Cooking things?"

"Yeah. I watched a few episodes of cooking competitions and read some articles about chefs.

No big deal. I just wanted some information to start a conversation with. Side note: the culinary world is full of drama, and I didn't see it coming."

A giggle burst from me. "Not as much as the hockey world is."

Ethan's head came up like a shark scenting blood. He stepped closer to me until his arm pressed against my side, and I had to crane my head up to meet his glittering eyes. "And what would you know about the hockey world?"

I rolled my eyes at him and stabbed him in the side with my elbow. The only reaction he had to my boney jab was to smile wider, all teeth and triumph.

"Milly, did you Google us?"

"I Googled the team and saw some interviews you guys did. And maybe I watched some of your videos and perved on a couple photoshoots. But I drew the line at looking up your personal information. It felt weird."

Ethan's sharp smile softened, and a tender look took over his face. His mouth opened.

A stomach growled through the air, and Ethan's cheeks, which had just lost the last of his embarrassment, darkened again, his mouth snapping closed.

I laughed and took his hand in mine.

"Come on. I know a place around the corner. That is, if you're up for it."

He raised his eyebrows in confusion at the dare in my voice but went willingly as I dragged him down the street.

"Come on. You have to admit that was good."

Finished with his last slice of pizza, Ethan threw his trash in a bin as we passed by and continued aimlessly down the street.

Ethan's lips twitched and he patted his abs. "Maybe. But I'm going to have to run a marathon to work the calories off."

I took a sharp left at the end of the street. "We can do that."

Ethan's brows scrunched but he followed me.

"Damn, woman. Where are we going now? I need a nap after that much grease."

"There." I pointed, and one of Ethan's signature smiles lit up the slowly darkening afternoon. I cataloged the hitch in my sternum when his head spun and he directed that gorgeously sharp grin my way. My answering smile was involuntary.

"Oh, hell yeah."

Ethan picked up his pace until he was practically skipping ahead of me. The pedestrians he passed didn't even glance at his odd enthusiasm. Welcome to New York.

With a laugh, I rushed after him. Looked like his food coma was gone.

Before I knew it, we were at our destination.

"Wait." I came to a halt on the sidewalk. "Maybe going into a New York park right before sunset is a bad idea."

"It'll be fine," Ethan said, having come to a stop before the entrance to the park to wait for me to catch up.

"You would say that, large man."

Not offended, Ethan took my hand. "Well, this large man promises to protect you."

I shouldn't have felt the need to squeal and giggle at the promise, but I couldn't help it. What I could help was not letting the sounds out, though. Biting my lip to keep myself composed, I entered the park, Ethan by my side.

We were only walking for a minute or so before I saw it. The squeal that I'd managed to hold in earlier escaped, and I abandoned Ethan to run to the children's play area ahead of us.

The empty children's area was sectioned off from the rest of the park by a short fence. The gate to enter was on the other side, but I had no patience. I jumped the fence, the rusted metal harsh on my hands.

The deep rumble of Ethan's laughter followed me, and I looked back to see him trailing at a more sedate pace. How the tables had turned. Now I was the one skipping in excitement.

I stuck my tongue out at him and continued toward my goal—the swing sets.

I was already seated and pumping my legs wildly when Ethan caught up to me and dropped into the plastic swing seat beside me. Quickly picking up speed, I laughed into the air, letting the wind rip the sound away from me, and leaned back. My hands white-knuckled the metal chains as the blood rushed through my head.

The sky, painted in hues of blue and pink by the setting sun, blurred above me. I swung for a while longer, letting my momentum carry me back and forth until the world blotted out from my eyes and I had to sit up or risk falling backward.

My boots dropped with weight and dung into the dirt. I jerked to a stop and glanced around as my vision returned to me. My dizzy gaze crashed into Ethan's, and if I wasn't already out of breath, the air would have rushed from my lungs at the look in his eyes.

16

Ethan

*M*illy's hair flew around her like she was caught in a storm, her brown waves whipping in every direction and obscuring her joyful face. She leaned so far back on the swing that I was terrified that she would tip over at any moment, but she kept her tight grip on the chains, laughing into the sky.

I had never seen her this carefree. The wind seemed to strip away all the obvious stress that was weighing on her, leaving the fun and loving woman whom I had seen glimpses of but had never fully met. She was beautiful.

Milly skidded to a stop, her boots throwing up dirt in a cloud around our ankles.

"What?" she panted out, her eyes not entirely focused on me.

I smiled at her until her deep-water eyes cleared of dizziness. "Just wondering how old you are," I teased, my feet not leaving the ground as I rocked on my swing.

Milly tucked the crazy mass of her hair behind her ears, leaving her bangs free, and shot me an amused look.

"Hey, I haven't been on a swing set in years."

"Years?" I asked. "I would have guessed more like decades."

"I'm not that old. And one night in Lyon, a friend of mine and I ended up in a park like this and found a couple of swing sets. We spent the night swinging. Of course, this time, the company is better."

She rested her temple against one of the metal chains and shot me a smile.

I returned it. "Your dates sound much more fun than mine."

Her furrowed brow peaked out from her bangs, and her red lips part in question. "It wasn't a date. But what do you mean you don't have interesting dates? Aren't you some big-shot athlete? I figured you took helicopters across the city to eat at the best restaurants or took your yacht out for moonlight boat rides."

I snorted. "I don't know how rich you think I am, but you're way off."

The corner of her eyes creased with her smile. The toes of her boots walked in a circle. The chains twisted around each other. Then she picked her feet up, and her chains unraveled, whipping her around in circles. Her giggles rolled across the park, and my chest ached.

"Then what do you usually do on your dates? I assume mediocre pizza and walks in the park aren't your usual go-to."

Absolutely not.

While I may have considered a walk in a park, pizza of any kind, mediocre or not, would be completely out of the question. I was still amazed that she was able to talk me into having a couple of slices. Not that it took much convincing, just a bat of her pretty lashes and a pleading smile. I gave in with only perfunctory resistance and destroyed my diet in thirty minutes. But I couldn't bring myself to fully regret the food; I hadn't had a cheat day in months, and it wasn't like letting loose one or two times would kill me or my career, right?

"Maybe they need to be because I've had more fun in the past couple of hours than any dates I've ever been on."

A blush crept up Milly's shy face.

I pushed off the ground and swung back, the metal chains squeaking under my weight. "My usual dates are pretty boring. We go to fancy restaurants or museums or even hockey games—as if I don't get enough of those already."

"The restaurants and museums don't sound too boring, though."

I shrugged and swung back and forth. "You're right. The dates were fine. It was the company that I had a problem with. Women who only wanted me because I could afford to go to the best restaurants and buy them the newest trinkets.

Hell, I once had a woman date me because she wanted season tickets for the Blizzards. For my entire career, every woman I've ever dated has only wanted me for what I can give them access to rather than for me."

Milly's swing came to an abrupt stop, and her face pinched. "That's awful," she muttered, gaze on the ground.

"Oh, no," I sputtered. "I didn't mean you. I know you're nothing like that. You didn't know anything about who I was when we met and have never asked me for anything."

Her apathy toward me at first was actually one of the main reasons I'd even looked at her twice. Had Milly recognized me that day in the kitchen break room and fan-girled over me, I would have been put off from her.

Like my mother drilled into my and my brothers' heads, I went into every relationship with the intent to find the person I wanted to spend the rest of my life with. But since high school, I could never find out what I was doing wrong. And my mother refused to tell me. While my father was the one to push me and my brothers to do the best we can in sports, our mother was our emotional rock. By her own admission, she was a hopeless romantic and made sure that each of her three boys followed in her footsteps.

And we did. Every one of us were unapologetic momma's boys and had a vested interest in finding the perfect life partners like our mother had with our father. Unfortunately, it took me dating fans and a few puck-bunnies for way too long to realize the problem with my dating habits. While my mother wanted us to find the right partners as much as we did, she let us make our own mistakes. Since then, I hadn't dated anyone, which has done wonders for my hockey game, but I think I've finally found a good one with Milly Chambers. I mean, I ate pizza for her; I must be completely gone on her.

For a moment, the only sound between us was the creaking of the old metal chains as we swung lazily. Then Milly looked back up from the ground, her smile a touch forced. I soldiered forward to dissipate the weird energy between us. I didn't know what I said wrong, but I didn't like the look it put on Milly's face. Maybe she had problems with people using her as well.

"What about you? What were dates like in France? I assume it was all street cafes and croissants in the morning."

Like a switch was flipped, Milly came back to life with a laugh. She twisted the chains of her swing, spinning about softly, and shook her head with bemusement. "I wouldn't know. I never went on a date in France."

I gaped at her. "How is it possible no one asked you out? Have you seen yourself?"

The pink sky lit up the blush playing across her face. "People asked me out, but I always said no. I didn't have the time for things like that. Kitchen hours are long, and by the time I got off a sixteen-hour shift, I just wanted to pass out."

"I didn't know you worked shifts that long. I haven't worked a nine-to-five since high school but that seems a little rough."

"No. That was actually the part I loved. I basically lived in kitchens across France, creating whatever I wanted and living my dream. I don't miss much about working in professional kitchens, but the fire in the people, the passion of the chefs there, was inspiring."

Her eyes drifted off to the side as if she had disappeared into the past.

"Then why did you leave?" I asked.

Her gaze refocused. Then turned dark. She attempted to tuck her already tucked hair behind her ears.

"Because with passion like that, there are always downsides. Chefs don't only expect perfection and genius from themselves, they expect it from everyone around them as well. You know those shows you watched? The ones with screaming bosses and terrified chefs? Those are tame compared to precision kitchens in France."

"And you couldn't take it," I guessed.

She shrugged. "I could at first. But as time went on, it didn't seem worth it."

"So you left."

"*If you can't take the heat, get out of the kitchen,*" she said in French, her accent perfect compared to my southern take on the language.

I considered her. She wasn't telling me the whole story, but it wasn't the time to push. I'd already driven some darkness into her eyes, and

I couldn't stand the thought of putting more remembered pain into those deep waters. I pivoted away from the subject, but I didn't forget the look on her face that reminded me of when I'd asked Kingston if he really loved playing hockey or if he was just doing what was expected of him.

"Well, I, for one, am glad you left," I said.

Her eyebrows shot up under her bangs. Red lips twitched. "Oh, yeah?"

My hand darted out, and I grabbed the chain of Milly's swing. I yanked, and we collided together. Milly laughed at the sudden jerk. Keeping a grip on both of our swings, I rocked us side to side. To keep her balance, Milly grabbed onto her chains, her giggles floating through the air.

"Yeah," I said as her laughter died down and we spun off-axis. "Because if you'd never left, I wouldn't have met you. And that would be a tragedy."

Milly sobered, staring into my eyes, then leaned in for a kiss that left me reeling.

My back slammed into my front door, closing it with a bang. I barely had time to breathe before I was cradling the woman crawling all over me. I ran my hands down her delicious curves, my palms practically twitching with need after spending the drive home firmly on the wheel and away from the woman radiating need in my passenger seat.

I'd barely managed to hold it together in the elevator, not wanting to give Mr. and Mrs. Bergman a show. Apparently, Milly was holding herself back just as much, because the second we were safely in my penthouse, I was being attacked. And I fucking loved it.

Memories of the last time I'd had her lips on mine that morning at her place flashed through my mind, and my hands slid down her waist to grip at her leather-covered thighs. I couldn't wait for another taste of that delicious pussy.

Then a thought crossed my brain, and my hands stopped groping. I pulled away from the lips I had become obsessed with since the first time I'd seen them.

"Wait, wait, wait," I gasped out, and Milly immediately pulled back, ripping herself from my hands.

She took three steps back, putting herself out of my reach. With the back of her hand, she wiped her lips clean of saliva. Her lipstick didn't budge. Then, with a deep breath that did nothing to quell the lust in her eyes, she took another step back.

"What's wrong?" she asked.

Her voice was full of gravel, and she was an octave away from growling at me. I had to hold in my answering rough sound.

"We need to stop."

Hurt flashed across her face, followed quickly by embarrassment.

"Wait, no! Not that I don't want this, and you. I mean, goddamn … look at you." I caught myself drifting into fantasy, dreaming of all the things I wanted to do to the amazing woman standing before me and forced myself to snap back to reality. "But you still haven't given me an answer."

"About what?"

"I know you're hesitant to put a label on us, and I don't want to rush you, but the only person I want to sleep with is my girlfriend. And if that means holding off on sex until you're ready to be her, I'm perfectly willing to do that."

Milly shook her head with a fond smirk.

"What's that look for?" I asked.

Without answering, she reached for the hem of her short top and pulled it over her head. A bright-red lace bra, the exact shade of the lipstick that I was coming to find synonymous with Milly Chambers, lovingly cupped her pale, full tits. Oxygen fled my lungs. I had never been so jealous of a piece of clothing before. I remembered how those tits felt in my palms, warm and hefty, and I longed to feel her thick curves again and watch as she denotated into a million pieces around me. Before I could get too carried away, my gaze snapped back up to Milly's face as she spoke.

"Okay, I'll be your girlfriend. I'll even put it on my Facebook to make it official."

"Really?" I barely had time to ask before her bra was gone, her beautiful tits springing forth, and the crimson underwear was being flung in my direction.

I caught it on instinct. Amusement fluttered through me. I'd never had someone throw a bra at me. I may be famous, but I wasn't a rockstar. Then Milly stalked toward me, and I felt less like a rockstar and more like a god. A god blessed with the most gorgeous woman in the world.

I dropped the scrap of lace to the floor, and my hands went to her waist. A grunt escaped me as her soft flesh warmed my palms. I dug my fingers into her sides and pulled her the rest of the way to me until she was plastered against my chest.

"Yes. Really," she purred into my ear.

I didn't do her the disservice of questioning her again. Instead, I grabbed her by her plush thighs and heaved her up. She let out an adorable squeak and wrapped her arms behind my neck as her legs wound around my waist. Our new height difference put her tits right in front of me, so I immediately buried my face in them. I breathed in, and vanilla filled my nose.

Then her chest trembled, and I picked my head up to find Milly laughing at me fondly. She smiled down at me.

"Take me to bed, boyfriend," she ordered.

"Sure thing, darlin'."

I was across my apartment and kicking open my bedroom room before I realized I was moving.

Crossing the length of the room took seconds, then I was dropping Milly onto my navy comforter. She immediately flopped down and made a snow angel on the soft bed.

"Nice."

I smirked down at her, marveling at how sexy she looked only half-dressed. I'd seen her fully nude, yet somehow having her here on my bed in only her skin-tight leather pants and boots was turning me on more than anything had before. Said boots lifted off the edge of the bed and hung in the air between us. She wiggled her feet.

"You mind helping me out of these?"

I stepped forward until her boots rested on my thighs. I had the laces undone in a flash, placed her shoes off to the side, then laughed at the way Milly was squirming on the bed, fighting her pants.

"What are you doing?" I asked between chuckles.

Milly stopped wiggling and gave up on pushing at the top of her pants. "These pants have glued themselves to me."

"Need a hand?"

"Yes, please."

I bent over Milly, kissed her hard, grabbed the tops of her pants, and had them off with one good yank. Once free from her clothes and only in a lacy thong that matched the bra laying somewhere in my entryway, Milly sat up and reached for my hips.

"Your turn," she said.

I stepped between her spread thighs until I ran into the bed. She grabbed onto my hips to pull me closer and tugged eagerly at the front of my belt. While she did that, I undid the top buttons of my shirt until it was loose enough to pull over my head then whipped it off. Then my pants were undone and being shoved down my legs with my boxer briefs. My cock sprang free from its tight confines and greeted Milly eagerly.

Deep-water eyes widened as I finished kicking off my pants.

"Holy shit," Milly breathed out.

I shifted my weight, and my cock bobbed along with me. At eight inches long with a hefty girth, I knew I was bigger than average. Silence stretched for a moment as Milly seemed hypnotized, and I felt the uncomfortable urge to apologize. Then her hand reached out and grasped me. A moan burst from me at her touch, and I flexed my stomach to keep from immediately thrusting into her sure grip.

"Damn, darlin'."

With a playful look shot my way, Milly's knees hit the floor.

I held my breath.

A pink tongue ran up the length of my cock, and I almost lost my footing.

I watched, enraptured, as red lips parted and wrapped around my cut head. Warmth, hot and tight, surrounded me. Then Milly added suction into the mix, and I was lost. She bobbed up and down, working herself farther down my length on each stroke, her painted lips a sight against my dark cock. Just when I thought I'd reached the back of her throat, she pushed farther, and I sunk down her esophagus. My hips jerked forward of their own volition before I could stop them. I stuttered out an apology, but Milly just moaned around me, gripped my ass, and pulled me back down her throat. Her free hand went up to play with my balls, and I swore I blacked out for a second. My lungs heaved erratically as warmth rose through my stomach and up my spine, sending tingling sensations across my whole body as Milly sunk down again, her dark hair falling around us. I gathered the curtain of her wavy hair in a loose grip, not wanting to miss a second of the magnificent show that Milly was putting on.

She popped off my cock and glanced up at me from under her disheveled bangs. Water had pooled in the corner of her eyes, and her chest heaved. "Harder."

I obeyed, and she moaned as I pulled her hair.

The hand on my ass disappeared. I glanced down blearily to see Milly shoving away the crotch of her soaked panties to bury her magical fingers in her pussy. My thighs clenched in an aborted thrust. That was it; I couldn't take any more. With my grip on her hair, I pulled Milly off my cock with a wet pop. Saliva bubbled at the corners of her lips, and her red lipstick had worn off slightly. A surge of pride swelled in me at the sight of her infallible lipstick smudged.

"I need inside you," I growled.

Milly's thighs spread further, her fingers still playing with her clit, thong pushed to the side. "Then get in here."

I almost tripped over my pants in my haste to fish a condom out of my bedside table. By the time I turned back to the bed, condom victoriously in hand, Milly had stripped off her panties and crawled to the top of my bed, lounging against the black headboard like a queen. All at once, Milly was gone and only Chef Chambers remained, so at ease in her surroundings and confident in her abilities that I almost believed my bedroom had turned into a kitchen.

"You're the most gorgeous woman in the world, darlin'," I breathed out in awe from the foot of the bed.

She tilted her head, and her hair fell to the side, exposing the long line of her throat. "Yeah? Then you should get a closer look."

She didn't have to tell me twice.

I exploded forward with every shred of power I'd trained into me over the past decades, grabbed her by the ankles, and pulled her away from the headboard. Arousal radiated from her every molecule as she allowed me to drag her down the bed until I was kneeling between her legs and she was staring up at me. Her dark hair billowed out around her head. I crawled up her body, caging her between my arms. She stretched out under me, her back arching and pushing her eager nipples into the air. The space between us filled with anticipation.

Bracing one hand beside her head to hold myself up, I brought my free hand to her face. Her lashes fluttered as I traced the ridges of her cheekbones. I trailed my hand down her body, dancing through the valley between her breasts, over her padded stomach, and across the sharp jut of her hips. Goosebumps rose in the wake of my fingertips until they stopped just short of where she wanted me. I tapped over the trimmed patch of hair and waited.

Three, two, one…

"Please."

My smile was more of a baring of teeth as I parted her lips with the ghost of a touch over her clit and plunged a finger into the pussy I'd been dreaming of for the past seventeen nights. Milly's back left the bed as a moan tore through the air. I pumped my fingers and brought my thumb into the fun by playing with her clit.

"Yes! Yes! Yes!" she screamed and reached up to claw her nails into my shoulders. She clung to me as I inserted another finger into the tight heat of her and flicked her clit. Suddenly, a hand was darting out and the condom that I'd set aside on the bed was being slapped against my chest.

I paused, taking a moment to appreciate the view blessing my eyes as my fingers continued to pump into silky, tight heaven.

"Wow." The exclamation slipped from my lips on an exhale.

A buffet of flawless ivory skin spread out before me, mine to touch, taste, and worship as much as I pleased. From her flushed face all the way down to the feet locked behind my waist, Milly had given herself over to me. It was a trust so profound that I could do nothing but deliver to her everything she desired. And right now, that was me.

I hovered over her, ignoring the pain in my abs from the exertion of our activities, and rained down kisses like prayers, worshiping my queen.

"Ethan," she moaned.

I couldn't wait any longer. I drew my hand out of Milly, tore open the condom, sheathed myself in the latex, then settled at her entrance. My fingers clenched onto her thick thighs as I held them open for me, flesh bulging around my knuckles. Her body rippled under me as if a wave was rolling through her and pushed her pussy onto the tip of my cock.

Deep-water eyes obscured by blown pupils glared up at me. "Ethan motherfucking Jones, if you don't get inside me this instant I'm going to kill—Fuck!"

I bottomed out in one smooth thrust.

Dual groans rent the air, joining together in glorious harmony. Then the higher-pitched vocals turned into a whine as I stilled inside of the juiciest pussy I'd ever felt. My molars ground together as my lungs stalled. Fire lanced up my abs. If I moved even a centimeter, I was going to be done for. Unfortunately, Milly didn't seem to share my problem.

Her heels dug into the back of my thighs and urged me on like a stallion. I had no choice but to draw out, light-headed from holding my breath, then slammed back into her. By some miracle, I held back my release and drove into her again. Her nails left gouges down my biceps, and I welcomed the pain that kept me grounded. I pounded into her, wordlessly encouraged to continue on harder and harder by her symphony of moans and breathy screams.

Sweat beaded on my forehead. I wiped it away absently, entirely focused on the woman writhing in ecstasy below me. She thrashed about, only my tight grip on her keeping us connected. I chanced dropping a hand from her thigh and reached between us, feeling for that little nub. My fingers homed in on it with unerring accuracy.

"Scream for me, darlin'."

I tapped her clit, and, as if I'd pressed her self-destruct button, Milly exploded around me. The cry she let out lanced my eardrums, but I listened to every sharp sound as her clenching body rode out the last of its orgasm on my throbbing cock.

By the time she came down, her screams turning to whimpers and her pussy fluttering weakly around me, I couldn't hold back anymore. Two more thrusts, and I was spilling into the condom, electricity shooting up my spine while blackness painted the edges of my vision.

I barely registered pulling out of Milly, keeping a grip on the base of the condom on pure instinct. Then I was on my back beside her, chest heaving as my over-heated body tried to cool down. Beside me, Milly's head flopped to the side, and I was graced with a glazed look of satisfaction as thanks for a job well done.

I couldn't stop the love-struck smile that cut across my face if I wanted to. And I didn't want to.

17

Milly

With more effort than I expected, I heaved myself up as Ethan ridded himself of his condom into a tissue. After shooting the wadded-up tissue into a trashcan in the corner of his huge bedroom—and fist pumping the air when it sailed effortlessly in—Ethan collapsed onto his back and found me sitting cross-legged beside him. I laughed at his ridiculousness.

"I'm an athlete," he defended himself.

I giggled again, and he pouted.

Still sprawled out before me like a delicious buffet that was all for me, Ethan pursed his lips. "Having someone laugh at you after sex is hard on the ego, you know? I may never recover from this."

Sobering, I unfolded my legs, swung one over Ethan, and shifted until I was straddling his diaphragm. His hands automatically came up to my thighs to steady me.

I smirked down at him. "That's a shame," I purred. "I was really hoping you would bounce back fast."

Lust reignited in Ethan, turning his brown eyes from puppy dog to predator. "Like I said, darlin'. I'm an athlete. Don't challenge me if you're not ready for the consequences."

My hips rolled. "Oh, I think I'm ready."

The hard planes of Ethan's muscles flexed underneath me, and I braced for him to shoot up.

Ring. Ring. Ring.

The noise came from somewhere under the bed. Ethan groaned and swung an arm over his eyes.

"Always being interrupted," he grumbled.

The ringtone was mine, so I dismounted Ethan and hopped off the mattress. "At least we got through round one," I teased while fishing for my pants that had been kicked deep under the bed.

When I popped up, cell in hand, I was greeted by Ethan glaring balefully at me. I smirked at him and answered the phone.

"This better be good, Thea, or I'm hanging up on you."

Hang up, Ethan mouthed.

"Don't hang up," Thea's tinny voice demanded.

I waved off Ethan and sat on the edge of the bed, putting my back to the gorgeous man. If I looked at him any longer, I would jump him.

A high-pitched whine came from behind me, but Thea took my attention.

"I'm sending you an address. Get there as soon as you can."

My brow furrowed as my cell dinged with a new message. "Is everything okay? What's going on? It's"—I pulled the phone away from my ear, checked the time, and blinked in surprise—"almost ten."

"Nothing's wrong. I just need you to come to the address."

"I'm a little … busy at the moment."

A pause. Thea's voice turned secretive. "Are you with Ethan?"

I debated not telling her for a second but knew there was no use hiding it from her. "Yes."

A squeal about burst my eardrum.

"Really, Thea?" Usually Thea was a hard-ass, but when it came to relationships, she melted.

"Sorry." A throat clearing came over the phone. "But I need you to come. Ditch him or bring him. I don't care. Just get here."

With that, she hung up. Abrupt and rude; there was the Thea I knew.

I dropped the phone to my lap and chewed off my lipstick. *What the hell was that about?*

"Are you okay?" Ethan asked, his voice cracking. It almost sounded as if he was holding back tears.

I turned to find him sitting up, his navy comforter pulled over his lap. His brows were furrowed, and pain swam in his eyes, turning their usual light brown into a dark umber. Startled, I checked him over, my heart kicking in my chest. I knew we had been a tad bit rough, but I shouldn't have done any damage to him. From what I could see, he didn't appear to be injured. Only light scratches from my nails decorated his arms, but it was nothing too serious.

"What's wrong?" I asked, phone call forgotten.

"I need you to tell me the truth," he pleaded.

I tensed. Where was he going with this?

Hesitantly, I nodded. "Sure."

"Did I hurt you?"

"Huh?"

His hand shot up toward me but came to an abrupt halt before his fingertips touched my bicep. His fingers wavered in the air. Then, with the greatest care, he laid his hand on me and, his pressure feather-light, turned me around so he could see my back.

"Di... Did I do this?"

I still didn't get it.

"I swear it wasn't on purpose. I didn't even notice until you turned around to take your phone call. Does it hurt?"

A touch brushed across my back, and a sharp jolt of pain lanced through me, bringing under-standing. *Oh. Oh, shit.*

I twisted around sharply and grabbed his shaking hand with both of mine. Squeezing his large hand between mine, I looked deep into his eyes. Pain and shame had darkened them.

"Ethan. You did not hurt me. I promise."

"But your back is covered in bruises."

"You're a hockey player. I'm sure you've seen and had your fair share of bruises before. How old do these look?" I gave him my back again, allowing him another full view of the mottled bruises that I knew were decorating the whole of my left lat. I barely registered the pain of turning around, used to the sharp pangs after getting hip checked too hard into the track railing a couple of practices ago.

Silence reigned behind me as Ethan studied the sickly colors. Barely-there touches sprinkled down my back.

"These are at least a few days old, if not a week." There was no relief in his tone.

I faced him. "See? You didn't hurt me, Ethan. I'm okay."

"Then who did this to you?"

I pulled back, his hand dropping from me and my walls going up with a resounding *bang*. There was no way I was telling Ethan how I got injured. There was no way I was telling anyone outside of my team. I couldn't risk it. Not when I had already lost one passion by daring to change up my routine. Roller derby was the only thing I had left that was completely mine, and I refused to let anyone taint it.

"It's okay, Milly. You can trust me. I would never betray you."

Just like that, my walls crack under the sledgehammer of Ethan's sincerity. Before I knew it, I was off the bed and booking it, fully nude, to the ensuite bathroom in the back corner of Ethan's bedroom.

"Milly?" he called to my retreating back, but I ignored him.

The door slammed shut behind me. I didn't bother locking it; I knew he would give me the space I needed. He always seemed to know what I needed. And, as he said, he would never betray me or my trust.

I slumped against the door. *Not like I'm betraying him,* I thought acidly.

And I was. I was lying to him. I was using him just like all the other women he's dated had. He may have thought I was different, but I wasn't. The guilt that had been buried under my lust came roaring back.

Suddenly, I was back on the swing sets in a random park in the middle of Queens, listening to Ethan pour his heart out about all the women who have hurt and used him and knowing I was no better. Knowing I was hurting this kind, gentle, loving man for my own gain.

I looked up from staring at my toes, seeing Ethan's bathroom for the first time. Like the rest of his apartment, everything was oversized. From the enormous tub that I would love to have a soak in, to the glass shower and walk-in closet that hung open, everything was sized for a man twice Ethan's size. And, considering how huge he already was, that was saying something.

I paced across the space, the floor cold on my bare toes.

My mind raced as I stared blankly at my surroundings. The concrete floor and black cabinets reminded me of his kitchen. The kitchen where I'd been cooking for Ethan, not because it was my job, but because he was my unwitting muse.

A jar of coconut moisturizer lay on the counter. I opened it, and the scent that I'd begun associating with Ethan bombarded me. I closed the lid and made my way to the shower, a memory tingling at the back of my mind. I peered through the glass panes, and there it was—a jar of coconut oil. The man really loved his coconut. For some reason, that brought a smile to my face.

I turned to the mirror and shook my head at the reflection of the smiling, sex-mussed woman with crazy hair. Just the thought of Ethan could cheer me up and rescue me from my own head. I couldn't do it, I decided all at once. I couldn't betray him. But … I needed time to do this right.

The smile flaked off my face like old paint.

I had to do this carefully. Because, as I was coming to discover, I didn't want to lose Ethan. Not because he was the key to my success in the kitchen though. But because I found the thought of a world without him in it to be dull and lacking the light that Ethan seemed to embody.

I shifted my weight as I considered how to do this, and a hot soreness radiated through my back. A lightbulb went off somewhere in the chaos of my mind.

I couldn't tell him the whole truth just yet, but I could let him in like he had let me in. All it would take was risking the one thing that I still had passion for. *No pressure.*

I splashed some water on my face, patted it dry, then exited the bathroom.

I didn't know how long I had been having an existential crisis, but I knew Ethan would be waiting for however long he needed to.

I was right.

At the sound of the door, Ethan pivoted around from where he stood in the middle of his room. He had put his slacks back on but nothing else. The sight threatened to distract me, but I held onto my resolve. I strode over to him, determination in my step, and gathered my pants and panties on the floor beside him.

"Come with me," I demanded and left his room to find my shirt and bra somewhere in his entryway, knowing he would follow.

He always did exactly what I needed him to.

"This is where people die," Ethan commented casually as he navigated the dark road. "Am I about to die?"

I blinked.

Ethan had been silent the whole drive, patiently waiting to see why I was giving him random directions to a run-down, semi-industrial area on the outskirts of Manhattan.

"Well, if you're about to die then so am I, because I have no idea where we are." I looked at the GPS on my phone. "Turn left here."

Ethan obeyed, and the street we turned onto looked marginally less sketchy.

"Does Dr. McKenna usually call you out to random parts of the city in the middle of the night? And do you usually just go without question."

I shrugged. "Not really. But she tends to have good reasons for whatever she does. And I have a vague idea who we're meeting."

We took another left and ended up in the crowded parking lot of a short rectangular building. A sign with a pair of neon roller skates lit up the lot in pink.

My suspicions were confirmed. But instead of being relieved, a wave of nervous energy flowed through me, making my leg bounce on the rubber mat of Ethan's SUV. There was no turning back now. Ethan was about to see a side of me that I hadn't shown to anybody outside of my team before.

Ethan studied the building, taking in the neon sign and the mass of cars that was odd for the time of night. "I've been meaning to ask you since we first met. How do you know Dr. McKenna?"

I nodded at the building. "You're about to find out."

Ethan put his SUV in park, and I hopped out.

I recognized most of the cars surrounding me. Confident we weren't about to be attacked and mugged in the sketchy parking lot, I waited for Ethan to get out, and we headed toward the neon sign and the front door. As we reached the building, I kept an ear out, but the inside of the building was dead quiet. Through the frosted plexiglass door, I could see no lights. They were up to something.

I pushed open the doors.

"Surprise!" two dozen women screamed at me as the lights flipped on.

I stepped back from the sudden noise and ran into Ethan.

He steadied me then dropped his lips to my ear. "Is it your birthday?"

"No," I mumbled back as my eyes adjusted to the fluorescent lights. "I have no idea what's going on."

I looked around the inside of the roller rink. Ethan and I stood in the lobby area, a ticket booth and a skate rental bar to our right. In front of us, congregated on a carpeted lounge area, my entire derby team smiled at me. Most of them were in their skates, obviously ready to jump onto the wooden roller rink to my left that took up the majority of the building. Everybody stared at me, huge smiles of anticipation on their faces.

It was obviously a party, but I had no idea why.

Thankfully, the lady with all the answers separated from the crowd and wobbled over to me, the carpet making her skates useless. "Congratulations," she screamed as she came at me, a sparkly vision in her sequined, black tank top and booty shorts that were inappropriate for the weather.

"Congratulations!" The girls echoed.

"Nice going, Chopkick!" someone cheered, and the girls broke into chants of my derby name.

My laugh ended with a dozen question marks.

"What's going on?" I asked Thea over the noise as she finally made it over to me and Ethan.

Thea glanced behind her then let out an irritated huff.

"Guys, the sign," she shouted and pointed with a sharp finger.

A few girls quickly jumped off the half wall encircling the rink, revealing a banner. "O captain, my captain!" it read.

Everything clicked together.

Oh my God.

Thea turned back around, a proud smile on her face, and I launched myself at her. I enveloped her in a lethally hard hug.

"Are you serious?" I screamed into her ear.

"The vote was unanimous. You're the new captain of the NYC Killers."

I squealed and squeezed her tighter until she tapped out.

"Ready. Steady. Go!" Skate Winslet shouted, and five girls took off down the roller rink. The rest of the girls cheered as the racers made the first of

their two laps around the rink. I didn't bother with more than a curious glance. I knew who would win the race; Trauma Queen was undefeated.

I returned to the wall of rental skates with a grimace. Had I known we were heading to a roller rink, I would have insisted on stopping by my apartment to grab my skates.

"Just grab whatever. Lady MacDeath's girlfriend owns the place and told us to have at whatever we needed. As long as we put everything back, of course," Thea said beside me.

With a nod, I finally grabbed a pair of size nine skates in the most hideous muddy orange that had ever cursed my eyes, then we rounded the rental counter to head back to the main area. Carpeted benches lined the half-wall of the rink. I popped a squat and kicked off my boots.

Thea dropped down next to me, looking around conspiratorially. "So, you brought him, huh? I didn't expect that."

I glanced over my shoulder to make sure Ethan was still at the snack table and out of earshot. He was. Still, I leaned toward Thea and dropped my voice.

"Well, I figured what was the point of hiding this from him."

Thea's ginger brow furrowed. "What do you mean?"

I sighed. "I'm going to tell him about why I started cooking for him. About him being my muse or whatever."

"What? Why?"

"Because I don't want to use him anymore. I don't want to be that person."

"What if he breaks up with you?"

The thought stung more than I anticipated. "If that's what he decides to do, then so be it. But I've made my decision."

Thea's lips pursed. "What about your job, though? What will happen when you can't create new recipes anymore?"

I shrugged. "It's not like I need the job to survive."

"Maybe not monetarily. But can you handle losing what is left of the dream you've had since you were a kid?"

My silence spoke volumes, and a hint of selfish doubt flared to life in my brain.

"How about this," Thea continued. "Wait until you're done making the team menu then tell him. At least that way, you have some extra money. Your savings must be running a little dry after not working for six months. And who knows, maybe by then you'll have learned how to create again without him."

The suggestion was tempting. But could I do it? The guilt of using Ethan had grown exponentially since I'd slept with him. And that had only been a couple of hours ago. Who knew how much worse I would feel if this continued on at its current pace? Our relationship was getting serious—more serious than I had expected. It couldn't continue like this, not if I wanted it to last. And, as I was finding out, I did want it to last.

Unfortunately, once Ethan found out, it wouldn't matter what I wanted. And with his history of girlfriends using him, I had a strong feeling about which way his decision would lean.

A shot tore through me.

"Ok," I breathed out. "I'll put it off for a little longer."

"I think that's the right decision, Milly."

It had to be. I didn't know what I'd do if it wasn't.

18

Ethan

I walked up to Milly as Dr. McKenna left her sitting alone on the bench to finish tying up her skates. A troubled look had settled over her face as she tied her laces into bows then tucked them into the top of her dull-orange rental skates that she had to resort to wearing because she didn't bring her own, unlike the rest of the girls. From what I had seen, she and Thea had just finished a deep conversation, but I didn't overhear what it was about. Whatever it was though, it had left a look on Milly's face that I didn't like.

"Hey, Chopkick," I chirped as I dropped down beside her, carefully placing my flimsy paper plate full of food on the other side of me.

Milly looked up from her feet with a playful grimace, and I smiled to see the dark thoughts gone from her ocean eyes.

"And you had the nerve to make fun of my nickname," I continued my teasing.

"Hey. Yours is objectively worse. At least mine has some flare."

"Fine. You may be right. So, who picked it out, because I know it wasn't you."

Milly chuckled. "Thea did."

I gaped at her for a second then looked around the roller rink, trying to spot Dr. McKenna. I found her on the rink, dancing on her skates to the music blaring from the speakers hanging over the rink. It was only the second time I'd seen her so carefree, the first being the day I'd met Milly in the kitchen break room.

I turned back to Milly. "Dr. McKenna is *punny*?"

I wouldn't have believed it a day ago, but after all the new information I was learning today, I shouldn't have been surprised.

"Oh, yeah. She's the worst."

"What's her derby name?"

"Dr. Jekyll."

A laugh barked out of me. "Sounds about right."

Milly giggled.

I picked up a slice of pizza from my paper plate and took a huge bite of cheese and pepperoni.

"More pizza?"

I shrugged and swallowed. "It's the only thing they have."

Milly's voice filled with gravel. "And after we just finished working off the extra calories of our last meal."

Flashes of our strenuous bedroom exercises raced through my mind. My bite of pizza went down hard. "I guess we'll just have to burn off these calories as well."

Lust flared in Milly's eyes, and an evil grin pulled up the corners of her lips. "I guess so."

I fell into her deep-water eyes and lost time. It wasn't until a cheer was let out on the rink that I snapped out of the trance my woman had put me into. Our gazes broke apart, the electricity that was streaming between us dissipating but leaving a lasting effect. I shifted on the bench, my pants tighter than they should have been, and silently thanked the interruption. I had been seconds away from jumping Milly in the world's most scandalous PDA ever seen.

I cleared my throat, unsuccessfully attempting to rid myself of the lust choking me. "So," I practically growled. "Roller derby, huh?"

Milly nodded, clearly trying to get ahold of herself as well, and reached over my lap to steal a slice off my plate. She bit, chewed, and swallowed. "Yeah. I've been playing since I got back to New York."

"Is that how you met McKenna?"

"The other way around. Thea is my neighbor and invited me to join the team when I was in the middle of moving into my apartment on my first day back in the city. I didn't know if I would like it at first, but I've grown to love it."

"And you must be good at it. Otherwise, you wouldn't have been made captain so early."

A blush spread up her cheeks. "I don't know about that."

"Well, I do. I was talking to some of your teammates earlier, and they wouldn't stop singing your praises."

"I'm sure they were exaggerating. And you're a team captain, too. You know it's about more than skill on the field. It's about passion and teamwork. And about being friends with and caring about your teammates for more than just what they can provide for the team. But also, at the same time, not overwhelming them and letting them come to you with their problems. The support that these girls give each other is like nothing I've ever experienced before." Her face filled with life as she spoke about the game that she obviously had so much love for.

I watched her in awe. It was the same expression that I'd caught brief glimpses of in the kitchen when she was in the throes of a new recipe.

Then something in her words registered.

Let them come to you?

I froze. Could it be that easy? Did Milly just solve my problem?

"It's nothing like being a chef," she continued on, not realizing the lightbulb that she'd set off in my brain. "I'd never experienced what being on a team was like before joining the Killers. I mean, sure, theoretically everyone in the kitchen is on the same team, but in actuality, it's a dog-eat-dog world and everyone is out for themselves. Joining this team made me realize that. And made me understand that wasn't what I wanted to surround myself with. No matter what happened afterward, I don't regret leaving the culinary world."

She stopped abruptly, eyes wide as if she just realized she went on a bit of a tirade and shoved more pizza into her mouth.

I grinned. Damn, she was amazing.

After swallowing her bite, she cleared her throat. "But of course, you know all of that. I've seen you with your team. You're a great captain."

"I'm sure you'll be just as fantastic as me, if not more so."

A flush of pink erupted on her cheeks. "I don't know about that. I think I got the position because I'm friendly with all the girls and try to help them out in any way I can. But you're different; you've got that strategic brain. You would probably be a great coach too."

Wait. What?

Three days later, Milly's words still pinged around my mind like the puck being passed around on the ice in front of me. From the bench, I mindlessly watched the rubber disk as Frey came up with it and shot toward our opponents' goal. Three Ottawa Polars sped after him, but Frey put on the burners and broke away. On the other side of the ice, Little matched Frey's speed and dodged around some stray Polars. Little made himself open, and I caught the considering look Frey threw him. Then with a stony face, Frey dismissed Little and took the shot at goal on his own. The puck hit the goalpost and deflected directly into the goaltender's glove.

Frey deflated at the missed attempt, and the crowd sighed along with him. Then the Blizzards' home team crowd clapped, encouraging Frey to get them next time. If there was one thing about our city that I loved, it would have to be the loyalty our audience showed us. Even when we went through a rough patch for a couple of years as our team suffered injury after injury, they stood by our side, encouraging us to keep going, celebrating our wins and mourning our losses with us.

That was the great thing about this sport; the camaraderie and the support that was inherent in both the teams and the fans. It was why I was so passionate about the game. And my teammates felt the same. Which is why there was one person more disappointed about Frey's missed shot than Frey himself—Little.

On the other side of the opponent's net, Little looked like a kicked golden retriever. I sympathized with him. Not only did he know he wasn't on his best game, everyone else did as well. Especially Frey, his linemate. And to have your linemate not pass the puck to you because they didn't trust in you and your abilities must have stung.

A whistle blew from behind me, followed by a command in a deep voice, and my team-mates on the ice headed to the benches for a switch. Coach Hansson hadn't called for my line, so I waited as my teammates jumped over the half-wall separating us from the ice. Once the players switched and a new line was setting up for a face-off, I heard a deep sigh beside me. I turned to find Mick Little beside me. He did not look happy, but I couldn't tell if it was because of Frey snubbing his help on the ice or because he ended up sitting next to me on the bench. Braced like he was expecting to get hip-checked into the boards, Little kept his stare firmly on the ice and away from me, dimples gouging angry craters into his cheeks.

A few days ago, I would have immediately started up a friendly chat with him, trying to get him to open up to me.

"Nice hustle," I said. Then, I turned back to the ice to watch the face-off, leaving it at that.

I felt Little glance at me as if he was expecting more. No more was coming. No more would ever be coming, in fact, because I was taking Milly's advice. Or more accurately, I was taking Milly's throwaway comment. I wasn't sure if she even noticed during her little speech the other day about why she loved roller derby that she had solved my Mick Little problem.

The solution to getting him to open up wasn't to stay on his ass, it was to ease up and let him come to me. So I was doing just that. And it seemed to be working.

"Thanks," Little grumbled, shoulders relaxing under his pads.

I almost smiled but managed to hold it together. A few days ago, he would have just ignored me, maybe even switched seats. Now, he only threw me a suspicious look and settled in to watch the face-off.

I should be watching our team with him, but my attention was drawn to the other thought that Milly had embedded into my consciousness.

"You're up next, Jones," Coach Hansson said in my ear as he passed behind me, pacing up and down the length of the benches.

I glanced at him as he reached the end of the bench and turned around for another lap, clipboard in hand and intensity in his eyes. For the majority of the game, while his eyes were glued to the ice, mine were glued to him.

Is Milly right? Would I be a good coach?

It seemed absurd that I hadn't thought about it before, because now that I considered it, it was the perfect position for me after I retired.

For a while now, I figured my next step after retirement and taking a long vacation would be to jump into commentating with both feet like my father had after his football career. Hell, I had been watching and studying game tapes and commentary for years now. I knew what the sportscasters would say before they even did. Putting my knowledge of the sport to good use seemed like the next logical step. But I never considered that there was another way to do that.

Not even after occasionally helping out with Kingston's charity and coaching peewee hockey teams. I had fun then, teaching the kids simple drills and plays and watching them improve. But the thought of doing that forever seemed like a dream.

I immediately knocked the end of my stick against my helmet. I had never not chased a dream before.

What the hell was I doing?

Little must have had the same question because he gave me a weird look at the action.

I went on ignoring him as per my plan to reel him in with silent support.

Maybe I shouldn't be a coach if it took me so long, and help from someone else, to understand how to get through to a teammate. I'm sure Coach knew the whole time that my previous method was shit and that Little would never respond to it.

At the thought, I glanced over at Coach again, who had finally stopped pacing to glare at the rink as a Polar stole the puck from our offense and took off down the ice with it. I pictured myself standing where he was, and I liked the image. A spark of determination went off inside of me, familiar and persistent, and my mind was made up.

I was going to become an NHL coach.

Once again, Frey broke away from the pack of Polars and skated down the ice like his life depended on it. The kid had been on fire lately. One would think he was trying to prove something to the world after becoming the first active NHL player to come out as gay, but in actuality, he had always been an aggressive player. The other aggressive player on Frey's line seemed to have regained some of the spirit that had been just out of his reach before and sped after Frey. Little dodged around a stray Polar, more life in his skates than I've seen since he was traded to our team.

A defenseman appeared in Frey's path, big and unmovable. There was only one person available to pass to. Frey passed to Little who got control of the puck immediately. The expanse of ice before him was free and clear.

I leaned forward, eyes glued to the puck. This could be it. The score was tied, and we needed another goal to stop the game from going into a shootout. The puck danced between the blade of Little's stick as he played around with it. His movements were confident and quick. The Polar goalie crouched in his net, ready. Little's stick drew back, and I held my breath as he let it rip.

The black disk flew to the left. The goalie dove for it, glove outstretched. The puck hit the glove, tipped off the edge, and ricocheted into the goal, the white net billowing out with the force of the impact. The goal horn blew, and the audience erupted around us.

"Nice, Little!" Coach roared behind me.

Little looked over at us and met my eyes.

I nodded.

He nodded back then turned his attention to the teammates congratulating him on the ice.

Damn, I thought with a vicious smile. *Milly was onto something.*

My grin turned anticipatory without my permission.

I knew just the way to thank her.

Milly

"**W**here are we going?" I asked Ethan as he guided me across his apartment. When he said he had a surprise for me, I expected to head into his bedroom for some fun. Instead, he towed me by the hand out his front door and … to the end of his hallway?

A metal door that read "roof access" popped open as Ethan typed in a passcode to the keypad beside it, and a flight of stairs appeared ahead of us.

I hesitated. "Why are we going to the roof?"

"Come on. You'll like it, darlin'."

I wasn't so sure about that. I was likely to have a heart attack before I enjoyed anything on a roof. But I could never resist Ethan. I took a deep breath, let it out in a controlled stream of air, and let Ethan lead me up the stairs without complaint.

Well, without verbal complaint. Internally, I was losing it. My heart raced, and my palms started to sweat where Ethan's fingers interlaced with mine. He didn't even notice, too excited by whatever this surprise was. He practically hauled me up the stairs until we were at another metal door. I didn't have time to hesitate again before the door was open and the brisk noon air rushed into the stairwell, blowing up my pigtail braids and bangs around my face. Then I was being pulled outside, and my fear of heights disappeared under the astonishment and pure excitement at what I saw.

"Is that what I think it is?" I squealed.

"Do you like it?" he asked.

The roof was a simple thing, not decked out with furniture like some others in the city. But this roof had something that I had always dreamt of having. In the otherwise empty space, a black-framed structure stood like a mini house in the middle of the roof, the spaces between the metal posts wrapped in what I knew was polycarbonate plastic.

It was a greenhouse!

"How?" I managed to ask.

"I called in the guys who renovated my apartment. They put the greenhouse up in less than an hour."

I stepped toward the house, letting Ethan's hand fall from where I was crushing it in my excitement. "What do you have growing in it?" I pressed my face to the plastic, hands cupped around my eyes, and saw it was empty except for some raised beds and a table. "Nothing?" I asked before Ethan could answer and rounded the little house to find the door in the thick plastic. The hinged door was secured with a padlock, and I turned around to see Ethan holding up a key with a wide smile.

"I figured we could pick out things together since I don't really know what would be best. You must have some ideas, though." He came over, unlocked the door, and pushed it open.

I stepped inside the surprisingly roomy greenhouse and grinned. "Oh, yes. I have a few."

I estimated the space to be about twenty by ten feet. Along the perimeter of the plastic room, raised wooden beds stood waiting to be filled with the variety of vegetables I was already making a mental list of. Under the beds were dozens of plastic bags of soil.

It was the most extravagant yet intimate thing anyone had ever done for me. But what really made me melt in my boots was what sat wrapped in cellophane on the wooden table as if Ethan felt the need to get me more than a whole fucking greenhouse.

I turned to Ethan who stood in the entrance, his wide shoulders filling the doorframe. "You bought me roses?" The tremble in my voice matched the one in my chest.

Ethan smiled that contagious smile. "I know they're not the nicest ones, but I saw them at a bodega and thought of your lipstick. I have a vase inside if you don't think they'll survive the trip back to yours on your bike."

Words escaped me. In all my years of dating, including some Frenchmen who were supposed to be the most romantic men on the Earth, I'd never had someone do anything like this for me. Not only did Ethan remember the little comment I'd made that first day shopping with him, he also remembered the exact shade of the lipstick I always wore.

If I hadn't already decided to come clean to him about my original intentions when I started seeing him, this would have cinched it. Because the colorful feelings swirling in my heart wouldn't allow me to deceive him much longer. But before that...

I took a rose from the cellophane bundle filled to bursting, snapped off half the stem, sauntered to Ethan, and stuck the rose behind his ear. The flower bloomed by his temple, and his brown eyes lit up with mirth. I looked up at him with a satisfied smile, so close to him that I felt it when his chest rumbled with his deep chuckle. Reaching up, I twined my arms behind his neck, rose onto my toes, and pressed a light kiss on the corner of his grin. His beard was soft under my lips, and the silky petals of the crimson rose brushed across my cheek.

"Thank you for the greenhouse. It's amazing," I murmured against his mouth.

He put brief pressure into the kiss then eased back. "You're welcome. There's a garden store about twenty minutes from here where we can go pick up some plants if you want."

I pressed feather-light kisses across his bearded jaw. "I'd love to. But first, I want to properly thank you."

I ran a hand across his shoulder, down his arm, then threaded my fingers with his. I tugged. His lips tugging up at the corners, he followed like he had no choice under my weaker strength, and I led him fully into the greenhouse.

The high-altitude wind slammed the door closed with a clang, and we were shut off from the world inside our little plastic house. The New York City skyline was blurry but visible through the thick plastic, and I knew that our silhouettes would be just as barely discernible to anyone in the neighboring buildings who happened to glance out of their window. That didn't stop me.

I pivoted, dragging Ethan in a circle around me until his back was to the center of the greenhouse and the very sturdy wooden table. I took a step closer to Ethan and plastered my front against his. Then I took another step, forcing him back until the back of his thighs hit the polished table. With a finger against his chest, I pushed. He chuckled darkly but allowed himself to be guided until he was perched on the edge of the table, the wood holding his weight effortlessly.

"Pants," I ordered Ethan, then stepped back, giving him room.

His laugh this time was filled with more amusement than lust. Still, he worked his pants open and slid them down his legs while managing to stay seated on the table.

"What?" I asked as I undid my shirt.

"Nothing." He kicked off his slides, jeans, and boxer briefs. His plain white shirt was tugged off his hard torso in a flash. "You're just bossy."

I paused, my black button-up blouse hanging undone and giving Ethan a peek at my emerald bra. His eyes flashed down for only a second before they returned to my face. I had to give him credit; he made an effort to look me in the eyes during a conversation even when I was undressing in front of him.

My control wasn't as strong as his. My gaze raked down his body, across his broad chest, past the deep grooves of his Adonis belt, and landed on the thickening cock that hung heavy between his thighs. A moan caught in my throat as I remembered how every inch of his body felt on top of me. I barely managed to tear my eyes away from Ethan's naked form, the miles of smooth, hard, black skin mesmerizing.

I let the blouse fall off my arms and puddle around my feet.

"Does bossy scare you?" I asked as my bra followed my blouse.

A savage grin cut across his face as his southern accent came out in full force. "Not at all."

The words flowed over me, and my nipples tightened in the heating air of the greenhouse. Ethan's eyes flicked to the hardened nubs, and he bit down on his plush bottom lip. I couldn't help but picture replacing that lip with my aching breasts, almost feeling the sharp nibbles across my tits and around my nipples. The hunger in his gaze filled me with a confidence that I rarely had during sex, because Ethan was right—I was bossy. Most guys didn't tend to enjoy that. But I was quickly learning that Ethan Jones was not most guys.

I dropped my pants and panties in one swift movement and kicked them off with my shoes. The air trapped in the greenhouse, borderline blistering compared to the icy breeze outside the plastic walls, brushed past my bare skin, raising goosebumps across every inch of my body. I shivered. Then Ethan pushed off the table, grabbed me by the waist, and I shivered for an entirely different reason. He tugged at me, and our bodies collided together with a delicious slap of bare skin on skin. Ethan hummed in delight as I instinctually wrapped my hand behind his neck. His big palms slid up and down my sides, soothing away my goosebumps. I arched into him, the scent of coconut filling my nose.

"In fact," Ethan murmured in my ear. "I think I'm growing to love bossy."

A smirk tugged at my lips as I fiddled with the rose that was one wrong move away from falling from his ear. I secured it back in place and gave the lobe of his ear a nip.

"Oh, yeah?" I leaned back and looked up into Ethan's glowing face. "Then get on the table," I whispered against his lips.

Heat filled his gaze, his pupils expanding until only tiny rings of rich brown were left of his irises. Without another word, he followed my direction. His thick arms flexed, veins popping out against his dark forearms as he heaved himself up and sat on the tabletop.

"More," I said with a smirk as I pushed against his rock-solid chest.

He scooted further onto the table until he was in the center, his arms propping up his upper half as he looked down his splayed-out body at me. I took a second to soak in the sight of him, laid out like a feast for my eyes. I stalked toward the buffet before me until my thighs hit the edge of the table. With a satisfied hum, I placed a light kiss to one of Ethan's calves. Then his knee. Then his thigh. Through my lowered lashes, I kept my gaze locked on his as I worked my way up his body. His eyes watched my every move, face filled with silent anticipation, but he kept his hands to himself, letting me do my thing.

Once I finished exploring one leg, I ignored the weeping cock begging for attention, and turned my attention to the other leg, giving it the same treatment. By the time I finished teasing Ethan within an inch of his life, his cock was soaked in pre-cum and flushed with blood. At some point, Ethan had laid back fully on the wooden table, head tilted to keep me in his view. One hand rested behind his head, while the other absently played with one of his nipples.

I squeezed my thighs together at the sight, wetness slicking them. The pressure squeezed my clit, sending electricity reverberating up my spine, and a moan escaped me. As much as I was teasing Ethan, I was also teasing myself. And I'd about had enough. I climbed onto the table, knees straddling his parted legs.

Ethan's dark brows rose at the change of pace. A low grumble vibrated his chest as I prowled up him, finally giving his cock a single wet lick as I passed by it, then kissed up his abs. A hand reached for my face then pulled me up from worshipping the dips and curves of chiseled abs. I pouted for a second before I found myself looking down at a grinning Ethan, straddling his abdomen, his hard cock pressing against my ass. I turned my face and pressed a deep kiss to his palm.

"Hi, darlin'," he whispered up at me, his thumb caressing my cheek.

I beamed at him, and I could practically feel the sparkles of humor in my eyes. "Hi, cowboy."

"Huh?"

I shook my head. "Nothing."

His eyes narrowed, and his rough hands landed on my hips with evil intent. A half-scream, half-laugh tore out of me as I tried to wiggle out of his grasp, but it was useless.

"Stop. Stop!"

The tickling fingers ceased their torture. "Only if you tell me what you were smiling at."

Coming down from my laughing fit, I smirked at the man between my thighs. I considered holding out for a moment but decided to give in lest I have to endure another tickling session.

"Did you know that your southern comes out when you're turned on?"

Ethan blinked. "What?"

"It's not noticeable usually, but whenever you're flirting or aroused, you're suddenly all 'y'all's and 'darlin''s." I tried to mimic his drawl. From his amused but pained expression, I missed the mark by a mile.

"No, I'm not," he protested.

"Yes, you are. It's cute, though. Makes you seem like a cowboy. All you're missing is the hat."

His rough hands slid down my waist and gripped the tops of my thighs. Texas infused his voice. "If anyone needs a cowboy hat 'ere, littl' darlin', it's you."

The deep drawl fried my brain for a moment before I realized what he said and the position I was in on top of him. A smirk cut across my face, and I rolled my pelvis while scooting back on his hips. My ass settled along the length of his shaft.

A groan tore out of his throat, and the hands on my thighs cranked down.

"I wouldn't mind a hat," I mused aloud, not stopping my grinding. "Maybe some boots." I braced my hands against his ribs, leaned down, and pressed my lips to his ear. "And nothing else."

A growl vibrated Ethan's chest, the image I'd put in his mind practically flashing across his dark eyes. Then I was weightless and clutching at Ethan's shoulders to keep myself from sliding off his body and onto the floor as he reared up.

"What?" I squealed.

Ethan swung his legs off the side of the table then hopped down, holding my weight as if was nothing. With a sharp pivot, Ethan spun us around. My nails dug into his traps as I held on for dear life. Next thing I knew, I was taking Ethan's seat on the table, my legs wrapped around his waist, feet hooked together behind his back, as his mouth descended on mine.

I moaned as his tongue invaded my mouth, and I immediately gave as good as I got. His hands came up to my face and titled my head, getting a better angle to plunder my mouth. Then one of those hands trailed down my torso, leaving a trail of fire in its wake, and landed with the force of a bomb between my thighs. Two fingers slid through my slick folds and shoved into me. I cried out into Ethan's mouth, arching against him as if even my body, along with the rest of me, couldn't get enough of him. Thick digits pumped into me, stroking my insides, while his tongue fucked my mouth the way I wanted his cock to.

"Ethan," I whimpered, words other than his name escaping me.

Thankfully, he knew what I wanted.

After one last pump, his fingers withdrew from me, and the hot length of Ethan parted my pussy. My walls clenched, ready. The head of his cock teased my entrance for a second. My breath hitched, my lungs burning with anticipation. Then, with one long thrust, he bottomed out in me.

Our groans echoed through the greenhouse in a harmony of lust.

The next minutes were lost in a blur of thrusts and moans as Ethan drilled me into the table. With every pump of his hips, the heavy wooden table screeched across the floor an inch until Ethan grabbed onto the edge and pulled it, and me, back toward him. Our hips met with a wet slap, and the breath was driven from my lungs. My muscles liquified under the intense pleasure ricocheting through my body, and I collapsed backward onto the table, spreading out underneath Ethan. I reached up and grabbed the edge of the table above my head, grasping onto anything I could to keep myself grounded in the moment when all I wanted to do was drown in the ecstasy taking over me with every plunge of his thick cock. I writhed against the smooth wood as my eyes crashed into Ethan's. A gasp burst from me at the raw heat in his gaze. Sweat beaded at his temples, and his biceps flexed with every tug against my pelvis as he dragged me to meet each of his thrusts. My thighs squeezed his waist, heels digging into his back as I met his passion, thrust for thrust.

"Fuck, darlin'," he groaned and reached up to roughly pet my cheek, his face full of wonder as he dedicated every bit of himself to my pleasure.

I was lost.

I broke into a million pieces around him, a scream erupting from my throat as I clenched down on the length inside of me and whipped around in ecstasy. Time lost its hold on me as I let the waves of my orgasm wash over me. Only his gaze kept me pinned in place as I finally came down to earth just in time to watch as every muscle in Ethan's body flexed with the force of his own orgasm. His thrusts lost their relentless rhythm. He hunched over me, eyes squeezing shut in pleasure, and stilled as a rush of warmth filled me. My ankles lost their grip behind his back and fell apart as the last of my muscles turned to jelly.

Strong hands crashed down beside my hips, the only things keeping Ethan's heavy body from collapsing onto me. Not that I would have minded taking his weight.

With a satisfied hum, I ran my fingernails up the rippling ropes of his arms until I reached the back of his head and lightly scratched his scalp. Ethan practically purred, and I smiled lazily up at him. The rose I'd tucked behind his ear had managed to stay on against all odds.

His lips parted into his signature smile as his eyes melted.

"You're amazing, darlin'."

I blinked.

"I'm serious. I want to say I've been looking for you my whole life, but that would be a lie. Because I never knew someone like you could exist. I never thought I could meet someone and feel like I've known them my whole life. I didn't believe my mom when she told me. Yet here you are, in the flesh, perfect and all mine."

My face heated, the intimacy of his words rivaling the sex we just had tenfold.

Before I could make my gaping mouth move in a feeble attempt to put the sensations clenching my heart into words, Ethan reached off to the side. A crinkling of cellophane tickled my ears before Ethan straightened up. A rose was in his hand, the flower torn off the stem. He rubbed the bloom between his hands, then separated his palms.

Blood-red petals rained down on my naked body, each one landing against my skin with the weight of a loving kiss.

20

Ethan

With all the confidence that I didn't feel, I knocked on the door looming before me. My heart rate, which had just calmed down from practice, shot back up. I could have waited until I had at least showered off the sweat and grime, but my nervous excitement had forced me to forgo changing, leaving me in my ripe compression pants and long-sleeved shirt. I hadn't even put on shoes for the trip across the arena, and I knew Milly would be making fun of me for walking around in my socks again if she were here.

"Come in," a gruff voice called.

With a deep breath, I entered the office and stopped in front of an oversized desk. Sitting like the king of the castle, Coach Hansson cocked his head at me, his depthless, dark eyes taking in every detail of my awkward stance. His shorn hair only enhanced his drill instructor-like vibe.

I locked down my body, fighting off the urge to shift my weight under his heavy gaze. My eyes refused to meet his and flicked around the room as if I were seeing it for the first time. Unfortunately, there wasn't much in the room to distract me.

Coach kept his office as no-nonsense as he was. Behind the large desk made of some kind of dark wood, the beige wall contained nothing but a sky-blue flag with the team's logo—a silhouette of a wild tornado with a large snowflake embedded into it— hanging dead center. Beside the flag and desk, a corner of shiny filing cabinets was the only thing in my eyeline.

Before I could turn around to peruse the bookshelves that took up the entire back wall of the office, filled to bursting with DVDs because he was old-school and liked to have physical copies of our old games to review, Hansson rapped his rough knuckles against his desk.

"What's going on, Jones?" Hansson asked, breaking the uncomfortable silence that had been building since I stepped foot in the office.

I cleared my throat. "Do you have a second, Coach?"

Without a word, he picked up the remote on the edge of his desk, pointed it over my shoulder at the upper corner of his office where his television hung, and pressed pause. The television had been near-silent, escaping my notice.

Coach's eyes flicked over my shoulder then back to me. A smirk danced on the corner of his lips, and the sun-tanned crinkles around his eyes deepened in mirth.

I glanced behind me, and a snort escaped my nose at what was paused on the television.

"Really, Coach? Football?"

"Hey, I was born in San Francisco, and the 49ers will always have my loyalty."

"Fair enough," I conceded.

"And I like to keep up with most sports. But I don't have time to watch every game, so I leave the highlight reels and commentators running in the background. And this guy is my favorite." He gestured to the television with the remote.

I rolled my eyes, the tension draining from my shoulders, and flopped into a chair across the desk from Coach. Over my shoulder, my father's face, frozen mid-word as he dissected last night's football game, watched over the room. It was both irritating and comforting.

"Eh, he's alright," I dismissed with a laugh.

Hansson leaned back in his leather office chair. "Don't worry. You'll be up there in a few years, and I have no doubt you'll be an amazing commentator. Hell, you'll be just as good, if not better, than your dad."

I hummed. "You think so?"

"Of course. You definitely have the personality for it, and you've got a good head for the game. Plus, with the way you deal with the press, you've got a way with bullshit, something all media personalities need. You'll make a perfect commentator. Just like your father."

My chuckle shredded my throat. "Yeah. I guess I was going to follow in his footsteps, even without picking football."

Maybe that was why I thought being a commentator was the next logical step after retirement—I was simply doing what my father did. I didn't know how to feel about that. While I loved my old man, I've always wanted to pave my own path. Distancing myself from my family's football legacy wasn't the only reason, or even the main reason, I chose to pursue hockey, but it was certainly a factor. And now I was diverging from my father's path again.

"Was?" Coach asked.

I finally met Coach's eyes. "Yeah. Was."

Hansson scratched at his clean-shaven jaw and considered me. I held still under his gaze, but the nervousness that had accompanied me into the office had disappeared. I was Ethan fucking Jones—first black captain of the New York Blizzards, Stanley Cup winner, and now, a future NHL coach.

"What are you going to do instead when you retire?" Coach questioned me.

"I was thinking of taking your job." Blunt. True.

A beat.

Another.

A smile split across Hansson's flat face, lighting him up like the sun was shining through his tan skin, and a deep guffaw echoed around the office. His huge chest trembled under his Blizzards' zip-up as if an earthquake was rumbling through him.

I blinked. Coach rarely laughed at all, let alone this hard. I let him get it out of his system, knowing he was laughing at my audacity, not at my dreams. He would never do that.

When his chuckles finally petered off, his eyes had a wet gleam to them. Then, like a switch had been flipped somewhere, one of the biggest and baddest centers to have ever stepped foot on the ice was staring me down. Hansson was infamous for his intimidating presence on the ice, and while he was no longer a player, he still had the thousand-mile stare that made goalies freeze in their skates when they saw him barreling down at them. His back snapped straight in his chair, and he seemed to fill the entire room.

I held his steely eyes and waited.

"Well, it's about damn time."

My brows slammed down.

Coach lurched forward and braced his forearms on his desk. He about vibrated with excitement, and he leaned closer to me. "I was going to give you one more season to figure it out, then I was going to start hiding whistles and playbooks in your shit until you got the fucking hint. You're practically a faux coach on this team already with the way you treat your teammates. Sure, it's part of your job to help them out and give advice, but you go above and beyond. You always have."

I huffed out a laugh in bemusement. "And that would make me a good coach?"

"You think every captain cares as much as you about their teammates? Hell, I saw you going over game tapes with Nicks the other day."

I shrugged. "He needed help closing a hole in his defense. He made a couple of errors last game."

"I know. And why were you reading a book on hockey strategy on the plane the other day? It couldn't have been for fun. I've read that one, and it's drier than my wife's Christmas cookies."

"Why not?" He was right, though; I fell asleep twice reading it. It had some interesting insight about team mentality though, so it wasn't a total loss.

"Because your gameplay has been flawless since your rookie year, and you're years away from retiring. You don't need to do either of those things. In fact, that's my job."

I opened my mouth to question him again but paused, realizing I was fighting against my own interests. I was arguing about things that I'd figured out over the past couple of days just because I was a little irritated that Coach Hansson had seen what I had been blind to for years. In fact…

"Why didn't you bring this up before, then?"

Coach returned to leaning back in his chair. "It's something you needed to figure out yourself, and I knew you would figure it out eventually.

Looks like Little and his yips problem was the key after all."

"Little?" I asked, wincing at the y-word. You didn't say that word in the arena lest the hockey gods hear you. But sometimes there was no other way to discuss the issues athletes had when life was getting in the way of their ability to play, and Coach had never been superstitious.

"I admit, it was a gamble, bringing on a player that had been having obvious problems for weeks, but I knew whenever you got through to him, he would become the Mick Little that was an unstoppable force on the ice again. And I was hoping he would be the final push that made you realize what I already knew—you want to make each one of those men the best player they can be, and not just for the team but for themselves. That's what a coach is. It's not just about winning; it's about bringing out the full potential of every player and not just churning out hockey robots. First, you have to care about the person and the team; the winning comes after."

My mind spun with information, flying thoughts escaping my grasp. But one thing kept on coming back around—Milly. This was all because of her. It was Milly that made me even consider coaching, not Little. And if it wasn't for her, I don't know if I would have ever gotten through to Little. Before her, I was just driving Little away with my obsessive need to help. Her advice to give him space and silent encouragement and trust was the only reason Little had relaxed around me and on the ice.

For the past few days, Little had been playing better than he had since he'd joined the Blizzards. His goal a couple of games ago was only the beginning. He had stopped fumbling pucks and making rookie mistakes as often and was starting to play like his old self again. No doubt, I wasn't the only thing that was helping him out, but each time he scored a goal or pulled off a perfect play, I gave him a slap on the back and hearty, but short, words of praise. Slowly, his icy exterior was melting. It was only a matter of time before he was a puddle.

"But I don't know about taking my job," Coach said with a smirk.

I let out a shy chuckle, the corners of my mouth creeping up. "Maybe that was a tad dramatic."

His eyes narrowed in consideration. "Maybe. Maybe not."

"What the fuck is that?" Warren asked in horror as I entered the mostly empty locker room.

The other two people left in the room looked up at me.

"What you've never seen a book before?" Travis Hall, our starting goaltender and Warren's mentor chirped at her as he finished tying his shoes.

Beside him in her neighboring locker, Warren flipped him off without looking, and raised her eyebrow at the loud *thunk* that emanated from the tower of books as I dropped them onto the bench of my locker. The stack wobbled, but I managed to stabilize it before it could tip over.

Berg flinched back from the books like they were going to bite him. "Jesus," he rumbled. "You going back to college or something? I hate to tell you this, bud, but I don't think they let in meatheads with 1.0 GPAs."

I scoffed. "Fuck you. I graduated high school with a 3.5, unlike your 2.0-having ass."

Berg rolled his eyes, his mouth quirking through his billowing blonde beard.

Warren stood and crossed the room, taking down her blonde ponytail and shaking out her sweaty hair while she avoided stepping on the team logo in the middle of the locker room. She came to a stop in front of me and Berg and picked up the first few books off the stack of thirteen.

"*Psychology of Sport. Team Mentality. History of Hockey Strategy*," she read off the titles. "What the hell?"

"Homework from Coach," I said, keeping my answer short. I didn't want to reveal my future plans to anyone for a while.

"You don't have to write essays, do you?" Berg asked, his horrified look returning.

"Dear Lord, Jones. What did you do to deserve such hell?" Hall cried.

Warren shook her head at her idiot team-mates and balanced the books back on top of the tower. "Thank God you guys are pretty and can handle a hockey stick."

"Hey," Hall protested. He got up from his locker and swung a backpack over his shoulder. "I went to college before I was drafted, which is more than I can say for you asinine lot."

"Ohh, 'asinine.' Bet that got you a nice SAT score," Warren shot back, finally joining in on the ridiculous chirping flowing through the locker room.

"Ninety-fifth percentile."

Not missing a beat, Warren returned verbal fire, and the two were off.

A chuckle built in my chest as I watched the two goaltenders snipe at each other. They were a trip. While Hall was almost forty years old, I'd only ever seen him act like a teenager. Warren, in her early twenties, was infinitely more mature than him. Yet, whenever she was around the older goalie who had been assigned as her mentor this season, her childlike side came out.

"I'm off. Make sure to do the reaction exercise I showed you. I'm sure your *boyfriend* won't mind helping you out," Hall said as he backed toward the door, apparently done riling up Warren, but getting one last jab.

Warren sighed after him, reluctant fondness written all over her face.

"How much longer are they going to milk that for?"

Berg stood and shrugged on his denim jacket. "Only for a couple more … years."

A growl built in Warren's throat, but I knew she wasn't truly mad.

Over the weekend, after months of gradually increasing their public outings as if they had just started dating instead of being together for almost a year, Warren and Kingston had announced their relationship online. The reaction of the public was as expected. The press had exploded with questions, and the online comments were insane with speculation. But Warren and Kingston had been dealing with the media for their entire careers and were ready for the uproar the news of their relationship had incited.

What they couldn't prepare for was the reaction of the team, and as much as she tried to hide it, I saw how nervous Warren was. But she had never been one to back down from anything.

This morning, she walked into the locker room, head held high and Frey flanking her like a bodyguard, to face the men who had seen the news plastered over every social media site and newspaper. Silence had reigned in the room for a few moments before the first chuckle slipped out of Berg. Then, like the starting gun had been fired, the room erupted into friendly laughter. Warren rolled her eyes but sat at her locker as the team teased her. She endured it all with an annoyed look on her face, but her relief was obvious. The team was treating her like they would any other team member with a new girlfriend. The respect that she busted her ass to earn hadn't been stripped away because she was sleeping with the team's old assistant captain.

Unfortunately for her though, the teasing wasn't going to end anytime soon.

With a deep chuckle at her expense, Berg disappeared out the door, leaving me alone with Warren.

I looked at her in confusion. "What are you still doing here, by the way?"

She shrugged her shoulders, and I finally noticed that she hadn't showered yet and was still in her leggings and undershirt like I was.

"I figured you'd want to stay late to practice that new deke you're working on."

I shot Warren a sardonic work. "Right. And you're not at all trying to avoid the mob of reporters hunting for you in the halls."

Her hand fluttered to her heart. "Of course not. I just want to help my friend fight off the impending ravishes of time that affect old athletes like yourself. You're no spring chicken, you know. We've got to make sure you can keep up with all these new young rookies."

"Well, thank you for volunteering your time so selflessly, Warren. But I'm not staying today. Milly is playing her first bout as captain of her team in a few hours."

Warren fluttered her eyelashes at me. "Oh? Are you going to offer her pointers about leading a team? You're such a good *friend.*"

My brain told my mouth to purse at her in annoyance, but the neurons must have misfired because I found the corners of my mouth stretching across my face at the thought of Milly Chambers. I knew I looked like a love-sick fool, but I couldn't stop it.

Warren's eyes softened, and I knew she wanted to pat me on top of my head like she often did to Frey when he was being cute and/or stupid. Thankfully, before her hand could reach out, the far door to the locker room swung open.

I paused as Mick Little strode into the circular room, confused. Little hadn't stayed after practice a single time since he joined the team. At the first chance he had to escape the arena, he took it. So, what was he doing here?

Warren must have had the same question. "What's up, Little? You're not usually here this late. You need something?"

Little shifted in his sneakers, eyes bouncing around the room for a moment before landing on me. His dimples danced with his erratically flexing lips. "I was just stretching in the gym." He paused and visibly forced out the next words. "Do you have some time, Jones? I wanted to slap some pucks around with you."

The planet must have gotten sucked into a black hole, and we were in an alternate universe. It was the only logical explanation. There was no way Little was voluntarily asking to spend time with me, but Warren's look of astonishment told me this was happening.

I fought to keep my hand glued to my side and not victoriously pumping in the air.

"Sure." I kept my voice even. The last thing I needed now was to scare him off.

"Cool." Little grabbed his skates and gloves then headed in the direction of the rink without another word.

Warren snorted. "And another one bites the dust. I swear, Jones, you could make friends with a brick wall."

I gestured to the door Little left through. "I basically had to, with that one."

I was grabbing my skates from my locker one moment, then froze the next.

Milly's bout.

Shit.

My hesitation must have been evident because Warren's hands went up in an "I got nothing" gesture. She knew as well as I did that it was my job to go after Little. If I blew him off, the chances that he would open up again were infinitesimal. This was the only shot I had to get through to him and to show Coach I was committed to this team and its players.

I checked the clock hanging on the wall by the main door. If I made this quick, I could still get to Milly's bout in time to catch most of it.

I raced after Little.

Milly would understand.

21

Milly

"What's got you giggling, Captain," Lady MacDeath, a veteran blocker on the team, asked as she collapsed onto the bench that separated the rows of metal lockers on either side of us. She stretched her legs out in front of us, rolling her skates back and forth on the concrete floor, her thick, colorfully tattooed thighs flexing with each movement. Her lashes, coated in black and dramatic against her pale skin and light eyes, batted at me. It would have been cute if every other inch of her didn't scream "fuck off." Not everyone went full out on the makeup for bouts, but Lady MacDeath, like her namesake, had a flare for the dramatic.

I rolled my eyes at her and put the phone I had barely managed to tear my eyes from into my locker. "I don't giggle," I deadpanned.

She didn't buy my bullshit. "Bitch, please, I'm surprised you're not kicking your feet." Her skates scissored faster for emphasis. "Cartoon hearts are about to explode from your eyes."

The image made me grimace. "And here I thought I would be free from this when Thea quit."

A sly smirk crossed her black-painted lips.

I narrowed my eyes. "She told you to harass me, didn't she?"

"Made me promise actually. Pinky swear and all."

"That fucking woman."

"Don't act like you don't love her."

I blew a raspberry in the air but couldn't help the smile that tugged at my lips. I did love her, but that didn't mean she wasn't a pain in my ass.

My phone dinged, and my skates almost slipped out from underneath me as I lunged for it. MacDeath laughed. I silently cursed out the app notification on my screen.

MacDeath shook her head at me. "Just call them."

It only took me a moment to relent.

"Alright. One second."

I left MacDeath and the rest of the team at one end of the locker room and skated to the shower area, where the only sound was the awkward *thump thump thump* of my wheels rolling over the tiles. After checking to make sure I was alone, I settled underneath a showerhead in the communal space and finally called the number I had been waiting to pop up on my phone for hours.

"You've reached Jones. Leave a message."

"Hey, Ethan. I'm just calling to see if you made it here yet. Remember to take the second right like I told you; the turn-in is hard to miss." I paused and my voice softened. "I'm really nervous about today. When Thea and the team chose me to take over as captain, I wasn't sure it was the right decision. I've only been on the team for a little bit, and I'm terrified that I'm going to fuck it up. I don't want to let the girls down. Were you nervous your first time as captain? What did you do? You probably just put a big smile on your face and got to work, huh?" I huffed out a laugh. "You always know what to do. I, on the other hand, am a mess. Maybe I should try to channel you, but we already know I can't pull off the accent."

"Where's Cap?" a voice hollered across the locker room.

"I've got to go; they're calling for me. I guess it's time to pull on my big girl panties. I'll see you after the bout, and I expect victory sex. Or condolence sex. Either is good with me." Words that weren't ready to see the light of day danced on my lips, but I cleared my throat. Not yet. Not over the phone and not until I told him the truth. "Bye."

"Chop?"

I looked up from my phone. "Hey, Rockem. Sorry. Is it time to go?"

"Yep. I think they want you to give a speech to kick off your captaincy."

I groaned but got moving, Rockem at my side. "I suck at speeches. I absolutely blow."

"You can't be *that* bad."

"Oh, yeah? Do you remember Thea's birthday party?"

She bit down on her smile. "That's not the best example; you were drunk."

"Not really. The next day, Thea promised me the Maid of Honor position whenever she gets married, but on one condition—that I never touch the microphone or try to say more than a few sentences at a time for the whole day." Not that she's getting married anytime soon; she'd have to find someone to put up with her crazy, red-headed bullshit first.

The laughter she had been trying to repress escaped Rockem's lips. "Maybe keep it short and sweet then."

We rolled to a smooth stop behind the girls who were gathering around the open space of the locker room to wait for Coach Sheila. Chatter filled the air as everyone got settled against various benches, lockers, and walls.

"Hey," Rockem whispered, all humor suddenly gone from her voice. "You may have flubbed a speech here or there, but you've given at least one good one."

She stared softly into my eyes, and I remembered our talk a few weeks ago when she'd asked me for advice about quitting her job. I wouldn't have called what I said a speech per se, but at her words, the tension drained from my tight shoulders.

"How did that go, by the way?"

"You were right; my parents didn't get it at first. But then I showed them this." She whipped out her phone, tapped at the screen a few times, then turned it around.

"Holy shit!" I leaned in closer for a better look. "You painted this?"

On the small screen was a picture of one of the most brutal and beautiful paintings I'd ever seen. I didn't know much about the finer arts, but even I could tell that Rockem's art was amazing, the details as close to picture-perfect as the human hand could produce. The canvas must have been at least seven feet tall and just as wide, dwarfing Rockem who stood next to it for scale. But it was the subject of the painting that took my breath away.

Decked out in full derby gear, a woman crouched in the center of the enormous canvas. In her stance, balanced on the toe stops of her skates and fist raised, ready to explode with energy the moment the referee's whistle let her off her leash, the woman snarled at the world with eyes that bored into my soul. The layers of paint and glass couldn't protect me from her challenging glare.

Throughout the painting, a rainbow of colors fought angrily for dominance, muddy yellows pushing at the edges of the highlights on her face, deep purples creeping from the shadows cast across her body, and every color in between swirling through and against each other, dipping into every painstakingly placed detail. The rainbow palette that should have sanded down the rough edges of the subject only served to draw attention to the blood dripping through the cracks of her teeth, the blossoming kisses of deep-tissue bruises decorating her bare arms and peeking from her tiny shorts, and the grease paint that smeared down her face to join the deep red of her lipstick.

If I had been standing next to the painting in all its full-sized glory, I would have been struck dumb in awe. As it was, I could only draw together a few lame words that didn't come close to expressing the amazement I felt. "That's amazing, Rockem. You're a fantastic artist."

I finally drew my eyes away from the phone and was once again struck with awe, this time at Rockem.

Her almond eyes that showed her Korean ancestry swam with pride that I'd never seen on the usually shy woman before. "Thank you. My parents thought so too. I'd never shown them my art before, and I was terrified at what they would think, but they couldn't have been more proud. Just like you said."

She glanced at her phone, smiled at the payoff of her hard work and passion, then tucked it away into the waistband of her black spandex shorts. Her back straightened as if held up by her pride, her face practically glowing.

A bittersweet grin creased my lips. I missed that face staring back at me in the mirror, full of self-confidence and the contentment that came with knowing you were following your dream. Looking back, it had been missing for a year before I noticed its absence and finally acted on it. Then, right as I'd accepted its disappearance, I met a certain hockey captain who I wanted to cook for like I had never wanted to do before in my life. And just like that, a glimpse of Chef Milly Chambers appeared in the mirror, coaxed into revealing herself by the night-light smile of Ethan Jones.

It was everything I had ever wanted, but I knew it couldn't last forever. I would have to tell Ethan about my deception soon, and I knew as well as I knew how to make my favorite meal that he would leave, taking the fire that had just started to blaze back to life again with him.

But worse than losing my love for cooking again, Ethan would be gone.

Rockem chattered happily beside me as I worked my way through my teammates to get to my locker. I tried to pay attention to her, but it was all I could do to focus on breathing past the anvil someone had dropped on my lungs.

Bzzz. Bzzz. Bzzz.

I scrambled for my phone.

"Damnit," I grumbled. Ignoring the random number calling me, I tossed the damn phone into my locker, grabbed the last of my pads, and slammed the metal door shut.

"Boy troubles?" Rockem asked.

I grunted and tugged on my wrist pads.

A clap echoed through the locker room, silence following in its wake as the girls shut their mouths and turned to Coach Sheila in unison. We rolled forward, ears open.

"Alright, ladies. We've studied every bout the Babes have played for months. You know what to do. Trust yourselves, trust your team, and trust that the derby gods are looking out for us." Coach stepped back. "Any words, Captain?"

"Short and sweet," Rockem said with a slap on my back that pushed me into the middle of the semi-circle of girls.

The anticipation of the coming bout was rolling off the team like a heat wave, distorting the air around them.

I stuck my arm out and braced.

A dozen palms crashed down on top of my hand, plastic wrist pads clanking together. My arm burned as I fought against dropping it under the weight of the team's hands.

"Killers on three! One, two, three!"

"Killers!"

As our hands broke apart and flew into the air, I shook off every thought that wasn't about wiping the track with the Brooklyn Babes and led my team out.

Well, that lasted about five seconds, I thought sardonically as we took our opening laps around

the banked track, my vow to put Ethan from my mind broken the moment my wheels touched the smooth track. I should have known better; not once in the two months since I'd met him had I been able to distract myself from him.

Without my consent, my head whipped around, searching the crowd for a familiar large frame as I flew around the track, bypassing girls from both my team and our opponents'. Under the colorful strobe lights, it was near impossible to make out a face in the mass of shapeless bodies.

By my third lap, I'd given up hope of spotting him in the packed crowd pressing up against the barriers of the oval track. Instead, I came to a screeching stop in front of the unmistakable head of fiery hair I spotted amongst the audience.

I leaned over the padded, boob-high railing, pulled a body out of the crowd, and hugged as tight as I could.

"Hey!" Thea shouted over the roaring and jeering of hundreds of people.

"What are you doing here?" I shouted back into her ear then snorted as her ponytail tickled my nostrils.

Thea pulled out of my embrace and turned to show me the back of her black NYC Killers jersey. But instead of her derby name plastered across the shoulders, mine stood out in bold white. My lucky/favorite number, thirty-seven, sat in the middle of her back.

"Where did you get that?" I asked when she turned around. The team didn't sell replicas of our jerseys, only shirts with the team's name on them.

"I asked Shelia to order me one. Gotta rep my girl."

I pulled her in for another hug until I heard her ribs groan.

A body squeezed past Thea, the right height and build. I arched my neck to follow the figure. He turned, revealing a strange white face.

"Ow." Thea shoved me away and rubbed at her temple. "Watch the helmet."

"Sorry."

Thea grunted.

I found myself scanning the crowd again. "Hey, have you seen Ethan?"

"He's coming?"

"Supposed to but I haven't seen him. He said they had late practice today and he would have to rush to get here."

Thea's ginger eyebrows furrowed. "Really? I came straight from the arena, and his SUV was still in the lot. But I'll keep an eye out for him. He'll be here soon, but you have to get going." She gestured at the girls gathering at the bottom of the track.

"Shit." I gave Thea one last hug for luck then rolled down the track.

The teams and referees got settled, a whistle blew, and the bout was on.

I grimaced at the scoreboard. A nine-point deficit wasn't great, but it was recoverable.

"Chop, MacDeath, Winslet, and Trauma, split them down the middle," Coach said and tossed the fabric helmet cover emblazoned with a star to Rockem, marking her as our jammer.

"You heard Coach, let's clear Rockem a path and get some points on these bitches." I popped my mouthguard back in place, wiped at the grease paint and sweat dripping down my face, and took my place at the line on the track.

The rest of the blockers from both teams settled into position around me, the jammers crouched at the ready a few yards back. Rockem stared down the pack from her position, her face a perfect reflection of her painting.

The pack of blockers shifted, and we each found an opponent to mark. A hush fell over the girls, a stark contrast to the roaring crowd, as anticipation built with each second the starting whistle wasn't blown. Like every time I lined up at the beginning of each play, my gaze was drawn to the cloud of red curls at the end of the track. Thea shook her head.

Be here soon, my ass.

If Ethan didn't arrive in the next twenty minutes, he would be showing up at an empty warehouse.

My eyes were still scanning the crowd when the sound of the first whistle pierced the air.

Shit.

My mind snapped back to the bout, and I scrambled to get my skates under me. The pack pushed forward, gaining speed and dragging my stumbling ass along with them. By the time the second whistle blew, releasing the jammers, I'd managed to find my balance but was trailing at the end of the pack. With a burst of strength from my exhausted thighs, I shouldered my way through the mass of clashing bodies, putting every ounce of my weight into each push off my wheels.

Unfortunately, when that amount of momentum hit a body, making contact from shoulder to knee, it went down hard. The force of the impact reverberated through my pads as I landed on my knees and slid, trying to control my fall and steer away from the track.

I was a millisecond away from being clear when a hip hit the back of my shoulder, sending me spinning into the concrete headfirst.

Blackness.

Ethan

"We're inviting Berg and Frey next time. Maybe Warren and Hall too. You're a tough opponent but I want to see how it feels to work with you instead of against you."

Through the open window of the taxi, Little nodded silently.

Where I would have taken his silence as indifference before, after spending a couple of hours together on the ice and a few more downing low-calorie beer at Satan's Place—a bar a lot less sinister than it sounded—I now recognized the happiness in the minuscule wrinkles around his eyes.

I answered with a cheek-hurting smile. "Alright. See you later."

I smacked the roof of the taxi, and the driver pulled off into the night, the streets around Milly's apartment empty at this time of night.

I checked my watch and winced.

Five hours late.

Milly had every right to murder me after missing her first bout as captain, but I was hoping she would understand that I had no choice. She knew how hard I was working to get Little to open up, and when the chance finally came, I had to take advantage.

At first, I had thought it was all for naught. For two whole hours on the ice, Little hadn't said a word outside of suggesting plays and drills, leaving me to fill the silence with casual chatter while watching the neon red clock taunt me with each passing minute. I would have called it a night there and hauled my ass to Milly's bout, but something held me off.

For the first time, Little was actually listening to me. I jumped from topic to topic with no logical connection—hockey, video games, team gossip, football. No matter what I said, Little paid attention when he would have told me to shut the fuck up not even a month ago. So I prattled on as we battled the puck from each other in a light game of one-on-one until we were dripping sweat and our muscles were jelly.

I rushed through my shower, barely stopping to dry off before pulling my clothes on, the fabric sticking awkwardly to my damp skin. But I had no time; if I didn't leave immediately, I would miss more than the first fifteen minutes of Milly's bout.

I only made it a step outside the locker room when Little's deep voice stopped me with words I'd never thought I'd hear from him. I was pretty sure Little offering to get a drink with anyone, let alone me, was the first sign of the apocalypse. But the hard glint in his eyes told me he was serious, and his lips, which had been glued together on the ice as if to keep secrets firmly locked behind them, were beginning to loosen.

I wanted nothing more than to ask for a raincheck and run to Milly. Instead, I broke my alcohol limit and had a few beers with the man who looked like he wanted nothing more than to talk.

And after a few beers of his own, talk he had. For hours.

Now, with a bouquet of cellophane-wrapped roses clenched in my hand, I could only hope that Milly would let me explain. With a deep breath, I hit the buzzer for Milly's apartment.

No answer.

I pressed it again. "Milly? You there?"

No answer.

"I'm so sorry for missing your bout. And for not calling. Shit, I should have called you. Milly?"

I tugged my phone from my pocket and cursed at the notifications on the screen. One voicemail followed by two more missed calls, all from Milly.

I hit the voicemail first, bringing the phone to my ear.

Milly's choked voice greeted me. With each word she spoke, a spike of pain lanced through me, guilt following on its heels. The pleasant buzz of a few beers was suddenly gone, leaving me exposed.

"Oh, darlin'," I murmured into the air. What had I done?

The other two missed calls had no voicemails, so I hit her number, my thumb trembling with nerves. I slumped against the brick facade of the building and chewed on my lip as the phone rang in my ear.

No answer.

"Ethan?"

My head snapped up. "McKenna?"

I blinked, but the sight of Dr. Thea McKenna getting out of a cab didn't change. My brows scrunched in confusion before I remembered. McKenna and Milly were neighbors.

I lurched off the wall and hurried up to McKenna. "Dr. McKenna. *Thea.* Can you let me in? I need to talk to Milly. It's important."

Green eyes narrowed at me. "More important than her bout?"

I winced.

McKenna glanced down at the sound of crumpling plastic and raised a brow. I followed her gaze to the roses being pulverized in my fist. Great. A pained sound escaped me, and I must have looked more pathetic than I felt because McKenna took pity on me.

"Milly's not in her apartment."

"Then wher—"

The back passenger side door of the taxi opening cut me off.

"I mean, who plays true crime in an ER waiting room?" Milly stumbled from the car, and, in an uncharacteristic display of clumsiness, had to catch herself from falling with an arm against the cab.

I rushed around the car before her words processed in my brain. They only registered when I saw the sling holding her left arm to her side. My feet stuttered to a stop before her, and my hands were reaching for her to check for more injuries before I told them to stop. They froze in the air.

"What happened?" I choked out.

Milly's glassy eyes fluttered before she finally seemed to recognize me. A bright smile split her face, and she stepped into my arms, her free arm looping around my neck. "Ethan! There you are! I've been looking for you!"

Joy radiated from her every pore as she snuggled into me, and I wrapped my arms around her, careful of my strength. A loud snuffle beside my ear was followed by a giggle.

Did she just smell me?

"Mmm. Coconut."

Over her head, my wide eyes met McKenna's.

She gestured us over to the sidewalk then mumbled something to the cabbie.

With a gentle hand, I steered an uncoordinated Milly behind the cab and out of the street. She went willingly with a little hum.

McKenna was talking before I could get the first question out, rattling off what happened with medical efficiency.

"She's fine ... mostly. She took a pretty bad hit and was clipped again on her way down. Her shoulder caught most of her weight before her head hit the concrete. She only lost consciousness for a few seconds and has no concussion, but her shoulder dislocated. I went with her to the emergency room. They shot her up with some morphine, popped her shoulder back in without surgery, and sent her off with a pain prescription. She's very high, but otherwise okay. Three weeks in the sling and a few months at minimum before she can play again."

Milly made a grumbling noise before her head shot to McKenna with her loopy smile out in full force. Her uninjured arm wrapped around my bicep and squeezed in excitement. "But..." she prompted McKenna.

McKenna sighed in exasperation. "But we won the bout."

"Yeah, we did!"

McKenna shot a fond look at Milly then turned to me. In the blink of an eye, a steel door clanged shut over her face and her expression was back to the apathetic, and slightly sadistic, look that every Blizzards player unfortunately knew too well.

Dr. Jekyll was gone.

"Bring her up to her apartment and take care of her," Mr. Hyde said. The "or else" was implied but unnecessary.

My head dipped sharply.

After one last chilly look, McKenna returned to the cab that was still waiting at the curb. "I'm going to pick up her bike and prescription. I'll be back."

The taxi door slammed shut, and McKenna was off.

"Did you get me more flowers?"

"I think they're a lost cause, darlin'."

"No." Milly shuffled the roses around more, one-handedly straightening out the bent stems and fluffing up the crushed petals. "There. Perfect."

I cocked my head at the sad vase of roses on Milly's kitchen island. They still looked like an idiot giant mangled them in his paw, but I wasn't about to let down Milly again. "Yep. Perfect."

Milly beamed at me.

I returned her smile, praying she wouldn't see the guilty strain of it. The drugs must have affected her perception because she bought it and centered the vase on her island, satisfied.

Suddenly, a lightbulb flashed behind her deep-water eyes, and she spun around in her stool. I rushed around the counter to help her down lest she fall. Again.

She tried to bat my hands away from her waist, but I didn't release her until her bare feet were firmly on the ground. With a huff, she readjusted the black satin pajamas that she insisted on changing into the moment we entered her apartment. Knowing not to bother arguing with a high person, I helped her change out of her derby uniform, fixed her sling when she was redressed, and wiped off the rest of the grease paint on her face that she had obviously tried, and failed, to remove at the hospital.

"What are you doing?"

Milly had rounded the island and was digging through a cabinet. She pulled out a metal mixing bowl and slammed it too hard onto the counter. "What does it look like?"

"It looks like you're cooking. But I know that can't be the case because you're high off your ass and only have one working arm."

She waved her uninjured arm over her head. "It's fine; I'm right-handed. I'd only need two hands if I was going to chop things, and Milly Chamber's World-Famous Pancakes don't require any chopping."

Despite the mood that had taken hold of me at the sight of Milly hurt, I couldn't help but chuckle at her. I don't know how, but she was even cuter when stoned. It was like the drugs had dulled that perpetually hard edge of hers. "Oh, yeah? How are you going to mix the batter?"

She pouted in thought. "I know! You can do it."

"What, burn down your building? Because if you leave me in charge of your stove, that is what's going to happen."

"Hey, you've cooked here before."

"That was just an omelet and some turkey bacon. A kindergartner could make that. Plus, I'm pretty sure I burnt that turkey bacon."

Her look told me I was right, but she soldiered on. "I'll help you out. You just have to be my arms."

I doubted I would ever be able to say no to Milly again. With a huff, I stepped up beside her. "Okay, but don't say I didn't warn you when the firefighters are hauling your ass out of here."

"Please. You would have me over your shoulder and on the other side of the borough before the firefighters ever got here."

"Try the other side of the city."

"Okay, but you have to make sure you grab my knives on the way out." She pointed to the fabric roll of knives on the far side of her island that she took to and from the arena every day.

"I promise."

She raised onto her toes and pressed a sweet kiss to my cheek. I turned my head to meet her lips with mine, but she slipped away before I could make contact.

"First, flour." She spun toward the cupboard, opened it, and produced a plastic canister of the white powder with barely a look. "Sugar." Another canister. "Baking powder." A jar.

She bobbed around the kitchen, naming ingredients like she was reading them off a mental recipe card and pulling containers out of various cupboards. The clumsy movements brought on by the drugs lost in the fight against Milly's muscle memory.

She moved like a one-armed ballerina across the space. Though I made sure to keep close should I need to catch her, I didn't offer to help. She would ask if she needed it. With a last trip to the fridge where she returned holding a cartoon of almond milk and the pockets of her pajama pants stuffed with eggs and a stick of butter, she had all the required ingredients. She gave up her pocket eggs and butter then considered the pile on the island with a hum. Her head turned to me then back to the ingredients.

"What?"

"I'm trying to remember if I have protein powder. We can put it in your batter so you won't have to eat all this sugar."

"It's fine. You don't need to do that. I'll risk the calories."

Milly's brows descended from her curtain of bangs. "Are you sure? If I don't have any, I can run next door to Thea's. She definitely will."

"But then I wouldn't get to fully experience Milly Chamber's World-Famous Pancakes."

Milly grinned, and I helped her hop onto the island.

"Alright, we ready?" I asked.

"We will be once you wash your hands."

"Yes, Chef."

"Okay," I admitted. "These are the best pancakes I've ever had."

Milly somehow managed to send me a victorious look even with a mouthful of pancake and syrup. She quickly chewed and swallowed. "They would be even better if you put syrup on them."

"I would, but there's only so much I'm willing to do for you," I lied.

She scoffed and shoved another forkful of food into her mouth. "Liar," she called me out around her mouthful, displaying atrocious table manners, especially for a chef. "You cooked something other than eggs and bacon for me. I'm pretty sure that means you would chug that whole bottle of syrup." She swallowed her food. "Don't actually do that though, because that maple syrup costs two hundred bucks."

I gaped at the glass bottle. "Seriously?"

She shrugged. "Yeah, it's pure barrel-aged maple syrup. But don't worry; I'm not crazy enough to spend that much money on syrup. It was a gift."

I breathed out a sigh of relief and ate another piece of pancake with only some jaggedly sliced strawberries as a topping.

Milly watched me. "It's a shame you don't have a big sweet tooth."

"How do you know that?" I asked then remembered a second before Milly answered.

"Your palate test. You don't mind sugar, but it's not your favorite. You're more of a savory guy. Spinach crepes are probably more up your alley."

She was right; that did sound good.

A thought that had fluttered through my mind came into focus as I contemplated my decimated pancakes. "Not that I would have been able to pull it off, but why didn't you have me make crepes instead? You're a French chef, right? In fact, you barely cook any French meals at all. You'd think after all your years in France, that would be all you made."

Clang.

My head snapped up as my eyes widened.

Milly stared unseeingly at the fork lying in the puddle of syrup that was her plate.

"Milly?"

"I just don't anymore."

"Why not? I thought you loved French cuisine. Isn't that why you moved all the way to Europe?" I questioned hesitantly.

Her mouth twitched down. "Yes, it was."

"But you quit to move here."

"Yes."

"Why?"

The glare Milly shot me would have made me flinch back, but the anger swimming in her deep-water eyes was aimed inward. My fingers twitched with the need to caress her cheek until the fury tightening her face dissipated. I held back though as her rigid body prepared to flee the island stools we sat on.

"Because I couldn't hack it," she spat. "Because I am a pathetic excuse for a chef. Because I'm a coward. Because I gave up."

She slid from her stool, grabbed her plate, and fled to the kitchen sink. Water ran ineffectively over the sticky syrup. Milly cursed and reached for the soap with her other hand only to find her arm in a sling. She cursed again.

I got up with measured calmness, took my plate to the sink, relieved Milly of hers, and scrubbed them both clean. Milly watched.

Once the dishes were placed in the drying rack, I turned to the woman radiating anger and frustration. This time, I didn't hesitate. I reached for her face and brushed a few strands of wavy brown hair behind her ear. She watched me cautiously from under her bangs, not relaxing in the slightest.

"Bullshit," I said softly. "Why did you really leave? Tell me the truth."

"I told y—"

"No. You told me what you've convinced yourself was true, not the actual truth."

She batted my hand off her face and backed away, the anger that tormented her starting to turn its attention on me. But there was something else hiding behind all that rage.

"What are you saying?" she demanded.

"I'm saying that you, Chef Milly fucking Chambers, are not a quitter. I don't believe for

a second that you gave up a career that you worked your ass off your whole life to get. At least, not because you were scared. I've known you for sixty-two days, and in that time, you've never backed down from anything. Not from an argument, not from a challenge, not even from me. I've never seen an ounce of fear from you. So why are you afraid? What are you afraid of?"

The words that had started off as soft as fresh snow ended as hard as black ice.

She stepped into my chest and growled, her deep-water eyes set aflame. "Fuck you."

"See? Not an ounce of fear."

Without another word, she stormed across her apartment and into her room. The slamming of the door rattled the windows.

23

Milly

"**W**e had a fight," I informed the unconscious body on my couch.

Ethan mumbled and rolled onto his back. The orange throw blanket that had barely covered him fell to the ground in a heap. Bright beams of morning light shone through the large windows of my apartment and caressed the high, bronzed planes of his beautiful and stupid face.

"Wha?" His long lashes blinked open, and his pupils dilated in the sunshine, lighting up the deep mahogany of his irises. Immediately, he let out a groan of pain and raised a hand to shield his eyes.

I stepped into the path of the light so that my shadow fell over him.

He let his hand drop and gazed up at me. The smile he let out eclipsed the early sun. I had to fight off the urge to copy Ethan and cover my eyes as well.

"Hey. Good morning, darlin'."

I retrieved the blanket from the floor, folded it, and threw it over the back of the couch. "Good morning. We had a fight."

The popping of joints as Ethan's arms stretched over his head was deafening. Then, with a sound I'd only heard when we were both naked and horizontal, he heaved himself into a sitting position and crossed his legs under him, still smiling at me as if I were the most delicious thing he'd ever laid eyes on. "Yes, we did."

"We had a fight, then I locked you out of my bedroom. That usually means you're no longer welcome."

"Usually, yeah. But I wasn't about to leave you here hurt, high, and alone."

I pursed my lips. The incandescent rage that had driven me last night had evaporated as I slept. Now, I was just left with my misery and a painful shoulder.

Like always, Ethan read my mind. "There are pain pills on the counter along with your bag, helmet, and the keys to your motorcycle. After she dropped you off with me, McKenna got your stuff from the track and parked your bike in the garage."

"Remind me to thank her for that. And then remind me to punch her for leaving me with your ass."

Chapter 23

I rounded the couch and headed to the kitchen, not able to summon the energy to stomp like I wanted to. The pills were right where Ethan said they were. I bypassed the pile of my things and snatched up the orange bottle, only to be stopped in my tracks by the childproof lid. I shook the bottle with a little growl.

"Here. Let me." Ethan reached around me, took the pills, and used his two working hands to pop the lid. After a quick read of the label, he shook out two pills and handed them over.

"Thanks."

"No problem."

It only took a second for me to step to the sink, stick my head under the faucet to get a mouthful of water, and swallow the pills, but it was a second too long. Now, I could only pray the pain relievers kicked in fast.

"I'm sorry."

I turned around to find Ethan folded into himself, shoulders weighed down and chin tucked into his chest. His finger danced against his hands where they were clasped together in front of him.

"I shouldn't have said all that bullshit. I was an asshole, and I'm so fucking sorry."

My lungs deflated with a sigh that was one part fondness and two parts relief. Of course, his apology would come with as many curse words as it did "I'm sorry"s. But I expected nothing else. Hell, I would have done the same.

In reality though, it didn't matter how he worded it, just that he apologized at all. Add in the sincerity radiating from every molecule in his body and I allowed the last bits of my anger to melt away. I stepped into Ethan's space like I had last night. But instead of cursing at him, I wrapped my working arm around his waist and buried my face in his soft grey shirt. The smell of stale beer invaded my nose. Odd.

Heavy arms rose to wrap around my shoulders and brought my head up.

"Does this mean you forgive me?" Ethan's smile couldn't hide the hint of genuine worry in his eyes.

"Yes, it does." A kiss to his lips underlined my words.

Ethan relaxed under the kiss and opened his mouth to return it. Our tongues stroked together. I canted my head to the side with a hum and put more pressure against his lips. His short beard scratched addictively against my cheek. Before we could really get going, Ethan pulled back, but my one-handed clutch at the back of his shirt kept him from going far.

"No, no. No funny business, darlin'. I've dislocated my arm before, and I know how much pain you're in."

"But the best part of fighting is the make-up sex."

"Darlin'," he chastised, but the Texan accent seasoning his admonishment gave away his desire.

I wanted to protest, but he had a point; the throbbing in my shoulder had yet to subside.

With one last peck, I gave in. "Fine. Go get cleaned up; I'll get out some food."

"Hey! No cooking!"

I swatted at his bicep. "Chill out. I can manage a box of cereal."

Ethan squinted at me.

I squinted back.

Slowly, he walked backward out of the kitchen. "Okay, but I'm watching you."

A smirk cut across my face. "You always are."

With a chuckle and a wink, he disappeared into my bedroom. When he returned, I was at my usual spot at the kitchen island. Ethan took his seat beside me, pulled his bowl toward him, and paused.

On top of his bowl of whole-grain cereal, sat a pile of freshly cut strawberries and bananas.

"Damnit, Chambers."

I batted my lashes and took another bite off my spoon. Cutting up fruit with one hand hadn't been as hard as I'd thought. Aside from a few slippery berries that slid under my knife, I'd managed to get even slices.

"You're a menace," Ethan chided but grabbed the almond milk and the ramekin of cinnamon.

We ate in comfortable silence.

"Oh, hey. You never told me why you didn't make it to the bout last night. Did something happen?" I gave him a once-over, but no injuries had appeared overnight.

Ethan's spoon clanked against the sides of his bowl as he gazed sightlessly into his cereal.

Clank. Clank. Clank.

When he finally looked up, the guilt that I'd wiped from his face only a few minutes ago was back in full force. "Do you remember Mick Little, my teammate?"

The name rang a faint bell. "The guy who looked like he was about to punch you in the arena hallway?"

Ethan scratched at his beard, his two-toned lips twitching through the dark stubble. "Yeah, that guy."

"You said he was avoiding your help, right?"

"Until last night, he was. But at the end of practice, he asked if I wanted to stay late with him for some extra training. It shouldn't have been a big deal; I would have still made it to your bout…"

"But?" I promoted.

The next words were visibly forced out. "But then he invited me out for drinks after. I couldn't say no; not while the breakthrough I've been working toward for months was finally within my reach. So I went with him, had a few drinks, and by the time we were done, your bout was over. I'm so sorry, darlin'."

Well, that explained the scent of beer coming from his shirt. "Did you get him to open up at least?"

"It took a couple of drinks, but once he spoke more than a few sentences, he didn't stop for hours. I feel like I should call and check up on him. That much talking probably shredded his throat."

I snorted. "Okay."

"Okay?"

"Yeah, okay. I get it; you had to put your team-mate and your team first. I understand. I just wish you had called or texted first. I was worried about you."

Ethan grabbed the edge of my stool and spun me until I was facing him. Our knees inter-locked, and he took my free hand in both of his. His palms warmed my fingers as I got locked in Ethan's intense stare.

His eyes flicked between mine as if to make sure I had his full attention.

Like there is anything in the world that can distract me from him.

"Yes, I should have called. But it slipped my mind, and I didn't see your missed calls because I forgot to unsilence my phone after practice. Then I listened to your voicemail..."

My face heated as I realized how pathetic I must have sounded. While my first bout as cap-tain didn't go exactly to plan—what with the dis-located shoulder and all—there was no need for me to be so nervous beforehand. Despite how much I'd hyped it up in my mind, it was just like every other bout I'd played.

My fingers wiggled between his palms, wanting to pull away.

"You were wrong, by the way."

My fingers stopped. "About what?"

Ethan's oaky cheeks blossomed with blood. "I didn't just put on a smile during my first game as captain. No, I was so nervous that I vomited my dinner up before I even put on my skates. Then, on the ice, I made three errors … in one play."

A giggle slipped from my lips.

"Yeah, it was bad." He sighed. "That's why I should have been there for you. I'm so sorry I wasn't."

I pulled his hand up and pressed a kiss to his folded knuckles. "You can make it up to me because the second my arm is fixed, I'm going right back on that track."

Ethan beamed. "I wouldn't expect anything less. And I'll be right there cheering for you even if I have to miss one of my own games."

We leaned closer.

Ring. Ring. Ring.

I slipped my hand from Ethan's and laughed with enough force to nearly tip me from my stool.

Ethan shook his head bemusedly. "Destined to be interrupted."

"Tell me about it." I slipped off my stool and found my phone set aside on the table by my front door.

I frowned at the strange number and let it ring through as I returned to Ethan.

"Who was it?"

I shrugged my good shoulder. My phone beeped with a voicemail notification. Curious, I checked my call logs and found another voicemail.

"Oh, yeah," I mumbled. "This number called me last night too."

I selected the first voicemail and held up the phone between us. A light voice speaking fluent and fast French filled the air.

"Hello, Chef Chambers. This is Charles Chavanne, the maître d' of Sunset on the Seine. I was given your number because we have decided to expand our restaurant to New York, and we are looking for a head chef. Your name was offered up by Chef Louis Janvier. We would love to set a meeting with you if you are open to the opportunity. Please call me back at this number at your earliest convenience."

Ethan and I shared looks of twin surprise.

"Coucher de soleil sur la Seine?" Ethan repeated the name of the restaurant in his adorable cowboy-accented French.

I nodded absently, mind still reeling. "It's one of the best restaurants in Paris. They specialize in putting modern twists on classic French cuisine, which is what I did in Lyon. They have two Michelin stars and are bound to get their last remaining one by the end of the year."

"And they want you to run the one they're opening here?" The astonishment and pride in Ethan's voice said he knew how big of an honor this was.

"It would seem so."

"Holy shit, Milly! That's amazing!" Ethan jumped off his stool and pulled me into a hug, being careful of my left side.

I smiled tightly. "Thanks."

"Go ahead and call him back. As much as I love having you around, you're way too skilled to just be one of the team's chefs. You should be running your own place. And this is perfect because you'll still be in New York. With me." His last words came out soft.

My heart melted at the shy happiness in his face. But…

"I'm not going to call him back."

Ethan's eyebrows scrunched as he pulled back to get a good look at me. "What? Why?"

"Because I'm not taking the job."

"You… You don't want to stay in the city?"

"No! Of course, I do! I just don't want to go back to working in a restaurant. Any restaurant. I told you last night; I couldn't hack it."

Ethan's face smoothed out, and an odd emotion frosted over his eyes. "So you're not going to try again? You're just going to spend the rest of your life working below your skill level?"

I backed up a step. Ethan watched me, and an unsettling aura suddenly filled the air. Tension flooded me.

"I guess I was wrong."

"About?" I gritted out.

"About what I said last night. Maybe you *are* just a quitter who gave up on your passion because it got too hard." Ethan spat out the words like he was accusing me of selling out.

"No, actually, you were right before," I blurted out before I could stop myself. But, by then, there was no going back. I pushed on. "I didn't leave because I was giving up on my passion. I quit to protect it. To protect myself."

That took the wind out of Ethan's condescending sails. "What?"

I took a deep breath. This was it; the truth was coming out. Despite what I knew to be true, I couldn't help but hope that he would stick around afterward. I let out my breath.

"I spent the majority of my twenties in France, creating new dishes every week, and I was one of the best *sous chef de cuisines* in Lyon. But, like I told you before, professional kitchens are not calm places. They are loud and violent and intimidating. I'm still not sure if that was the entire reason, but eventually, I grew tired of it. So tired, in fact, that I couldn't come up with a new recipe to save my life. And I tried. Oh, how I tried. But still, nothing. It was like my creativity, my passion, was gone overnight. Poof." I snapped my fingers.

"So you gave up?"

I shook my head. "Not immediately. At first, I thought I was just over France. So I moved back home and took a job at a well-known restaurant here, hoping a new city would spark my passion again. No dice. There wasn't a single new thought in my head. I was done. So, for the second time in my whole life, I quit, and I hated myself for it. But then last night, after our fight, I realized you were right; I was just afraid. Because despite all the bullshit, I still genuinely enjoyed cooking. Even if I could only remake the same food over and over again, that would have been enough for me. And the thought of losing that too was terrifying. So I ran while I still had some of my passion left."

By the time I was done, tears misted my vision, but I didn't allow them to fall.

Ethan, who had listened to my story with his full attention, frowned at me in confusion, and I knew he was recalling all the dishes I'd proudly presented to him, saying they were new recipes. The pieces of my story weren't entirely adding up. There was something I was leaving out, and he knew it.

"So your next logical step was to become a chef for a professional sports team?"

I cracked a rueful smile. "No, my next step was to play roller derby and do nothing until my savings ran out. Past that, I had no idea. But Thea, that wonderful bitch, would not get off my ass. She set up the audition at the arena, and I got the job. Then I met you, and the weirdest thing happened."

Ethan raised his brows for me to go on.

"I wanted to cook for you, something new. The day I met you, I ran home with recipe ideas running through my head."

"You're saying I fixed you?"

A cruel laugh tore my throat to ribbons. "I wish. When I got home and you were no longer there, it was like all the motivation you inspired was never there in the first place. I thought it was a fluke, but when I ran into you again, the feeling came back."

I watched as an understanding horror dawned on him. "That's why you wanted to be my personal chef. You just needed me around to see if you could create something new." He looked at me as if he'd never seen me before. "And did you, Milly? Did you make something new?"

I nodded.

A harsh snort broke out of him, and he lurched away from me as if the large gap between us still left him too close to me. He scrubbed harshly at the back of his head. "Jesus, Milly. So I was what? Some sort of fucked up muse for you?"

I could do nothing but nod again.

"No, that's bullshit. That's not what a muse is. You weren't *inspired* by me, you were just straight-up using me. Don't act like you don't know that."

"Yes, I do know that," I told him bluntly. After all I'd done, the least I owed him was honesty. "You were the only thing that woke up my passion, and I took advantage of that. Of you. And I am so fucking sorry. It was selfish, and while I know it's not an excuse, I didn't see how far this thing between us would go. I didn't know it would turn into an actual relationship or that I would feel this way. But the second I figured it out, I decided to come clean to you. I swear."

"And how long ago did you figure it out?" His hollow voice battered my heart.

I clenched my fist and confessed. "… a few weeks ago."

The numbers swam across Ethan's pain-filled eyes. "Before or after we had sex?"

"… before."

His lashes fluttered close, and his chest trembled. When he opened them again, I suddenly understood the terror his opponents must feel when he was staring them down on the ice.

"Right. So you slept with me, knowing you were using me for your own gain."

Just like everyone else, I heard in the following silence.

Searing tracks raced down my cheeks.

He took that as confirmation and bobbed his head, eyes unseeing and somewhere else. His plush lips thinned further with each excruciatingly quiet moment until they were just a slash across his face. Abruptly, his head halted, and his gaze crashed into mine. He'd made his decision.

I held my breath.

Ethan took a measured step, then another, until he was back at my couch. He retrieved his wallet and phone.

No. Please don't prove me right.

"Ethan," I choked out.

He tucked his things into the pockets of his joggers. "The team's leaving for a week of away games tonight."

"That's in like six hours, though." The plea in my voice didn't go unnoticed.

Ethan ducked his head to avoid my gaze and headed to my front door. "Yeah. But I wanna get some extra practice in before we leave, 'cause unlike some people, I actually care about my passion and don't wanna give up on it."

I distantly noted his accent creeping through. So it didn't only come out when he was aroused; it also made an appearance when he was furious.

He was almost at the door.

With a step forward, I reached through the air for him. Unfortunately, I reached with both arms. My left shoulder screamed out, and it took all my might to not do the same.

With a low grunt, I clutched at my shoulder, closing my eyes to breathe through the pain.

"Milly?"

I opened my eyes to find Ethan frozen, his body at war between leaving and checking on me. I made the most of his attention.

"I didn't give up on my passion," I gritted out through clenched teeth. "I did everything I could to keep ahold of it, including taking advantage of the man I love."

Ethan blinked.

I waited. The next part was up to him.

His jaw flexed, and he spun around. The door slammed behind him.

A sob broke free from me. My knees gave out, and I crashed to the floor, cradling my shoulder that didn't ache nearly as much as my heart.

24

Ethan

I stumbled off the team bus and threw a glare at the early morning sun. My retinas burned, but I held my staring contest with the ball of white-hot fire in the sky.

"Watch out, Captain," Hall called from behind me.

I blinked the white spots out of my vision and took a step further into the Blizzards' parking lot and away from the bus doors. As the team disembarked, Hall gave me a rough slap on the back in thanks as he passed. My eyes narrowed after him. As if he could feel my stony gaze on his back, he turned to throw me a wink before continuing down the length of the bus to retrieve his bag from where they were being hauled out of the storage compartment underneath.

Thankfully, the rest of the team wasn't as suicidal as him. They spilled from the doors and into the morning air, some quiet and tired, others in light conversation, but all avoiding the emotional mess of their captain standing apart from the team as they gathered around the pile of bags. The slight snub hurt, but I couldn't blame them; I'd been a temperamental asshole for the past five days. Which may not have been so bad if we were at home, but on the road to play a string of games, the team worked, ate, and basically lived on top of each other. It was impossible to avoid me.

A breath huffed out of me. I scrubbed at the back of my head. This wasn't me. I wasn't the guy that was avoided by his teammates or who let his emotions get the better of him. The side-eyes of my team and my scabbed knuckles disagreed.

Coach caught my attention as he exited the bus, the last one as always. "Jones. Head to my office before you leave. I'll meet you there in a few."

My instinctual protest died before it could pass my lips. While all I wanted right now was to take a searingly hot shower and climb into bed until the sun did a full cycle around the Earth, I had a job to do.

"Yes, Coach," I said, grabbed my bag, and made my way into the arena as the rest of the team hurried to their cars.

Security let me enter the building with barely a second glance, and I hurried through the hallways. The blue-and-white walls passed in a blur as I navigated the maze of an arena. I knew the paths through the halls of the Snow Globe Arena better than I knew the way from my bedroom to the kitchen in my childhood home. So how I ended up in front of the double doors of the kitchen instead of Coach's office, I would never know.

I cocked my head at the doors as if I'd never seen them before.

"Thank ya so much, Milly."

I jumped at the sudden New Orleans accent. Then the words clicked in my brain, and my heart rate shot up so fast I was sure my fitness watch was seconds away from alerting me of impending cardiac arrest.

Milly? Where?

I whipped my head around until I pinpointed where the voice had come from, and spotted Chef LaBeux exiting her office down the hallway. Following her out of the room was the woman I had been avoiding for the past week.

Before I could tell it to move, my body was already in motion. It only took me a millisecond to throw myself behind the corner of the hallway and press myself flat to the wall as if I could blend into the concrete.

A familiar laugh echoed through the tunnels.

Every muscle in my body braced. The tidal wave of her joy crashed into me, and my heart seized in my chest. It was the first sound I'd heard from her since our fight, and I would have rather she be cursing me out. Anything would be better than listening to her lilting laughter, so at odds with her black leather vibes, yet somehow fitting perfectly.

I twitched with the need to peek around the corner and get a glimpse of her crinkled laugh lines around the lips that I knew would be painted red. Because, for as many times as I'd seen them over the last couple of months, I hadn't been able to picture her laughing face recently. Every time I tried, all I could see was her standing in her apartment, the tears flowing unrestrained down her cheeks as her deep-water eyes spilled over and her shoulder clutched in pain—all ignored as she begged me with everything in her to stay.

The scabs on my knuckles screamed at me as my right hand clenched.

"I was just doing my job. No need for the thanks." Milly's voice floated to me, and like a balm had been applied to my soul, the tension fled my muscles as if it had never been there. The lungs that I hadn't noticed shutting down restarted.

"No. You went above and beyond," LaBeux told her.

With steps that wouldn't wake a mouse, I crept to the corner and peered out from my hiding spot. A sigh almost escaped me as I got a proper look at Milly. Unlike LaBeux, she wasn't in her chef uniform. Instead, she was rocking her jeans, and her leather jacket was thrown over her shoulders, partially hiding the sling that held her left arm immobile to her stomach. The way she kept shifting told me she still wasn't used to having her arm strapped down.

A shy smile crept across her face as she gazed fondly at LaBeux. My own lips unconsciously mimicked hers. I was right—her lips were coated in her signature red lipstick.

"Well, I'm glad you like it," Milly told LaBeux. She tucked her wavy brown hair, out of its usual French braid, behind her ear.

Suddenly, LaBeux pulled Milly into a hug, the short older woman having to reach up to wrap her arms fully around Milly. She must not have been very careful of Milly's sling, though; even from a distance, I could see the way Milly tensed in pain. Her already pale face lost what little color it had.

I took a step toward her but stopped myself before I could fully round the corner.

Visibly dismissing the pain, Milly wrapped her free arm around LaBeux. A few whispered words passed between them, then they let each other go. After accepting a grandmotherly pat on her cheek, Milly said goodbye to her boss and disappeared down the other end of the hallway.

I watched her go and wondered if she had felt the same pang in her heart watching me walk out of her apartment that I did seeing her get farther and farther from me.

My feet told me to follow her, to apologize for my harsh words, but I kept them glued to the floor. Despite the part of me that wanted to forgive her, I was still so angry at what she'd done. I'd never expected that kind of betrayal from her because for the first time in my adult life, I trusted someone with my heart. Then, like every other woman who had ever shown interest in me, she was just after what I could provide her.

Still, the genuine pain in her eyes when I'd backed away from her in her apartment hadn't just been from her injured shoulder.

"That you, Jones?"

I looked up and realized I'd stepped out from behind the corner unconsciously. I cursed my feet and grinned tightly. "Hey, Chef LaBeux."

She waved me over. After one more look down the empty hallway Milly had disappeared from, I walked up to her.

"What are you doing here? I'd think you'd be dead in your bed by now," she said.

"Coach wanted to talk to me."

LaBeux nodded, the pile of blue-and-white box braids on her head threatening to fall with the movement. "Uh-oh. Getting called into the principal's office, huh?"

An ounce of tautness left my face as my smile turned genuine. "I guess so."

"Well, no need to worry. Y'all played some great games. Beat those Tiger bastards into the ice. Congrats on the wins."

"Thanks. If we keep up this pace, I see the playoffs in our near future." At least, I hoped so. The Blizzards had been on a bit of a downward spiral the past few seasons, but we were finally starting to find our groove again.

"Good. I want to see that cup back in this arena." LaBeux said with the ferocity of a life-long hockey fan.

I scratched at my beard. It was longer than usual, but I hadn't had the energy to trim it the past few days. "You and me both. But don't worry; I'm going to have another sip from it before I retire. Count on it."

Her salt and pepper eyebrows furrowed at the hand on my face. "Not if you keep getting into fights. Having our captain in the sin bin and being one man down is not going to get us any goals."

I dropped my hand back to my side, hiding my scraped knuckles. My head bowed, and I shifted my weight uncomfortably. "Yeah."

"Are you okay, cher? You're not usually one to drop your gloves."

She was right. The only person more surprised by my gloves hitting the ice than the crowd was the unfortunate forward who had caught the brunt of my anger and my right hook. I made a note to text Mathers and apologize. While it was a clean fight, it wasn't actually about him or the cheap swipe he'd taken at me. It was about me and my personal problems. And I refused to be someone who took out their anger on others, especially with my fists.

"I was just having an off day, I guess," I mumbled to LaBeux.

She studied me for a moment before a bright grin broke out across her face. "It's okay, cher. We all have days like that." Her hand shot out and slapped me on the shoulder. I wanted to say it didn't hurt, but, like Milly, she had the upper body strength of someone who could chop a whole chicken in half with one swing.

"Ow," I whined like the little boy I turned into in her grandmotherly presence. "How come Milly gets a hug, but I get assaulted?"

"Because I'm going to see you again."

My smile froze in place then flaked off my face like decades-old paint. "What?"

She shrugged. "She just turned in the final team menu. And let me tell ya, she really lived up to her reputation. You boys are going to love it."

"But she's still staying with the team, right?" I barely heard my own voice through the ringing in my ears.

LaBeux considered me, concern evident across every inch of her dark face. I vaguely wondered what expression I was making to cause that reaction. She slowly responded to my question, every word measured and infused with curiosity. "I don't know. I originally hired her as a sous chef, but I never understood why she took the job in the first place. I always felt like she could just pick up and leave with no warning. With her commitment to the team menu complete, I have this naggin' feelin' that I'll never see her again."

Never see her again.

Never see her again?

The ringing in my ears cranked up to deafening levels.

For the second time today, I found myself staring up at a door with no idea how I got there. Not remembering the drive here should have worried me, but I had no more space left in me to feel anything else. As it was, my amygdala was at DEFCON 1, trying to handle the nauseating mix of panic and anger tearing through me like a rogue hurricane.

I knocked on the door, barely registering my trembling hand, and held my breath. Just as I was about to pass out from lack of oxygen, the handle finally turned.

"Jones?" Riley Warren asked around a mouthful of food.

"Hey."

Warren squinted down at me standing on the steps leading up to the brownstone. She was already a tall woman, but the new height difference made me look as small as I already felt. She took another bite of her chocolate bar. Twix, I knew. Everyone on the team knew. Not that anyone ever mentioned it, especially when she came in with a king-sized bar once a month. The guys just kept their mouths shut and stashed a bar or two in their lockers for her to steal whenever she needed.

"You here to yell at me again, Captain?" The New York in her accent warned me to consider my answer carefully.

I winced. "No. And I'm really sorry about that."

A beat.

Warren shrugged. "No biggie. I deserved it after fucking up that block. I haven't missed a shot that easy since peewee." Just like that, Warren forgave me for lashing out at her on the ice. Her ability to let things go still amazed me. But while she forgave, I knew she never forgot.

"Still, I was harsh."

She shrugged again.

I shifted my weight. "Is Kingston here?"

"It *is* his house."

"Don't you mean 'our'?'"

She squinted at me. "Are you in cahoots with him?"

I stayed silent.

Her brown eyes rolled so hard they turned completely white for a second. "You two are impossible." She stepped aside and held the door open. "He's in his studio."

I smiled gratefully and stepped inside, immediately heading to the stairs.

"Thanks," I called to Warren as I took the steps three at a time. The thanks wasn't just for letting me in, but also for the bit of weight she had taken off my shoulders with the thirty seconds of banter at the door. She never failed to loosen me up when I got too in my own head—a skill she shared with her boyfriend.

I didn't bother to knock as I entered the bedroom that Kingston had claimed as his hobby studio.

That may have been a mistake, I thought wryly as a yellow blur came flying at me.

I didn't have time to whip my hand up but managed to turn my face so the tennis ball slammed into my cheek instead of my nose. "Fuck!"

"Whoops," Kingston said with absolutely zero regret in his voice.

I rubbed at my cheek. "Damn, bud. Do you always throw them that hard?"

Kingston raised a dark eyebrow from his spot at his drawing desk. "Sure. But Frey and Riles' brother throw them even harder. If you were faster, it wouldn't be a problem. Maybe you need to work on your reaction time."

I flipped him off as I retrieved the ball from where it had landed after ricocheting off my face. My reaction time was fine. Warren's was just on a whole other level. It had to be, with her lunatic family chucking tennis balls at her every time she turned around. Even the team had gotten into the game that helped keep her reflexes quick enough to catch the speeding pucks that were shot at her every game. A basket of balls now sat in a corner of the locker room. Still, while she could take it and didn't even flinch at the rarely missed tennis ball to the face, the boys didn't get too rough. I was probably the most careful and was prone to lobbing an underhand toss rather than rocketing a missile at her.

But I wasn't as careful with Kingston, as I proved by slinging the ball back at him. He caught it with one hand an inch from his face and deposited it back into the basket of them sitting on the corner of his desk. He didn't even blink. Bastard.

With a sigh, I settled onto the couch pushed up against the wall perpendicular to Kingston's desk.

Silence stretched, but instead of the tension building with each passing second, I gradually relaxed into the shitty, blue linen couch. I picked at a white splash of paint staining the fabric. Like the expensive hardwood floors and white walls, the couch was covered in splatters of multi-colored paint. There wasn't a single surface in the art studio that wasn't smothered in the stuff. It suddenly occurred to me that I should have asked Kingston if any of the paint on the couch was wet before I sat down, but it was too late now. If my Blizzards' sweatsuit was ruined, I would just get another. Or maybe steal Kingston's in reparation.

"What are you working on?" I finally asked.

Kingston, who had settled into his desk chair to wait me out, held up the sketchbook he had been scribbling in. On it, a bouquet of flowers bloomed across the page in graphite. The style was different from the stack of canvases leaning against every wall of the studio. He tended to paint pop art, as he'd told me a million times. But the flowers looked as real as a picture and matched the ink that decorated his arms.

I was both impressed and infuriated. How was he so good at things he barely enjoyed? Like hockey, drawing and painting weren't what set his soul on fire. Yet the amount of pure talent in him seemed to override his lack of passion.

With an internal head shake, I let my envy go. I would never want to trade places with Kingston.

"Next tattoo?" I asked.

"Yeah. Daisies. Riley's favorite."

I nodded absently. He would probably get them inked across his rib cage—one of the only unmarked places on his upper body and close to his heart. An image flashed across my mind, and a desire I'd never had before reared its head. All of the sudden, I wanted to disregard my fear of needles and get my first tattoo. And I knew exactly what it would be—a bouquet of kissable red roses.

I cleared my throat. "You going to add color?"

"Of course."

I nodded again. Unlike the rest of the boys on the team who favored black-and-white ink, Kingston loved color. His lightly tanned skin was on its way to becoming fully covered in watercolor-like splashes.

"So…" I prompted but couldn't force more words out.

Kingston took the lead. "So… I hear you're an asshole."

A snort burst from my nose. "Warren told you?"

"*Everyone* told me. I've been getting play-by-play texts from the whole team for the last week."

I sunk into the couch. Damn, I knew I'd been an ass, but they didn't have to snitch on me to Kingston.

"Not that I wouldn't have figured it out after that fight. Haven't seen you go at anyone like that since your rookie season when you were still trying to deny your teddy bear personality."

I grunted.

"Did Coach rip you a new one? Heard he called you in."

"Nah. He did that after the game." It had been brutal too. Not that he yelled. No, when Coach got pissed, he got cold. All I could do was stand there and take the verbal dressing-down delivered in the deep bass of disappointment. But while he wasn't thrilled about the fight, he was more concerned about the way I was acting with the team. I'd been the very opposite of how a captain should be. And a coach.

Thankfully, he didn't say anything about no longer believing in my coaching future. In fact, he had mostly called me into his office to give me more homework. A box full of game tapes now sat in my car, waiting for me to watch them and write up a tactical analysis of each game. It looked like I hadn't been able to avoid writing essays after all. Now I just needed to find a DVD player to watch the ancient disks on.

"So not a hockey problem. That only leaves one option," Kingston concluded. With a sigh, he sat forward, his dark eyes full of the intensity that I'd only ever seen on the ice. "What did you do to Milly?"

"Ugh." My head dropped to the back of the couch, and I glared at the ceiling. Kingston had somehow managed to get paint on it as well. Then, with a burst of energy, I was on my feet. I pointed at Kingston. "You know what? I didn't do anything."

"Uh-huh." Kingston's grunt was practically drowning in doubt.

I threw my hands up in the air and stomped across the room. Paused. Stomped back. Kingston watched me pace as the fire inside of me that had only just died down flared up again.

"I didn't! It's what she did." Then I was ranting, spilling every ounce of anger, hurt, and pain at Kinston's feet like he had done with me when Warren broke up with him when they first started dating. Except this was different. Because *I* had left *Milly*. "And now LaBeux thinks Milly's going to leave. Which is just like her, and I should have seen it coming. She runs away from everything the second it gets hard. Why should this be any different?"

"Is that so bad?" Kingston asked, speaking for the first time since I'd started my filibuster-like tirade.

I paused mid-pace and turned to Kingston. "What?"

"I asked if her leaving is so bad? You broke up with her. Why should you care if she leaves the team?"

The gale force winds that had been propelling me forward at breakneck speed died, and my sails deflated. "I... I... Did I break up with her?"

A single brow rose at me. "Sure sounds like it to me."

"But if I broke up with her, I would never see her again."

"That's usually how breakups work."

No, of course, I would see her again. The very thought of never witnessing her deep-water eyes blink up at me from under her bangs, never ruining her perfect lipstick, and never tasting her heavenly food again was inconceivable. Of course, I would see her again. Right?

"Unless you decide to forgive her, that is."

My forehead scrunched. "After what she did? How could I?"

"Wow. I knew you were an idiot, but I didn't think you were a moron," a feminine voice said behind me.

I whipped around to see Warren in the open doorway. With a disappointed shake of her head, she walked farther into the room, bypassed me, and planted her ass on Kingston's desk. Suddenly, two pairs of eyes were staring me down, their thoughts on my mental prowess, or lack thereof, coming across clearly.

I growled. "Damnit, Warren! Don't you ever mind your own business?"

Behind his girlfriend's back, Kingston shook his head.

Warren shrugged and grabbed a tennis ball from the basket. The fuzzy, yellow ball danced between her hands like it was levitating. "I was curious. Plus, if this is the reason you've been a total dick all week, then it is my business."

I grunted but couldn't argue with that.

"So, do you stunted man-children want an emotionally intelligent woman's perspective?"

I exchanged a look with Kingston, who looked just as perplexed as I felt, then faced Warren again. "I would love that. Can you let me know when you see one because I know you're not talking about yourself. You know, the woman who broke up with the best man I know."

A rare soft smile crept across Kingston's face at that.

"True," Warren conceded. "That was not my best moment. But do you want help or not?"

I gestured encouragingly. "Sure. Why exactly am I an idiotic moron, Warren?"

"Okay, so that may have been a little dramatic. You're not a moron; you're just a hypocrite."

Warren's sudden seriousness snapped my spine straight. "Excuse me?"

"Don't forget, I was there when you decided to ditch Milly's bout to go with Little."

"I didn't really have a choice."

"Sure you did. There's always a choice. And you chose to put your career over Milly." Warren held up a hand as I opened my mouth to protest. "I'm not saying that was the wrong decision. You love hockey, and you love helping your teammates out with anything they need, be it professional or personal. Your passion is admirable, and I respect it. But you can't make a call like that and then get mad when Milly does the same thing."

"But I didn't use her like she did me," I countered, but it didn't have much force behind it. Warren made some good points, and I could already feel the anger slipping from my grasp. But I wasn't ready to let go of it just yet. If I did, I would only be left with one thing: the empty pit in my stomach that seemed to get wider every time I remembered Milly's crying face.

"Can you really blame her for that, though? She was drowning and grasping at anything to help her. Then you showed up like a life preserver. Of course, she grabbed onto you; I would have done the same thing. And so would you. Yes, it sucks that she used you, but she didn't know you then. All she knew was that you could help her keep ahold of the thing she loved most in the world. Aren't you all about passion? Shouldn't you understand, even respect, what she did?"

More anger fell through my fingers like sand.

"She's right, you know."

I turned to Kingston in desperation.

"We all do crazy things for our passion. That's what passion is; it's the thing that drives you crazy, out of your fucking mind."

"What would you know about passion, Kingston?" The second the words left my lips, I wanted to stuff them back in. But I couldn't un-ring that bell, and I hadn't said anything that I hadn't already thought before.

"Hey!" Warren's hand clenched around her tennis ball. I prepared to duck. I knew how strong her arm was, and I didn't want to take another hit to the face.

"It's okay, Riles," Kingston said and ran a hand down Warren's back. Then he turned to me. "And I know a lot about passion. Mine was just never my job. For a long while, I didn't think I would ever have anything I cared about as much as you obviously cared about hockey. I envied that about you. Then I met this one, and I found out that passion is just love cranked to eleven." Kingston petted Warren's spine again, and she about melted.

My chest hitched at the motion. A tingle zipped across my fingertips as I imagined running them over Milly's bare back, petting her as she slept beside me.

Kingston continued. "Trust me when I say, I would do anything to keep her. I would throw you under a Zamboni a million times over for her. Just like you would to keep playing hockey. Just like Milly did. She's a fighter. And from what you've said, she's fighting for you just as hard."

The last granules of rage sifted through my fingers and were carried off in the wind.

25

Milly

"**W**ell, this is absolute bullshit."

Thea and I stared down at said bullshit with suspicion and confusion, respectively. So carefully as to approach moving in slow motion, a spoon poked at the object. It screeched across the counter. Liquid sloshed threateningly. The spoon clanged to the counter, and Thea jerked back in her stool with a squeal.

The bowl of soup sat innocently between us.

Leaning on the other side of the island, my eyes rolled so hard I saw spots. "Dramatic much?"

Thea didn't take her eyes off the strange thing sitting on my kitchen island. "I don't trust it."

"It's not going to bite you. In fact, you're supposed to bite *it*. That's what you do with food." Despite enunciating clearly and only using small words, she still didn't understand.

"What if it tries to kill me?"

My jaw dropped. "Now that's just offensive! What do you think I am, some sort of toddler mixing together special potions in their parents' kitchen? I have never once in my life given anyone food poisoning."

"That you know of," Thea pointed out with a smirk. "Dead people can't exactly complain."

I sputtered.

Thea's laughter folded her in half over the island. Her red, curly hair puddled on the counter and covered her face. When she straightened, tears had gathered in the corners of her green eyes. She wiped delicately at her waterlines. "Oh, my God. You should see your face. Also, I don't know who you're trying to fool. You were totally the kid that made concoctions in your kitchen."

She had me there, but… "It's not my fault. My mom's a chef; I was just copying her."

"Fair enough," she conceded.

Suddenly, she jumped off her stool, rounded the island, and went over to rummage around in my fridge like she did every time she came over to my place. You would think that she had no food in her apartment with the way she scavenged my fridge and pantry.

I watched as she attempted to dig all the way to Narnia, hoping she wouldn't find the gourmet cupcakes I stored behind the pickles she despised. But what she came out with, holding up her prize in victory, was both better and worse.

"It's not even noon."

She shrugged. "But it's Saturday. And we have no games this weekend."

With a wave of permission, I let her go. At least my cupcakes were safe; I would need them later. Although Thea may have argued that point if she knew how many I'd eaten over the past week. I had already been forced to paint on extra concealer to cover up the sugar-induced break-outs across my cheeks.

The *pop* of the cork exiting the wine reminded me that there were worse ways I could be coping with the relentless ache that had nestled in and found a home under my breastbone. But even I knew not to fall into that trap, especially with the pain meds I was still taking for my shoulder.

The savory steam wafting off the top of the white bowl in front of me invaded my senses. My stomach growled. I ignored it, glared into the brown broth, and pushed away from the island in disgust.

My free hand twitched to do something, any-thing. I swept a few dirty dishes onto a vegeta-ble-covered cutting board, piled on some knives, and carried the whole thing to the sink.

"You're not going to taste it?" Thea asked in between sips from her full wine glass.

"No."

After pulling up the sleeve of my hoodie with my teeth, I managed to squeeze some dish soap onto a sponge with just one hand. I set a plate in the metal sink, pinned it against the corner, and scrubbed.

I didn't need to taste it. I knew it was good, even though I hadn't ever made it before.

That's right, it was a new recipe. And there wasn't a single hockey captain in sight.

"Well, I guess I'll brave the unknown," Thea volunteered.

I didn't need to turn around to know what she was doing.

The clinking of a spoon as it hit the side of the steaming bowl was followed by a blowing sound.

Three, two, one...

"Holy shit, Milly!" Her next words were muffled with another spoonful of soup. "What did you say this was again?"

The plate I had pinned slipped, and I fell into the sink as I was putting my whole weight forward. The forearm not strapped to my torso caught me but strained my injured shoulder. I mentally cursed up a storm in English and French.

"It's gumbo," I answered Thea through gritted teeth.

She hummed happily and slurped up more food, not registering my measured breathing as I fought to push past the pain. When it returned to a manageable level, I went back to the dishes.

I was rinsing out a drinking glass when Thea, she of horrible timing, finished off the bowl of gumbo.

"So, are you going to tell him?"

The sud-slicked glass slipped from my fingers. I jumped back to avoid any shards only to find myself assaulted by bubbles and the glass perfectly intact at the bottom of the sink.

A body slid up to me, the scent of an oaky red wine mixing with lemon soap.

Thea rested her ass beside the sink so she could face me. I stared into the dirty dishes and kept my expression locked down on instinct. I knew it wouldn't convince Thea that I was fine. Still, I had to try avoiding the topic at least one more time.

"Tell who what?" My voice fell flat.

Thea pursed her lips at me but went along with my bullshit. She was used to it at this point. Just like I was used to her eccentricities. "Are you going to tell Ethan Jones that you're fixed?"

My molars ground together, but it wasn't out of rage. No, it was the only thing I could do to keep the tears at bay. It worked; the salty drops stayed locked behind my eyes. I ignored my shaking hand. Everything was fine.

"Fixed?" I asked Thea.

She gestured over my shoulder to the empty bowl that she should have brought over to the sink. *Rude.* "Yes. Fixed. Cured. Found your mojo. Whatever you want to call it, it doesn't matter. You can finally cook again!"

Thea's freckles scrunched on her pale nose with her wide smile.

Only a couple of months ago, I would have been joining in on her excitement over my recaptured passion. Now, I simply retrieved the empty bowl from the island and rinsed it under the faucet. "Why would I tell him that?"

Thea ducked her head to the side and down to fully meet my eyes. Her face was a billboard of concern. "Because it means you don't have to use him anymore. He doesn't have to be your muse."

I sighed and abandoned the half-cleaned dishes. I would just throw them in the washer tonight. The therapeutic effect of hand washing had worn off. "It's not that simple."

Thea took a gulp of her wine. The large glass that had been filled to the brim was almost empty. "Why not? Go get your man."

"I can't!" The shout tore apart my throat.

Thea blinked at me.

I blinked back.

Neither one of us had expected that from me.

A beat.

A hiccup.

And there were the tears.

"Oh, Mills." Thea set down her glass and gathered me into a careful side hug, steering clear of my left shoulder.

"I can't," I sobbed into her silk blouse. I knew I was probably ruining it, but I couldn't stop. The floodgates that hadn't been opened since Ethan walked out the door had finally sprung a leak. My hiccupping cries sounded deafening in the concrete loft, and I cried some more for being such a pathetic crier. Why couldn't I be like Thea, who turned into a gorgeously sad Renaissance model when she wept?

She rocked me lightly, her heartbeat steady against my ear. "Why can't you go to him, Milly?" she whispered.

I pulled back, sniffed wetly, then wiped my face with the sleeve of the oversized Blizzards hoodie that I'd been wearing religiously around the house for the past week. The large twenty-four on the back left little doubt about who the piece of clothing originally belonged to. I hugged the fabric to myself, but the distinct scent of Ethan and coconuts had faded. As a consolation, I turned my head into the wall of my hair. I'd switched my usual conditioner to one that was coconut scented. *Mmm, coconut.*

"I'm the one who fucked up, Thea. Even if I'm 'fixed' now or whatever, it doesn't change what I did. I can't go to him. The ball is in his court. All I can do now is let *him* come to *me.* If he comes at all, that is."

Thea's face melted in sympathy.

Ring. Ring. Ring.

Thea and I share another confused look before the sound registered and set off a fearful hope in me.

Ethan?

I practically hip-checked Thea out of my way as I ran around the island, but her derby instincts must have kicked it because she was only a foot behind me, wine glass in hand again, as I grabbed my phone off my hall table.

The strange number on the screen crushed my spirit.

"Who is it?" Thea asked, peering over my shoulder like a curious owl.

"Probably the *maître d'* of *Coucher de soleil sur la Seine* again. He's already called a couple times to get me to reconsider his offer after I turned down the position." I considered the digits on the screen. "Although, I don't think that's the number he usually uses."

"Milly. I think that's the extension for the arena."

I hesitated a moment longer, then, with a one-shouldered shrug, brought the phone to my ear.

"Hello?"

"Good afternoon. Is this Chef Milly Chambers?"

"It is."

"Hello, Chef Chambers. My name is Theresa Argent. I'm the PR manager of the New York Blizzards. Do you have a moment?"

"The PR manager of the Blizzards?" I repeated for Thea's sake as she moved to my side instead of breathing down my neck.

She made grabby hands at my phone.

I put the phone on speaker and answered the woman as Thea took a sip of her wine.

"Hey, Captain! Could you help me out with this?"

I came to a sketchy stop on the banked track, my left arm unable to extend and provide balance. The stares that drilled into me as I wobbled for a millisecond were like a physical weight. But I hadn't expected anything less when I'd insisted on skating a few laps after sitting through a practice I wasn't allowed to participate in. Most of the women on the team were either moms, nurses, or both, so their mother-hen natures came out strong. Then my crazy best friend made the "Milly Protection Squad" even more dedicated to keeping me out of harm's way by threatening to take a stiletto to the foot of whoever allowed me to fuck up my shoulder more. After she'd finished her overbearing and threatening rant to the girls, they were about ready to tie me to a chair to keep me off the track.

Then I'd discovered the best perk of being captain; I only had to follow Coach's instructions. Since that discovery, I'd been entertaining myself by skating lazily around when I wasn't needed during practice. So as the team did their cool-down stretches, I made a couple of laps around the track, creating a wind that whipped my hair behind me.

But my duties as captain were never done.

As I got closer to Jaw Breaker, the newest girl on our team, I fell to my knee pads and skidded to a kneeling stop beside her spot on the ground.

"What's up, Breaker?" I asked, even though the answer was in her lap.

"Can you explain this to me? I don't quite get it." She gestured to the team playbook balanced on her knees, open to an advanced play that she probably wouldn't be ready to pull off for a few more months. Still, her eagerness was endearing.

I settled next to her and slid the binder over to rest between us.

"What do you not get, exactly?"

"Oh, I see," Breaker exclaimed excitedly. "So it's like the sled trick play but with the pivot instead of the jammer."

"Exactly."

Breaker flipped to another page in the binder. "What about this one?" she asked for the fifth time.

I ran my eyes over the page. "That's a good on—"

"Charlie!"

Breaker's head whipped up at what was presumably her given name. Lady MacDeath, who had brought Breaker onto the team, stormed up to us in tennis shoes. "Girl, if you don't get changed, I'm leaving without you."

A *meep* squeaked from Breaker, and in the blink of an eye, she was up and halfway to the locker room, her playbook binder clutched tightly to her chest.

"Damn, she's fast," I mumbled.

"Tell me about it. That kid makes me feel old. And I'm only twenty-eight."

"Preaching to the choir, girl." Though I was a smidge older than that.

MacDeath grabbed my reaching hand and hauled me up.

I scissored my skates back and forth as I straightened, trying to get my blood flowing again. My ass had gone numb after sitting on the hardwood of the derby track for too long.

"Hey, Chop?" MacDeath prompted beside me.

I looked up from my tingling legs. "Yeah?"

"Is that yours?"

I followed her pointed finger to the stands, and the oxygen froze in my lungs. The bleachers around the track were cast in darkness, but I instantly recognized the blurry silhouette of the love of my life anyway.

"Ethan," I intoned as if in prayer.

"I'll take that as a yes. He's been here all practice. He even helped some of the kiddos with their homework. But whenever he could look up, his eyes were glued to you..."

I didn't hear what else she said because my skates were rolling up the track. I was in a trance, and Ethan was my only anchor. From the stands, eyes that I could feel but not see clearly watched my approach. He made no effort to meet me halfway or move closer to the track at all.

Out of the blue, a barrier ran into my diaphragm, knocking a gasp out of me. I looked down and blinked slowly at the cushioned railing that encircled the perimeter of the track. I hadn't realized I'd gotten that close to the edge or to Ethan.

Speaking of...

I raised my head and fell into the sparkling mahogany eyes gazing at me. Silence stretched across the chasm between us, but I waited him out. I couldn't just jump him, as much as I wanted to. This had to go at his pace. *The ball is in his court*, I kept on reminding myself.

The eyes that hadn't left mine since I'd started skating to him released me and flicked away erratically. Ethan scratched at the base of his scalp.

I waited.

His hand dropped into his lap, and he peeked up at me through his lashes. "I'm sorry. I didn't mean to interrupt your practice. I just ... wanted to see you skate. The roller rink that hosted your captain party was too crowded for you to let loose, and I wanted to see you on your home turf where you're most comfortable."

I cleared my throat of the emotion stuck there with an awkward laugh. "Just as long as we're not on your turf, I'm happy. No matter how much you love the ice, I'll never get used to the cold."

A smile pulled up the corners of Ethan's plush lips, but his eyes had drifted off a little and landed on ... my hair?

He tapped the bleacher in front of him. "Come here."

I didn't hesitate. I went to him.

26

Ethan

*M*illy sat quietly between my legs, staring out into her derby track with her back leaning against my knees. She'd voiced no protest when I had directed her into the position, and it was like the first time we had sex. She was giving herself over to me, trusting me with her body and soul.

I raked my fingers through the waterfall of Milly's wavy hair, gently breaking up the tangles that must have formed while she was flying across the banked track. It took a few minutes, but with my constant combing, her curls untwined from each other. The soft strands wove through my fingers and left a ghost of their presence in the tingling on my palms.

Once I was pleased with my detangling, I buried my hands into Milly's roots. She immediately tensed but relaxed as I rubbed my fingertips across her scalp. A low moan vibrated her throat, and she swiveled her head to direct my hands where she wanted them most.

Her long hair draped across my arms as I continued the massage, and the soft scent of coconut drifted off her. Taking care of our hair was something that my mother drilled into the heads of me and my brothers. And her favorite thing to use was coconut oil. I sniffed quietly at Milly's hair and wondered if the fantastic smelling oil worked on Caucasian hair too.

"You should wear your hair down more," I muttered, finally breaking the silence.

"Really?"

"Yeah. It's much more wild when it's loose."

"And much more of a hassle," she pointed out. "It gets annoying."

"But you can't tie it up with your shoulder in a sling, huh?"

She snuggled backward into me more. "Yeah."

I opened my legs and let her lean back all the way into me. "Do you have a hair tie on you?"

She held up her hand and the elastic on her wrist.

"Perfect." I slid it off her wrist and onto mine. Then I got to work

A soft laugh escaped her. "Are you going to braid my hair?"

I started sectioning out the pieces I would need. "Sure. I used to do it for my mom and my brothers. Of course, we usually did cornrows, but I know my way around a French braid pretty well."

It took me less than a minute to wrangle all her hair into one rope and secure it at the end.

"There you go." I dropped the braid over her shoulder.

She immediately grabbed it, turning it this way and that to inspect my work. She straightened on the bench and turned to look up at me. I waited for her judgment.

"Well, you're going to be braiding my hair every morning from now on," she said with finality, then her deep-water eyes widened at the implication. Her grip tightened on the braid. "Uh, I mean…"

"You know," I said suddenly, stopping her desperate grasp for words. "That night at the Rockefeller Center was the day I discovered what passion was, but it wasn't in myself that I originally saw it. It was in my mother. That night wasn't just the first night I put on skates; it was also the first time I ever saw my mom on a rink. And she was breathtaking. She had this wild look about her, her eyes shining so bright I thought there must have been tiny little suns behind them, and her big goofy smile that she would have been self-conscious of had she known it was there. But she didn't; it was totally unconscious, like her body was just so happy that it was bursting with joy."

Milly gazed up at me softly.

I reached down, stroked my thumb down her cheek, then cupped the side of her face. "I thought I would never see anything as beautiful as her that night, but I was wrong. Because you out on that track, wind blowing your hair up around your face with your arms out and head tilted back like you wanted to soak in every ounce of freedom, about stopped my heart, Milly."

Milly's mouth opened, but I shook my head.

"I'm not done, because that's still not the most beautiful thing I've ever seen."

The skin between her eyebrows creased. I rubbed my thumb over the wrinkles to smooth them out and leaned over so we were eye to eye, blue and brown clashing.

"That honor goes to Chef Milly Chambers, the woman who can wield a knife like an extension of herself, who dances across the kitchen to get ingredients, and who is filled with breathtaking determination to show her love by providing for her family and friends. That is the most beautiful thing I've ever seen, and I could never take that from you. So if you need me in the kitchen with you to get a hold of that passion, that beauty, I'll be there every day."

Tears welled in Milly's deep-water eyes, and I panicked for a moment as I was thrown back to the last time I saw her cry. But these tears were different, softer.

She sniffled as she blinked up at me. "Why would you do that, Ethan?"

I cocked my head. "Isn't it obvious? I love you, and I want you to have everything you desire."

Milly gasped and clenched at my knee. "Say that again," she demanded.

"I love you, Milly Chambers."

Next thing I knew, I had a lapful of happy girlfriend.

"I love you too."

I pressed my lips to hers and worked my way down her neck.

Then she pulled back. "Oh, wait. There's something I have to tell you. Well, two things actually."

"Okay."

Nothing.

I waited.

Milly pulled her braid from behind her and played with the end while she squirmed on my lap.

"Milly," I prompted.

"Turns out, I'm actually … fixed."

"Fixed?" I repeated. I had no idea what she meant.

"Yeah. I made a new recipe the other night."

Before Milly's confession, I wouldn't have understood. But now I knew how big of a deal this was. "That's fantastic, Mills." I gave her a quick peck in congratulations. "What did you make?"

Her eyes shifted to the side. "Gumbo," she muttered.

I couldn't breathe through the shock, through the absolute betrayal.

I shot out of my seat, taking my girlfriend with me, and headed down the bleacher steps.

"Where are we going?" she asked with a giggle. But she didn't fight my hold, letting me take her wherever I pleased.

"Your house. Because you better have left-overs." I could only have authentic gumbo about once a year when I went to see my parents down south. And I knew as certain as I knew how to lace up my skates that Milly's recipe would blow everything else I've tasted out of the water. How dare she cook gumbo and not invite me over. She was lucky I loved her. I suddenly paused. Gently, I placed Milly on the floor, making sure she was balanced on the toe stops of her skates before letting go.

She immediately knew something was wrong and looked at me with questions floating in her deep-water eyes.

"Doesn't this mean you don't need me anymore, since you can cook without me?"

She reached out in an imitation of how I had earlier and cupped my cheek. "No, I don't think I need you anymore."

I held my breath, hoping with every fiber of my being that there was going to be more.

"But that doesn't matter because I *want* you."

I dropped my chin to my chest. Jesus, she'd about given me a heart attack with that pause.

"That is if you want me."

My head snapped back, mouth moving to answer immediately, but she held up a finger.

"Be careful before you answer that," she warned. "Because I'm not sure if you know this about me, but I'll do anything to hold on to the things I love."

I lunged forward, and our mouths crashed together. We ignited with the combined passion of a badass chef and a relentless hockey player.

Milly

"Look at how perfectly red this is! Isn't it amazing?" In my excitement, I held the tomato, freshly picked from my very own greenhouse, too close to Sebastian's face.

His eyes crossed as he tried to focus on it. "Yes. It is very red."

I pouted and pulled the tomato back into my loving embrace. "Ugh. Hockey players; they're horrible."

"Hey!" Riley shouted from Ethan's living room.

"Just the men, I meant," I called back.

"Better!"

With a snort, Sebastian went back to chopping the rest of the veggies for the salsa I was teaching him how to make for taco night. After taking my advice to prep before cooking, he had been enjoying it more and was even asking me for recipes. I watched with a careful eye and was impressed by the fast but smooth precision with which he held the knife. He must have been practicing at home. Or maybe Ethan hadn't been exaggerating when he said Sebastian could do literally anything.

From his seat at the island, Ethan picked up his head and closed the newest book Coach Hansson had given him to read. "You realize you've committed to spending another season surrounded by male hockey players, right?"

"Don't remind me," I groaned, but couldn't keep up the act for long. A smile broke across my face, but I restrained myself from dancing around the kitchen … this time.

The smirk on Ethan's face said he knew what I was restraining myself from doing.

I scrunched my nose at him. I would just have to wait until tomorrow to bust out my sick moves like I did every morning while I made breakfast. And Ethan would look on with fond amusement like *he* did every morning as he watched me finally enjoying myself. After having my memories of them tainted by toxic chefs, the kitchen had started to become my happy place again, where I could experiment with food, create new dishes freely, and provide for the family around me that had been steadily growing bigger.

A flash of ginger caught my attention as Thea came into the kitchen for a refill of wine.

"Bitch, please. All those boys love you," she said and emptied half a bottle of red into her glass.

"That's only because I feed them."

"True," Ethan and Sebastian said in unison then shot goofy smiles at one another.

I smirked. "It's my superpower. Just ask Ethan; all it took was me cooking for him for a few weeks before he was head over heels for me." I fluttered my lashes at my boyfriend. "Just think, babe. If you'd never asked me to be your personal chef, you would never have discovered how amazing I am and how much you love me."

Ethan snapped his book closed with a dull *thunk* and looked at me like I was a particularly cute moron. "Darlin', I never asked you to be my personal chef."

"What? I'm pretty sure you did. I remember because I was, you know, *there*. You asked me to make dinner at your place."

He crossed his arms and leaned back on the bar stool. I squinted at him. He looked a little too confident that he was right.

Thea took a sip of her wine, watching us over the rim like she knew this was going to be a good one. Over in the living room, Riley and Mason were twisted in half to get a good view of us over the couch. Even Sebastian, who usually couldn't care less about our squabbles, paused in his chopping to wait for Ethan's next words.

"No. I didn't ask you to make dinner, darlin'. I asked you *to* dinner. I asked you out on a date."

"No. You... You... Oh, my God." My brain ground to a halt.

But no one else was having that problem. Thea snorted into her wine, sending droplets out of the glass and over her face like tiny red freckles. Sebastian chuckled under his breath. I didn't hold out hope that he was making fun of Thea and not me. Riley and Mason were less subtle about their amusement and were practically folded over each other, their cackles echoing around the apartment.

My mouth flopped open and closed like a stunned fish.

Ethan watched without a word, content to let me spiral in embarrassment.

"You're an idiot," Thea summed up.

I snapped back to reality to bitch at my best friend. "You're one to talk. It looks like you're sweating blood." I threw a tea towel at her.

She wiped her face of the wine and turned to Ethan. "You'll have to watch out for her, Jones. This one can't recognize when people are flirting with her."

Ethan snorted. "Tell me about it."

"Hey," I protest. "Watch it, babe. Or you'll be eating unseasoned chicken and brown rice for a month."

He held up his hand, unarmed.

"That's what I thought."

"Aw, don't be mean to him, Mills. It's not his fault that you're emotionally stunted." Thea smirked.

I flipped her off, stole a diced piece of tomato from Sebastian's pile on the cutting board, and chewed petulantly. "Why did I agree to keep working with the Blizzards, again? For a second there, I was almost rid of you. Now I have to keep seeing you every day."

She shrugged. "I doubt you will, actually. I've got a feeling you're going to be too busy to even see your boy toy at work. You've got your work cut out for you with this cookbook."

At the mention of the cookbook, a familiar thread of terror tore through my stomach. But unlike the pure anxiety that I used to have at the thought of creating new recipes, a wave of anticipation dulled the edge of my fear. This was the first project I would be doing after "getting my mojo back," as Thea still called it, but this time it would be different. There were no screaming chefs or mean customers, just the men I'd come to know and love over the past season.

Men I would soon be getting to know even better because I was partnering with the Blizzards' PR manager to make a customized and nutritional cookbook for the team. They would also be sold to the public. There were already thousands of pre-orders, and the team hadn't even done anything more than announce the book's future creation. From the projections based on the last month of data, it was already looking to be a huge success.

Ethan looked up from the book he'd reopened when Thea and I started poking at each other. "You should think about hiring an assistant, darlin'."

I raised a brow. He may be right.

"Done," Sebastian announced.

I glanced at his finished piles of diced vege-tables. Every square of food was perfectly even.

Now there's an idea.

I stole another piece of tomato. "What do you say, Sebastian? Would you like to be my lovely assistant? I could get you a frilly apron and everything."

He blinked as if not registering what I asked. Then shock flooded his face, and he glanced around the apartment. Thea looked just as sur-prised as Sebastian. Ethan was filtering through too many emotions for me to pick out even one. But Riley was … considering.

I turned back to Sebastian.

His usual stoic mask was back, but I could practically see the gears turning in his head. Then, all at once, they stopped, and Sebastian faced me, back straight as if he were standing at attention.

"I would love to," he said calmly, but there was something hidden behind that cool exterior. His eyes beamed like a sun shone behind them, and the beginnings of an unconscious smile tugged at his lips.

I blinked and turned to Ethan. He met my gaze with intent; he'd seen it too—passion.

1. Should everyone strive to make their passion their job?

2. If you were Ethan, would you be able to forgive Milly for what she did?

3. Who do you think is the better captain? Milly or Ethan?

4. Would you want a Thea in your life, or would you not wish her on your worst enemy?

5. Can the thing that drives you forward also be the thing that holds you back?

6. Who was in the wrong during The Big Fight?

7. Would you rather skate on ice or hardwood?

8. Should Ethan have ditched Little for Milly's first bout?

9. Could you rock Milly's bangs?

10. Which character do you want to know more about?

About the Author

Mandy Fate is a new, young author trying to share her love of love with the world. She was born and raised in Houston, Texas with the most caring and supportive parents in the world and with the two most annoying, yet encouraging, big brothers.

Like every author, Mandy grew up with an addiction to books. And there was no cure. Especially when she (at an admittedly too young age) picked up her first romance book. She was hooked.

Now, fresh out of college and bright-eyed, she is wearing out the keys of her laptop with her excitement and ambition to become the author she has always wanted to be.